Praise for Jorn Lier Horst's *William Wisting* series

'Horst, a former Norwegian policeman, now produces classy procedurals with plotting, depth and humanity to rival the best of the Scandis.'   -*The Sunday Times* Crime Club

'Urban rather than natural settings are the stamping grounds of Jorn Lier Horst, whose *Dregs* is immensely impressive. Th writer's career as a police chief has supplie for the crime fiction form: credibility.'

    -Barry Forshaw, author of *Nordic Noir* and *Euro Noir*

'*Closed for Winter* is a piece of quality craftsmanship, bringing together an unexpectedly winding plot, highly intelligent characterizations and a delectably subtle noir mood to create a very engrossing crime novel.'   -*Edinburgh Book Review*

'Expertly constructed and beautifully written, [*The Hunting Dogs*] showcases the talents of one of the most accomplished authors of contemporary Nordic Noir.'

    -Karen Meek, The Petrona Award

'*The Caveman* is not just an intriguing, fast-paced thriller, but a thoughtful meditation on loneliness, and a moving testament to the value of human life.'

    -Nicola Upson, author of the *Josephine Tey* series

'Horst writes some of the best Scandinavian crime fiction available. His books are superbly plotted and addictive, the characters superbly reali∘d *Ordeal* kept me engaged to the end and I cannot wait f   Sigurdardottir

D1334179

Jorn Lier Horst is one of Scandinavia's most successful crime writers. For many years he was one of Norway's most experienced police officers, with the result that his engaging and intelligent novels offer a realistic insight into how serious crimes are investigated, and how they are handled by the media. The critically acclaimed William Wisting Series has sold more than one million copies in Norway, and is translated into thirty languages. Jorn's literary awards include the Norwegian Booksellers' Prize, the Riverton Prize (Golden Revolver), the Scandinavian Glass Key and the prestigious Martin Beck Award; *The Caveman* won the United Kingdom's Petrona Award in 2016.

Anne Bruce lives on the Isle of Arran in Scotland and studied Norwegian and English at Glasgow University. She is the translator of Jorn Lier Horst's *Dregs*, *Closed for Winter*, *The Hunting Dogs*, *The Caveman* and *Ordeal*, and also Anne Holt's *Blessed are Those who Thirst* (2012), *Death of the Demon* (2013), *The Lion's Mouth* (2014), *Dead Joker* (2015), *No Echo* (2016), *Beyond the Truth* (2016) and *What Dark Clouds Hide* (2017), in addition to Merethe Lindstrøm's Nordic Prize winning *Days in the History of Silence* (2013).

The William Wisting Series
Published in English by Sandstone Press

DREGS

Jorn Lier Horst

Translated by

Anne Bruce

SANDSTONEPRESS
HIGHLAND | SCOTLAND

First published in Great Britain in 2011
This edition 2017
Sandstone Press Ltd
Dochcarty Road
Dingwall
Ross-shire
IV15 9UG
Scotland

www.sandstonepress.com

This translation has been published with the financial support of NORLA.

The publisher acknowledges subsidy from Creative Scotland towards
publication of this volume.

ISBN: 978-1-905207-67-1
ISBNe: 978-1-905207-72-5

Cover by Freight Design, Glasgow
Typeset by Iolaire Typography Ltd, Newtonmore
Printed and bound by CPI Group (UK) Ltd, Croydon, CR0 4YY

In memory of Oddvar Lier Olsen

WILLIAM WISTING

William Wisting is a career policeman who has risen through the ranks to become Chief Inspector in the Criminal Investigation Department of Larvik Police, just like his creator, author Jorn Lier Horst. *Dregs* finds him around fifty years old, the widowed father of grown up twins, Thomas and Line.

Thomas serves in the military, in Afghanistan at the time of *Dregs*. Daughter Line is an investigative journalist based in Oslo, whose career frequently intersects with that of her father. Wisting, at first apprehensive, has come to value how she can operate in ways that he cannot, often turning up unexpected clues and insights.

Crucial to the series are Wisting's colleagues in the police. Audun Vetti is the arrogant Assistant Chief of Police who rubs against him continually. Wisting has more positive relationships with certain trusted colleagues: old school Nils Hammer, whose background in the Drugs Squad has made him cynical, the younger Torunn Borg whom Wisting has come to rely on thanks to her wholly professional approach and outlook, and Mortensen, the crime scene examiner who is usually first on the scene.

The setting is Vestfold county on the south-west coast of Norway, an area popular with holidaymakers, where rolling landscapes and attractive beaches make an unlikely setting for crime. The principal town of Larvik, where Wisting is based, is located 105 km (65 miles) southwest of Oslo. The wider Larvik district has 41,000 inhabitants, 23,000 of whom live in the town itself, and covers 530 square km. Larvik is noted for its natural springs, but its modern economy relies heavily on agriculture, commerce and services, light industry and transportation, as well as tourism. There is a ferry service from Larvik to Hirsthals in Denmark.

Dregs begins with a police report giving the place and time of the discovery of a training shoe washed up on the sand, still containing a severed foot from the victim's body, the introduction of CI William Wisting, and a first hint at his health worries. Soon a second shoe is washed up, but it is another left. Has there been a terrible accident at sea? Does it indicate the killing and dismembering of two victims? Is there a link with the unsolved disappearances in the Larvik area in recent months? In this gripping police procedural, Wisting gradually gets to the bottom of the mystery with the help of his all too human colleagues and his journalist daughter, Line.

1

The report was phoned in to the police switchboard in Tønsberg on Tuesday 22nd June at 09.32 hours. William Wisting had just left the doctor's surgery when the assignment arrived over the police radio. Now he was standing with fine-grained sand in his shoes, using his hand to shade the sunlight from his eyes, the third policeman to reach the discovery site.

Waves broke against the shore in front of him and rolled back to sea. Bare rock faces, smooth and slippery wet, sloped gently into the water on either side of the bay. Two uniformed colleagues had cordoned off the western side of the bathing beach.

This early in the morning there were only a few people around, a small group of onlookers comprising no more than twelve or thirteen people, mostly children. One of the policemen had taken aside a heavily built boy with red, bristling hair and a face full of freckles. The boy was trying to control a small black terrier on a lead with one hand, while pointing and gesticulating with the other.

Wisting let his eye rest on one of the few seagulls flying in wide, sluggish circles over the bay, as if he wanted to take a short break before filling his lungs with salt air and bringing his concentration to bear on another lengthy and demanding task.

A training shoe at the water's edge rolled backwards and forwards, looking as if it was going to be pulled out to sea each time the sand slid beneath it, only to be thrown back to shore with each new wave. Seaweed had entangled itself tightly around the laces, which were still tied, and the sole had a covering of brown algae. The remains of a human foot protruded from the shoe. Shrimp fry and other small forms of sea life crawled around, catching hold wherever they could. Wisting allowed his eye to take flight again, staring at the thin, grey line separating the sea from the sky. On the misty horizon he could make out the outline of a cargo ship.

A small van drove onto the grassy plain at the back of the shore, halting beside the police patrol car. Espen Mortensen stepped out, then leaned in again to pull out a camera case. Wisting nodded in welcome to the young crime technician. Mortensen reciprocated and opened the side door of the crime scene vehicle. He brought out a spade and a white plastic tub before approaching his colleague. 'Another one?' he asked, putting down the spade on the sand.

'Another one,' Wisting confirmed, squatting beside the macabre discovery while Mortensen got his camera ready. The foot looked as if it had been torn or pulled from the rest of the body at the ankle joint, but was still held tightly by the training shoe. Tendrils of thick, leathery skin unfolded on either side. Among the grey-white mass of flesh at the bottom of the shoe he could see pale scraps of bone and part of what might be a ligament covering the heel.

Wisting had seen it all before. This was the second severed foot that had been washed up in his district recently. He stood up and glanced at the crime technician. 'They don't belong together,' he said positively. Mortensen remained standing with a lens in his hand, looking down at the shoe.

'What do you mean? I think it looks exactly the same as the first.'

'That's the problem,' Wisting nodded. 'It's a left shoe. The first one was too.' He bent over and examined the contents of the shoe once more. 'Besides, this one has a white tennis sock. The first had a black sock.'

Espen Mortensen swore and hunched over the shoe as it bobbed up and down in the waves. 'You're right,' he agreed.

'I think this one's a couple of sizes bigger too. That means . . .'

They both understood what this meant. The body parts were from two unknown corpses that probably were still floating on the sea.

Mortensen took several photographs from different angles before putting the camera back into its case, gripping the spade and digging into the sand beneath the shoe. A little sand, a couple of shells and some seawater flowed with it into the tub.

The policeman who had been questioning the red-haired boy approached them, quickly summing up the boy's story of how he had found the shoe while walking his dog a short time earlier. 'We're organising a search of the shore,' he said. 'The rest of the body might float to land anywhere at all. There will be lots of children here today. The Red Cross has promised to come here with a search party within an hour.'

Wisting nodded his approval. After the previous foot had been found they had searched the coastline without any result. Perhaps they would be luckier this time. A large wave rolled far up the shore, and he had to take a few steps back to avoid getting wet. When it rolled back it wiped his footsteps from the damp sand.

He drew his hand through his thick, dark hair and looked out to sea again. He had experienced a great deal in life, but this time he could feel his heart beat a bit faster.

3

2

The map that lay unfolded over the conference table had a red cross on the outermost southern tip of Stavernsøya island. Wisting grabbed the felt-tip pen and marked a new cross on the bay beside the south-facing ramparts of the old fortifications and shipyard buildings in the old part of Stavern.

Nils Hammer was right at his shoulder. 'Another *left* foot?' he asked doubtfully.

Wisting nodded, pulling a bundle of photographs out of an envelope and spreading them across the map. All were of the same subject, a blue training shoe with an upper made of a synthetic material, padded edges and the manufacturer's name, Scarpa Marco. On both sides the shoe was emblazoned with red, contrasting stripes, faded after the time in the seawater.

What little doubt there had been was gone. The shoe that was found out on Stavernsøya island six days before was of the same make and model as the one that was now sitting on the metal bench in Espen Mortensen's crime laboratory. As the crow flies, there was barely a kilometre between the two discovery sites.

Wisting had delegated the first investigation and not involved himself closely. The detectives' principal theory was that the foot was from a boating accident in the Skagerrak. Forensics thought that it could have been in the water for between six and ten months. The work so far had consisted of charting all persons missing from this stretch of coast over the last year. The first thought Wisting had, when shoe and foot number two turned up, was that

4

they were a pair, but then it emerged that they were both left feet.

The coffee machine had not quite finished its work. Nils Hammer impatiently filled a paper mug while it was still sputtering. 'We're no longer talking about some kind of accident, are we?' he asked.

Wisting did not answer, but was in agreement that they had to come up with new theories.

Hammer swigged the warm coffee. 'A drugs reckoning,' he suggested.

Nils Hammer was in his mid-forties, with broad shoulders, a barrel chest and dark blond hair. He worked as leader of the narcotics division, and in his view most things were connected in one way or another with drugs crime. His dark eyes gave him a sceptical expression. Often it was enough for him to stare at a suspect to extract a confession, simply to escape that intense gaze.

'It doesn't need to be something criminal,' Wisting reminded him.

Hammer sat down and put his feet on the table. 'It's criminal to cut off someone's feet, whether they are living or dead.'

The coffee machine gurgled faintly and shot out a cloud of hot steam. Wisting fetched a cup from the cupboard and helped himself. 'It might not have been cut off by force,' he suggested. 'It's not unnatural for arms and legs to get separated from a body that has been in the water for a long time.'

'And just by chance it applies to a pair of left feet, wearing the same kind of shoe?'

Wisting shrugged his shoulders. He would not convince anyone by arguing against the facts, not even himself. He sighed. The fact was, they stood on the threshold of an extensive investigation.

Torunn Borg arrived at the door of the meeting room with a pile of papers in her hands. 'Another shoe?' she enquired.

'Another left foot,' Hammer corrected.

'A couple of sizes larger than the first one,' explained Wisting. 'But the same make.'

'A Scarpa Marco,' Torunn Borg nodded and sat down. 'A training shoe with laces,' she continued, leafing through the papers.

Wisting sat beside her. Professionally skilful, efficient and motivated, Torunn Borg was one of the most competent investigators in the section. She had been given the task of tracing the shoe type. 'Have you discovered anything?' he asked.

'It's produced in China.' Torunn Borg put down copies of order and production lists. '*Europris* imports around 15,000 pairs a year. Since 2005 they have sold just over 50,000 of them throughout the country.'

Wisting's telephone rang. Checking the display he saw that it was Suzanne. He switched the phone to silent and cancelled the call. She would want to talk about his doctor's appointment.

'The first shoe was size 43. 7,400 pairs of them have been sold.'

'That certainly makes it easier,' Hammer commented drily, biting into his paper mug. 'Who actually buys training shoes at *Europris*?'

'Sports shoes,' Torunn corrected him and held out a brochure that explained the shoe was made of artificial leather and had a moulded sole of ethylene-vinyl-acetate, which offered good shock absorption.

'Old people.' Wisting replied. 'My father shops at *Europris*. It's reasonably priced, and he's happy with the quality. The feet must belong to two of *The Old Folk*.'

The two others fell silent, knowing he was right.

The list of missing people during the past year was not a long one. It contained only four names. Wisting had them in front of him.

Torkel Lauritzen

Otto Saga
Sverre Lund
Hanne Richter

All four had disappeared within the space of a few days in September of the previous year.

The cases had caused a headache. Each year around fifty people were reported missing in the police district, but most were quickly located: teenagers who ran away from home, children who forgot the time and place, dementia sufferers who got into trouble, the mentally ill, berry-pickers and hunters. Usually these cases ended with happy reunions, although sometimes the missing persons were found as victims of an accident or with a farewell note. Only in a few exceptional cases did anyone disappear completely and without trace.

The first three names on the list were described by the division only as *The Old Folk*. Two of them lived in sheltered housing flats at Stavern nursing home in Brunla-veien. The third man was of the same age but still active enough to live at home in Johan Ohlsensgate in the middle of Stavern. Besides, his wife was still living.

The media had not been tempted to speculate about a connection, although they must surely have thought the same as the police.

Statistically speaking, these disappearance cases were practically impossible. There were about 6,000 permanent residents in Stavern. Barely four per cent of them were over 75 years of age and yet in the course of one and the same week, three had vanished.

The police had looked for connections and patterns in addition to age and residential similarities, but only discovered that the children of two of the missing were married to each other.

Torkel Lauritzen was a widower who had been head of human resources in the *Treschow-Fritzøe* group of companies. Two years earlier he had suffered a serious stroke. In the photograph that accompanied the case file, the corner of his mouth hung down on one side. The illness meant that he spoke indistinctly and in monosyllables, but rehabilitation at the nursing home had enabled him to manage by himself. He had partly regained the movement of his right foot and enjoyed going on short walks along the coastal path. Always precise and punctual, when he didn't come home for dinner after a walk on Monday 1st September, the staff became worried. Despite his illness he had not stopped smoking and both his blood pressure and cholesterol levels were high. They feared that he had suffered another stroke, and searched for him throughout the walking areas. He was never found, neither living nor dead.

Three days later Otto Saga went missing from Stavern nursing home. A retired wing commander he had previously been head of the Air Force officer training school in Stavern. After his wife died he started to write poetry and had issued a couple of collections through a local publishing company. Three years previously his family had started to notice the first frightening signs of dementia. Repeated minor infarctions or haemorrages in the brain injured nerve cells, leading eventually to the impairment of his mental faculties so that he forgot things and repeated himself. The family had successfully applied for a place in an institution, and their experience was that the staff not only achieved good relations with the old man but also communicated with him better than they did themselves.

He disappeared after breakfast on Thursday 4th September. The staff searched throughout the buildings, eventually widening the search to the area of the old shipyards and the abandoned military barracks where he used to work, and the residential district of Agnes where he had lived. He had got lost before and not been able to find his way back. When the evening shift came on duty he had still not been found. The police were alerted and the search continued all night: in parks and private gardens, unlocked storerooms and outhouses, town centre streets and boat harbours. After twenty-four hours there were no more places to look and the search was called off. 79-year-old Otto Saga seemed to have been swallowed by the earth.

Sverre Lund was an old schoolteacher who had ended his professional career as the head teacher of Stavern primary school. He was reported missing by his wife, Greta Lund, on Monday 8th September at 17.32 hours, according to the documentation. After explaining to her that he had a few errands to run he had walked off from his home at around eleven o'clock. His errands usually comprised of a cup of coffee, a Danish pastry and an Oslo newspaper at Baker Nalum's and, never far from home, he was usually back by one o'clock.

Both of the women behind the counter at the bakery shop knew Mr. Lund well, but neither of them had seen him that day. A chambermaid at the Wassilioff Hotel, who had been in the backyard having a cigarette, around twelve o'clock, thought she had seen the former head teacher getting into the passenger seat of a grey estate car outside the old post office. The driver had never contacted the police. All traces ended there and Sverre Lund was never seen again.

Hanne Richter was 34 years old, and had no connections to the others. Her case was different. A nursery teacher, she had been on sick leave for a long time before she vanished. For parts of that time she had been an in-patient at Furubakken, a regional psychiatric institution in Larvik. She was diagnosed with a paranoid schizophrenic psychosis, and had delusions that a foreign intelligence organisation was watching her and carrying out secret searches at her home, among other reasons to plant spying equipment. Anti-psychotic medicines suppressed her symptoms and allowed her to live independently in her rented house. When the community nurse visited on Wednesday 10th September, she was missing. The nurse had let herself in and searched through the house, noticing that the mail and newspapers from Friday 6th September had been taken in, but that the ones for the subsequent days filled the post box. She had expected to find Hanne Richter dead, either in her bed or in the bath, but couldn't find her anywhere, neither in the house nor in the surrounding area. The police published the name and picture of the missing person in the media, but it produced no results. No one had seen Hanne Richter or knew what had become of her.

Work on the four missing persons had taken up a large part of the police station's resources during the following weeks without leading to any explanation, and then they had had the case of the Night Man to deal with. Someone had decapitated a young girl and displayed the severed head on a stake in the middle of the town square, all their resources had been transferred and by Easter the four missing persons cases were deposited in the archives.

Wisting had taken them out again an hour ago.

3

Wisting closed the office door and sat on the chair behind the desk. He pushed away the piles of paper that were waiting to be dealt with, and put the files concerning the three missing persons in the middle of the desktop with an involuntary sigh.

In recent years his workload had grown while, at the same time, resources had decreased. Cases were left lying or only superficially investigated before they were shelved, to the despair of both the investigators and the victims. It did not have to be like this, if they only had the time that was required. If only they had more staff.

Truthfully, the time was approaching when crime would begin to pay. Criminality in the country was growing more strongly than ever, and he saw no sign of effective counter-measures. On the contrary, police and courts of law continued to be disempowered. The forces of law and order were in the process of capitulating.

He took a blank sheet from the bundle on the shelf by the window and again listed the names of the missing men in slightly clumsy handwriting. He sat back to study the short list:

Torkel Lauritzen
Otto Saga
Sverre Lund

Behind each name lay the hidden concern of their relatives. Worry, despair and sorrow. A void. A puzzle – and a solution.

The disappearance cases had already been investigated.

The family and acquaintances of the three men had been questioned and their last movements checked up until the day they vanished. The cases had dragged on without result. They had not been Wisting's responsibility, but he had watched from the sidelines before having to contend with the Night Man. After that he had been instructed to take a few weeks' holiday and, when he returned, the case files had been put away. Now he had to catch up with reading the extensive investigation material.

He was reorganising the folders, trying to take an overview of the three cases, when there was a knock at the office door. 'Come in!' he shouted.

Espen Mortensen stuck his curly head into the room. 'I'm off,' he said.

Wisting raised his eyebrows.

'To forensics,' continued the crime technician. 'I'm running tests on the reference samples from the family members, so that we can identify the feet.'

Wisting nodded approvingly. He had not managed to gather his thoughts properly yet, but of course it was important to have confirmation that the severed feet belonged to two of the missing persons. 'How have you done it?' he asked.

Mortensen took a few steps into the room. 'Of course, we've got Sverre Lund's DNA profile,' he explained.

Wisting pulled the top folder across the desk towards him and leafed through to a duplicate copy of the yellow ante mortem form. The old head teacher's wife had handed in his toothbrush, so his DNA profile was secured for the future and stored in the register of missing persons. It had not been as simple with the missing people from the care home. By the time the investigators realised that the cases were not going to have a quick resolution their rooms had already been emptied to make way for new patients. The files contained the usual information about height, weight, eye colour, length of hair and so on, together with details about

12

the state of their teeth and their general health, but no DNA profile. None of this information would be sufficient to identify a severed foot.

'It went quite well, really,' Mortensen elaborated. 'Otto Saga's daughter is married to Torkel Lauritzen's son. I went to their home an hour ago, explained the situation and took saliva samples from both.' He paused on his way out of the room. 'In a couple of days we should know who the feet belong to.'

Wisting gazed after him. Coincidental snags in an investigation, such as that two of the missing people were related, could lead to something. Perhaps it had nothing to do with the case, but it was a kind of unevenness that created a type of routine suspicion.

He let his gaze wander in the direction of the window. The office faced westwards, and the sun hung high above the horizon on the sea. Small boats with hoisted sails were crossing the fjord. He fetched himself a cup of coffee before once more settling and starting on the mass of material.

To begin with, he found it difficult to concentrate. He ought to phone Suzanne, but postponed doing so. It would be too much of an effort to discuss his doctor's appointment over the phone.

They had met just over six months previously. He had not thought to establish a new relationship after Ingrid died suddenly almost three years before, but the capricious accidents of life decreed otherwise when an unpleasant case involving two brutal murders brought them together. Without Suzanne it would not have been solved.

He fiddled involuntarily with his wedding ring, feeling the sense of guilt that always overcame him when thoughts of Suzanne mixed with memories of Ingrid. It came over him like a wave. The coffee in his cup was getting cold. He took a big drink and forced himself to become a policeman again.

In the course of several hours he went through the cases again, and by that time his body was filled with tiredness.

13

The air in the office was clammy and close and the sweat from his armpits had spread across his shirt.

His conclusion was that the investigation had been, to put it mildly, somewhat lacking. Several of the staff at the care home with a central role in the men's lives had not been interviewed at all. Most of the work was superficial. No searching questions had been posed. No trace of conflict among the missing men or the people around them had been discovered. No disagreements. No enemies or hostility. No family secrets had been uncovered.

The material gathered was like a smooth surface, but Wisting knew that somewhere underneath there was darkness. It was always there, as it was everywhere. It was just a matter of scraping thoroughly.

There was another knock on the door. Assistant Chief of Police Audun Vetti opened without waiting for an answer. 'A briefing?' he demanded, sitting on the visitor's chair.

Wisting leaned his forearms on the desktop and looked at the man in charge of prosecution services. Audun Vetti wore a newly pressed uniform with stars and hard edges on the shoulders, a signal that he held final authority. He reminded Wisting of the proud teapot in Hans Christian Andersen's fairytale. Self-centred and arrogant, it felt more important than the cups and saucers in the rest of the tea service because it had both a handle and a spout.

Audun Vetti was not the ideal team player. Little inclined to collaborative working or listening to the suggestions of others, he left when difficult decisions had to be made. He had flawed personal insight and was driven by his ambition to climb to the top of the career ladder. At the moment he had an application in for the vacant post of Deputy Chief Constable, and would need a case with a media profile, preferably with a speedy resolution.

Wisting didn't quite remember how the story of the teapot ended, but thought that it had something to do with broken shards of crockery. 'This is what we know,' he said

14

wearily. 'Three old men have been missing without trace for nine months. Two, who were related, lived at Stavern nursing home.' He paused and brought out the envelope with the pictures of the severed feet, spreading them in front of the Assistant Chief of Police before continuing: 'This week we have found two feet, from two different people.'

Vetti picked up one of the pictures and peered at it. 'Do we have a murder case?'

Wisting looked around as though he were afraid that someone was listening, sighed heavily and said, 'Between you and me and these four walls, without a shadow of a doubt.'

4

Line let her eye wander round the room once more. The small kitchen was equipped only with the basic essentials: cupboard, worktops, cooker and fridge. Two high windows looked out to the backyard. Pots of basil, oregano and lemon balm were growing on a herb rack on the windowsill, covering half of the window and the most of the view.

The man on the other side of the table had killed someone fifteen years before, but displayed no signs of guilt or remorse. He leaned backwards in his seat, with a gentle expression round his mouth. Clean-cut, he was well dressed and his hair was carefully groomed. His eyes were thoughtful, and he was breathing steadily. All the same, there was a kind of uneasiness in the room that made her feel uncomfortable, wondering if the whole interview project was a mistake.

The idea, to have conversations with six murderers, five men and one woman who had served almost 100 years altogether in prison, was a good one. She wanted them to talk about all those years of incarceration, the feeling of how time had run slowly past them. Of how each day had been a lost day, and gave them less time for the rest of their lives.

The journalistic angle was to show what punishment had done to them and whether they had become better or worse people. It would place a question mark beside how effective the use of prison as punishment actually is. In a time when the growth of criminality demanded more police with expanded powers, and shocking individual crimes were splashed all over the media, it was easy to call for more severe punishments. It was difficult for people who had not sat in prison to understand what it means to be deprived of your freedom year on year. Punishment was understood by society to be a necessary evil; but Line saw a paradox in this, when it also held the view that helping people in difficult situations, easing their pain and lessening their suffering, was fundamentally right.

Through this project she would question whether severe punishment had a purpose, by showing what happened to people who spent years behind walls. Her hypothesis was that a moderate level of punishment, a milder use of coercion by the state, could contribute to a more humane society.

The article had to be submitted to the weekend magazine by late summer. She had been allocated eight pages and two weeks to travel and conduct the interviews, and the number of pages could be increased if she produced good pictures. Since she was going to work on the project during her holidays as well, she would have five weeks in total. She had set her sights on having the article on the front page.

Henning Mørk was the first interview subject. The file of research material comprised mainly newspaper reports from the days in May 1994, when he had strangled to death a thirteen-year-old boy, Kristian Storås, who was his neighbour. Several of the articles described him as a child murderer. The case had aroused loathing throughout the country.

Henning Mørk had turned twenty six two days before he committed murder, the same age as Line was now. Today he was forty one years old. At the time he had been newly married, his wife was eight months' pregnant and he had a new job in a company that produced powder coatings. His whole future was in front of him. In secret though, he had started a relationship with a childhood sweetheart who had moved into the same street. The newspaper cuttings revealed that while Henning Mørk's wife had been at the maternity clinic the murder victim had discovered him and his lover *in flagrante* in the double bed at the house.

Line had been nervous in advance, but had not expected their meeting to be quite so distasteful. The piercing quality in his dark eyes, and the way he knit his brows and scrutinised her, scared her, quite simply. She could see that he was dangerous, that deep within him there was something dark and unpredictable.

This impression was in sharp contrast with his willingness to participate as an interview subject. He kept to the topic and gave supplementary answers. He was open and honest about life behind walls and the road from prison back into society. He talked about his life of isolation, and did not hide how bitter he was. Now she wanted to go deeper, closer to him.

'What are your thoughts about what you did?' she asked.

Henning Mørk looked at her with his dark eyes, his right hand tightening round the glass in front of him. Line lifted her own glass and drank, as though to take the edge off the question.

'It was a moment's impulsive action,' he answered, clearing his throat. 'It was all over before I could think. For that they took fifteen years of my life.'

'You think the punishment was too severe?'

He drank slowly, staring at her, before putting down the glass. 'I should never have been convicted.'

Line hesitated. 'What do you mean? You *did* commit the murder?'

'I killed him,' Henning Mørk nodded. 'The judge thought that was wrong of me. I disagree.'

Line squirmed in the uncomfortable silence that followed. 'I don't understand . . .' she began. 'Do you mean that it was right of you . . .' Afraid that a direct reminder of what he had done would be provocative she refrained from completing the sentence.

18

'Whether a murder is right or wrong depends on the consequences for those involved,' Henning Mørk elaborated. 'If the consequences, taken together, are good, then the murder is morally justifiable. If the consequences, taken together, are bad, then it's wrong.'

Line frowned. She didn't hide the fact that she had difficulty in following his train of thought.

'Think of a situation in which you could save two people by killing one person. Would it be right or wrong to kill?'

Line admitted to herself that she had not thought about this question thoroughly enough to give an answer. Instead she came back with an objection: 'But of course that was not the case . . .'

'What about avoiding great suffering?' Henning Mørk interrupted. 'Would it not be right to kill one person in order to save many others from long-lasting agony? Wouldn't the sum total of the consequences justify the murder?'

Line did not answer.

'Or think about a healthy person being killed so that his organs could save the lives of other people who need a heart, liver, and kidneys in order to survive. It isn't impossible that such a murder could lead to a better world with several happy lives, rather than a world in which those who need organs have to die instead. Isn't the killing of the healthy person then morally right?'

'Kristian Storås was thirteen years old,' Line reminded him, feeling provoked.

'He was a pain in the neck,' Henning Mørk said dismissively. 'The other children in the street were afraid of him. He bullied them. Beat them up and stole from them, forced the younger children to eat worms and beetles. He sneaked into neighbouring houses and stole money. That was how he ended up at our place. If I hadn't stopped him, nobody knows what kind of person he would have become, but the prognosis wasn't good. His mother had already given up on him.'

19

Henning Mørk leaned forward over the table, excited, his eyes gleaming triumphantly, as though he was convinced that, by killing a child, he had freed the world of a true sadist.

'But all the same . . .' Line continued.

'Wait!' Henning Mørk held up his hand. 'The problem isn't resolved. Exactly nine months after I was convicted, the boy's mother gave birth to a girl. A new child to replace the boy I took from her. She would never have been born, if it hadn't been for me. What about her life? She's 14 years old now. You might well have seen her. She was in one of those talent shows on TV. Played and sang music she had composed herself. Beautiful and clever, neither she nor her mother would have experienced that if her brother hadn't been killed.'

Line did not know what books of philosophy the man in front of her had read while he was inside, but he had an unpleasant viewpoint on life and death. She nodded, as if in agreement, and started to gather her belongings.

'As a journalist, you ought to adopt an impartial attitude,' Henning Mørk went on. 'If you're to be successful with these interviews, you'll have to try to stop seeing events from the murderer's perspective, from the victim's perspective, or from anyone's perspective at all. You must consider all interests to be equally valid and look at the case from the perspective of eternity.'

Line shook her head, but let her reporter's notebook lie. Henning Mørk's thoughts and opinions were going to make it easier for the project to hit the front page. It was going to raise the whole profile.

'I don't understand how you can defend killing a child in order to hide your infidelity,' she said quietly.

'Do you understand why the opponents of abortion in the USA think that it's right to kill the doctors who carry them out? Or why Muslim philosophers are against suicide, but nevertheless consider that people should sacrifice their lives in a holy war? In some countries it's legal to help the old and sick to end their lives, but in other countries you're punished for doing the same thing. Certain societies allow the head of the family to kill family members who have offended unspoken rules of conduct, while others reject that. Some individuals allow the killing and eating of animals, whereas others profess vegetarianism. Some permit the killing of enemies in battle, while others are against that too.'

Line nodded acknowledgement. People did uphold one morality in one area and a completely different one in another. Her facial expression, however, left no doubt about what she felt about using the double standards of the world to support your own actions.

'What about your father?' enquired Henning Mørk abruptly. 'Chief Inspector William Wisting.'

Line straightened up. She was obviously not the only one who had made preliminary enquiries. 'What about him?'

'Is he not also a killer?'

A sudden feeling of nastiness made her feel sick. She stood up to indicate that the interview was over.

Seven years earlier a murder case on which her father was working had ended in armed action. A man who had bestially tortured and murdered a pensioner created a hostage situation in which her father had shot and killed him. SEFO's investigation had absolved Wisting of all blame.

Line had always felt that she could talk to her father about everything, but this case had never been a topic. It was not a secret, but they had never discussed it. She didn't think that he had talked to anyone about it, not even her mother.

Henning Mørk was grinning at her. 'A life is obviously not sacred if you can kill to save your own and go free.'

5

The elm trees encircling the terrace stirred only slightly in the afternoon breeze. Sounds from the town floated up to them, muted at this distance. Suzanne had set the table outside. 'What did the doctor say?' she asked.

Wisting chewed slowly, postponing the discussion for a while longer.

'Hm?' she prompted.

Recently he had felt listless, tired and devoid of energy. He experienced mood swings, and became irritable without any good reason. He had problems concentrating, had lost interest in his work and lacked sufficient initiative even to consult the doctor. It had been Suzanne who finally made the appointment for him.

'The menopause,' he answered briefly and helped himself once again to the salad with pasta and ham.

Suzanne's eyes opened wide. 'The menopause,' she repeated, grinning.

'The doctor wasn't sure, but thought it could be that. It happens to men too. Apparently we produce less testosterone as we grow old.'

She spiked a piece of tomato and winked at him. 'I haven't noticed anything like that.'

Wisting returned her smile. 'In any case, it wasn't diabetes.'

'Did you get something to take?'

'I'll get the results of the blood tests in a few days, perhaps next week. Then I have to go back for a check-up in a fortnight. There are hormone supplements.'

'I can enquire at the health-food shop,' Suzanne suggested. 'They'll certainly have something there.'

Wisting shrugged his shoulders. 'Line is coming tomorrow,' he said, mainly to change the subject. 'I'll go home after work.'

'Very nice. Is she staying long?'

'I don't know. She's on holiday from next week, but is working on a series of interviews for *Verdens Gang*. Among other things, she's meeting a man who lives in Helgeroa. She'll be staying for a couple of days anyway. Tommy's coming home from sea on Thursday.'

'Perhaps we can go out for a meal one evening?'

Wisting reached for a slice of garlic bread. 'I don't know,' he replied, cutting it in two. 'I'm going to be fairly busy at work.'

'A new case?'

He nodded. 'We've found another foot.'

She glanced enquiringly at him.

'From another person,' he continued, sitting down again. 'I'm going to put together a team early tomorrow morning. A murder investigation team.'

6

Inspectors Nils Hammer and Torunn Borg and crime technician Espen Mortensen gathered round the conference table with Assistant Chief of Police Audun Vetti and Eskild Anvik, the Chief Superintendent. Most of the chairs were empty. There were no other people. The atmosphere was uneasy as the investigators leafed through their papers. A kind of tension was in the air, like the feeling that thunder and threatening clouds were on their way.

The Assistant Chief of Police was sitting with the local newspaper open in front of him. The discovery of a new body part was only mentioned in a couple of columns at the bottom of page five, illustrated by a picture of the beach and an archive photo of Audun Vetti himself. Wisting reckoned that he would cut it out when the meeting was over, and keep it in a drawer in his office.

The information that the case now concerned feet from two different people had been held back. The way the newspaper referred to the discovery of the previous day and the follow-up search suggested that none of the editorial staff suspected anything criminal. The find was linked to the disappearances of the previous year, and Audun Vetti was hoping that forensic examinations would confirm that this theory was correct. For once he had kept to what they had agreed should be released at this stage.

The purpose of the meeting was to share information, so that everyone who was going to continue on the case knew exactly where they stood. They had to agree on a plan and a goal. Their eyes turned to Wisting when he spoke.

'Something is going on here that we don't exactly grasp the consequences of right now,' he began. 'For the moment our starting point must be that the feet belong to two of the missing persons. This can't be down to coincidence. The next stage of the investigation should be set up on the basis of a worst case scenario.' A worst case scenario implied that they were embarking on a murder investigation. The others round the table nodded. 'It will be important to achieve three things over the next few days: identify the victims, find the rest of the bodies and determine the cause, or causes, of death.'

'When can identities be established?' the Chief Superintendent asked.

Wisting passed the question to Espen Mortensen.

'The samples were handed in to the forensics laboratory yesterday afternoon,' the crime technician explained. He pushed a copy of the request form across to Wisting, elaborating to the others how he had obtained reference samples for DNA matching from the relatives. 'We'll get an answer by tomorrow lunchtime. In addition we'll have a preliminary report from the pathologist by the end of the day.'

A ray of sunshine crept through the blinds and caught Wisting in the eyes. He went over to the window and adjusted them.

'What will we do about finding the rest of the bodies?' the Chief Superintendent asked as he sat down again.

'The beach searches are continuing today,' Torunn Borg explained. 'I've also got an appointment with a researcher from the Meteorological Institute.' She leafed through her papers. 'An Ebbe Slettaker. He's a specialist in floating objects.'

'You get specialists in that?' Hammer asked.

'They calculate the likely direction of drift for oil spillages, life rafts, cargoes, or people who have fallen into the sea. Slettaker is on holiday in Kragerø, but when he heard what it was about, he agreed to come.'

'When will he arrive?' Wisting enquired.

'I've made an appointment with him for twelve o'clock.'

Wisting nodded and made a note before leafing back a page. 'I've gone through the files of the three missing men,' he said. 'Originally we simply assumed that these were old folks who had got lost and involved in an accident. It will be necessary to do the rounds again with the close family. We'll require a thorough overview of their circles of acquaintances and to chart their last movements.'

Torunn Borg nodded and made a note. It was a task well suited to her ability to order and classify information.

'What about electronic traces?' Vetti asked.

'None of the missing persons had mobile phones,' Torunn Borg explained. 'Telecoms data from the fixed line network hasn't been collected, but is probably with the operators.'

'Strictly speaking we should inform the media too,' Audun Vetti said. He swept his hand over the newspaper page in front of him. 'We depend on tips and information from the public.'

'Let's gain some breathing space first,' Wisting suggested, gripping his coffee cup slightly more tightly. 'The feet have certainly been floating about for months. I propose that we hold back for one more day, so that we can obtain a better overview.'

The Assistant Chief of Police frowned his disagreement. 'We should consider going out in time to catch tonight's evening news,' he argued. 'You should in any case write a note concerning what we want information and details about.'

'We still lack an overview,' Wisting explained, setting his cup down abruptly. He could hear the irritation in his own voice. 'Let's see how the day develops,' he went on diplomatically, turning over a fresh page in his notebook. 'There's something unusual I've noticed in the case files. Several people mention that Camilla Thaulow, one of the carers at the nursing home, had good relationships with the

26

old folk, but she hasn't been interviewed in connection with the missing persons reports.'

'Shall I take that?' Torunn Borg offered.

Wisting shook his head. 'I want to speak to her myself.'

Chief Superintendent Eskild Anvik reached for the picture of Otto Saga that was sticking out from among Wisting's papers and held it up. 'Old men,' he commented. 'Who kills old men?'

No one could give him an answer. Wisting fixed his eyes on the man with thick, white hair in the photo. The eyes were almost black, beneath thick eyebrows, the face dark skinned and full of deep wrinkles and tired furrows. He had lived a long life, with plenty of space for the hiding of many secrets.

7

The waves rolled in on the white shore and glided slowly out again. The man at Wisting's side had researched the movements of seawater for more than twenty years. His eyes narrowed behind thick glasses, biting hard on his bottom lip, he seemed to be concentrating and speculating.

A fine mist blurred the air in front of them, and further on, the sea and sky merged together as though the horizon was a hallucination. A tent had been set up to shelter the search coordinators. Inside, two men stooped over a map, studying the shaded areas indicating the parts of the archipelago that had already been searched.

Wisting took a step back to avoid an approaching wave that was bigger than the others. The man by his side remained standing, following with his eyes how the sea drew it back again. 'One of the feet was found here?' he asked, directing his question to Torunn Borg.

'Six days after the first one,' she confirmed, pointing towards Stavernsøya island where a team of people in orange waistcoats were searching in a chain formation.

'There's a gentle current on the surface,' the oceanographer explained, 'but the speed of the underwater currents will vary greatly. The local underwater topography makes it difficult to calculate the tidal currents.' He pulled up the laptop bag that hung over his shoulder. 'I need to find co-efficients for turbulence exchange and bottom friction,' he continued. 'They will vary with tidal and sea bottom conditions but are, at the same time, characteristics of the movement itself.'

Wisting did not know what he was talking about. 'How accurately will you be able to determine where the feet came from?' he asked.

'It depends on the accuracy of the data I put into the model,' the oceanographer elaborated, patting his shoulder bag. 'I need as much information as possible about the shoes as well: weight, buoyancy, and shape.'

Wisting nodded at crime scene reports in Torunn Borg's hand.

'Water is not a homogenous mass,' the oceanographer continued, taking the papers. 'So there will be no guarantee that my results can be relied on.'

'Will the fact that the feet have been in the sea for nine months make the calculations more difficult?'

'Nine months?' The oceanographer raised his eyebrows. 'That certainly complicates matters.' He looked out to sea again. 'But when you come to think of it, in 1992 a storm washed several containers off the decks of a cargo ship in the Pacific Ocean. One of the containers opened up. It was packed with 28,000 bath toys, among them thousands of yellow plastic ducks. Ten months after the storm, lots of yellow plastic ducks popped up on the shores of Alaska. I used a dynamic, two-dimensional, depth-integrated numerical model to calculate the wave propulsion. In the data simulation, the bath ducks ended up on Knight Island far into the Gulf of Alaska, the same place that most of the ducks were found in reality.'

'Impressive,' Wisting said.

'It's reassuring to have theories confirmed by facts. We usually use buoys equipped with radio signals to study tidal flows, but they are expensive and have a tendency to disappear. Some of the ducks chose to continue their journey, floating very far north. Most were probably caught in Arctic pack ice. Some went in other directions. Six years ago, a yellow duck appeared on a beach in Scotland, and last year a couple more were found in England. It seems the pack ice carried them down the east coast of Canada to be captured by the Gulf Stream and carried to England. It's quite fascinating.'

'Have you found any in Norway?'

'No, but it's an absolute probability that they have reached here. If they've managed to travel on the Gulf Stream to Scotland, then there's nothing to stop them from drifting to the Norwegian coast.'

'Then the feet that were washed ashore here could therefore have come from completely different parts of the world?'

The oceanographer shrugged his shoulders. 'In theory, yes. They could come from a plane crash over the Atlantic Ocean, a shipwreck in the North Sea – or the tsunami in Asia for that matter.'

Wisting was going to say something aloud about how discouraging this information was for the investigation, but was interrupted when the policeman who was leading the search party approached them.

'A find has been reported,' he stated, lifting his police radio as though to explain how he had obtained the information. 'In Skråvika bay.'

'Where's that?' asked the oceanographer.

'On the other side of the peninsula,' Wisting explained, pointing westwards.

8

Dark pine trees with crooked, dense branches surrounded the great stretches of flat land above the small, cleft-shaped inlet. Twisted roots crept over the hillside and down towards the edge of the sea. From as far back as the 1950s, the area had been used for open-air concerts and, in a few weeks' time, stages would be set up once more for a festival which thousands of people would attend and would transform the idyllic place.

Wisting slammed the car door with a feeling of dejection and impotence. Normally a case like this would fire him up. He would be focused and concentrated. This time he didn't know how he was going to lead the team through the extensive work that lay ahead, he felt so tired and lacking in motivation. On his way to the station he stopped at a health-food shop to buy dietary supplements.

The beach had once been popular with bathers because of its fine-grained sand. However, when the sea decided to fill it with large, round boulders, people who liked to swim chose other places. The Red Cross volunteers sat in the shade of the trees. A thin, brown dog lay panting in the heat with its tongue hanging out of its mouth. Wisting ran two fingers around the inside of his collar. His hairline was becoming sweaty.

He had last been here seven years before. Three men had disappeared out of the inlet in a boat together with the 17 million kroner proceeds of a robbery and an important witness was brutally done away with before he could contact the police. Since that time Wisting had asked himself more and more often what was actually going on in the country. The annual number of crimes had more than tripled since he started in the police force and were frequently characterised by senseless violence.

On the boulder-strewn beach two uniformed officers stood in discussion with Nils Hammer. Wisting walked over to them with Torunn Borg and the researcher from the Meteorological Institute, noting the odour of salt sea and rotting seaweed. One of the police officers stopped in the middle of a sentence when Wisting caught his eye, taking a few steps to the side to reveal what the sea had washed ashore.

Wisting stopped. 'Bloody hell,' he cursed.

'Yes,' Hammer said, moving a toothpick from one side of his mouth to the other. 'Exactly. Bloody hell.'

In front of them lay another foot.

Driftwood, empty plastic bottles and pieces of rope lay along the water's edge and, tangled in a cluster of bladder wrack, lay a training shoe. Seaweed had covered and almost completely hidden it. At first sight the shoe did not look different from any other flotsam. Wisting sat on his hunkers and swallowed some phlegm. He had seen the same thing before: grey strings and shreds of skin hanging out of the shoe, fibres of flesh and severed tendons, but this was slightly different. It was a different type of shoe. This one was white, with the three black Adidas stripes along the side. At the same time, it seemed smaller than the two others.

Wisting cocked his head, studying it from slightly different angles to be sure. This, too, was a left shoe. 'Bloody hell,' he said once more and moved away. A nerve at his temple began to pound and he realised it would give him a headache if he didn't do something. He turned irritably towards the Red Cross team. 'What are you sitting there for?' he demanded.

'They've been working since seven o'clock,' Hammer explained. 'They need a break.'

Wisting regretted being so abrupt, but did not say anything further.

Ebbe Slettaker, the oceanographer, produced a little pocket camera.

'Is it okay?' he asked, holding it up in front of Wisting.

'Just don't let the photographs go astray,' he replied. 'Has Mortensen been alerted?'

'He's on his way,' Hammer confirmed.

The oceanographer first took a couple of landscape photographs, in which he captured the inlet and the sea beyond, before venturing nearer the water to take a close-up of the shoe.

'That's good,' he commented, making a note in a book. 'That makes my job easier.'

'What do you mean?'

'It creates more work, of course, but with more finds it becomes easier to reach a qualified conclusion. It's like taking a cross-reference bearing. The more reference points, the more accurate the answer will be.'

These comments made Wisting feel more favourably disposed to the world. In principle the oceanographer was right. The same applied to investigation work. Three murders were easier to clear up than two, with more chance that the perpetrator had left traces and clues. Tiny details connected to each individual discovery told a different part of a single story.

'Of course, I don't know if I can be of help,' the oceanographer went on, adjusting his glasses. 'Obviously I'll do my best, but the most logical explanation is probably that, somewhere out at sea, there's a bag of severed body parts that someone has dumped from a boat. The first parts have worked themselves loose but, in all likelihood, more will be washed ashore in the next few days. I'll have to be kept informed.'

Wisting turned to the group of Red Cross volunteers again, watching everything that the policemen on the shore were doing, but the search was not going to start again until they had finished their business. The thought of severed body parts floating around in the sea made Wisting feel unwell. It was 23rd June, St. John's Eve. The fjord would be filled with boats this evening. People would be gathering in lively company on all of the little islands and skerries, ready to light bonfires and celebrate midsummer. At the weekend, the trades holiday fortnight would begin. Summer cottage folk and camping tourists would double the population.

Espen Mortensen's crime scene vehicle swung onto the grassy area above them. The Assistant Chief of Police was first out, trotting down towards them, balancing on the round boulders, to stop about a metre from the severed foot. It looked as if he had difficulty controlling his facial expression. 'Another one?' he said finally, taking a grip round his own neck.

'I think the meteorologist is right,' Hammer said, nodding towards the marine researcher.

'I'm not a meteorologist,' Ebbe Slettaker corrected him, adjusting his glasses once more. 'I'm an oceanographer.'

'It's all the same to me,' Hammer smiled, spitting out a splinter of wood from his toothpick. 'But I think you're right.' He turned to face the sea. 'Somewhere or other out there there's a bin-bag full of body parts.'

The Assistant Chief of Police stood with an astonished expression on his bony face. Then he turned towards Wisting. 'I have raised the matter with the Public Prosecutor,' he said. 'There will be a press conference this afternoon. We have to release information about all this. Only by doing that will we get the responses we need.'

Wisting moved back a few steps to let Mortensen through with his equipment case. Right now he was not sure whether they had many more stones to unturn among the earlier investigative work, but he was not in disagreement. This case could well turn on an unknown someone coming forward.

9

Line parked on the stone-covered courtyard in front of the house in Herman Wildenveysgate.

She still thought of it as coming home, even though she had not lived here for almost six years. Moving to Oslo when she was twenty, she had begun studying media and communications but, after a year, had become fed up with schoolbooks and the curriculum. She wanted to gain practical experience and took a temporary job on her local newspaper back home. Finding a bed-sit in the town, she quickly realised that writing was what she really wanted to do.

The temporary post at *Østlandsposten* was like a door opening, just a crack, and she did not take long to step through. The profession of journalism suited her inquisitiveness and critical faculties. She got good responses to her work, her headlines increased in number and size, and quite soon she moved to another temporary post at *Verdens Gang* newspaper in Oslo. Her contract had been extended three times and, although newspapers throughout the country were cutting back, she hoped in time to win a permanent appointment. Someone, after all, would have to replace the sly old foxes when they eventually retired. She had already achieved one of *VG*'s 'golden pen' awards and, the year previously, she had been awarded the national SKUP prize for investigative journalism for her exposure of an international drugs network that used under-age asylum seekers for smuggling throughout Europe.

By taking a one-year course of study on the internet, she

had acquired a formal qualification, and after Easter had added to the sixty study points with a further course in features journalism. This aspect of the profession attracted her increasingly, not just the reporting of news but the telling of a story. Her talent for giving the material a personal voice had taken her into the features department.

She got out of the car and took out a bunch of keys on which she still had her old key. It always gave her a pang of homesickness to look at the brown-stained house with white window-frames. The garden had not been well looked after since her mother's death, but it was still growing, ivy still climbed the walls around the entrance, framing the front door.

When she was in her hometown she usually stayed at Tommy Kvanter's flat in the centre. They had been in the same class at times during primary and junior high school, but had not seen each other for ten years until they met again the previous autumn while Line was covering a murder case. Since then they had spent a lot of time together, but the relationship had not blossomed sufficiently to feel they were a couple. Work and studies meant she had to push such thoughts aside. Perhaps she also had to admit that they did not really suit each other so well. Tommy was impulsive and went his own way. He lived without worries and sometimes showed an unpredictable spontaneity, with a lifestyle that brought him into social circles that scared her. He had two prison sentences behind him, the longer of which was a year and a half for importing five kilos of hashish. In all likelihood, this was the real reason that she did not see a long future together.

His spontaneity was attractive and frightening at the same time. She envied his ability to live in the moment, and when they were together, many of her worries about the future disappeared.

Tommy worked as a chef on a Danish factory trawler that fished for prawns around Greenland. He was out for two weeks at a time. She had her own key to his flat, but she didn't like to stay when he was not at home. Neither of them was particularly happy about the commuting job that meant long spells apart. More often these days, Tommy talked about coming ashore and moving in with her in Oslo, where he could get a job in a restaurant. She didn't know if she really liked the suggestion.

Unlocking the door of the house she continued to think of as home she kicked off her shoes in the hallway. Her father had not installed a burglar alarm as most of his neighbours had done and she had mentioned it to him a couple of times. Last winter, she had worked on a series of articles about migrant criminals from Eastern Europe who broke into houses and helped themselves to everything of value. Next day they could be in a completely different part of the country, the stolen goods already far, far away. Her father's house was in a beautiful situation on the hillside above Stavern, and would probably interest that kind of criminal. Furthermore, it lay empty for most hours of the day and night. He spent a lot of time at work, and she knew that he also spent evenings and holidays with Suzanne Bjerke, whom he had met at the same time that she herself had met Tommy Kvanter.

It was clean and tidy inside the house, smelling just as she remembered. Her father had most likely spent a few hours the evening before tidying up, knowing she was coming.

She carried her bag containing a change of clothes up to her old room on the first floor and then went down to the kitchen. She got a glass out of the cupboard and filled it with water from the tap. Tap water here tasted cleaner and fresher than in Oslo, but then it was the water from the *Farris* spring. She cleared away a coffee cup her father had left lying and took out her portable computer and research file, as usual using the big kitchen table as a work area.

Her next interview subject was called Ken Ronny Hauge. It really was a typical name for a villain, she thought. In

38

many of the criminal cases she worked on, the culprit had a double-barrelled name – for one reason or another, the phonetics made her associate it with criminals. There was Ken Arvid, Roy Tore, Jim Raymond, and Tom Roger. Tommy was also a name that she had often come across in forensic reports, when she thought about it.

Ken Ronny Hauge was the most fascinating person on her list of interview subjects. On the night of 23rd September 1991, he had shot and killed a policeman. The case was one of Line's earliest recollections. Her father had bought all of the Oslo newspapers while the case was on the front pages and both parents followed the reports on television and radio.

The murdered policeman was called Edgar Bisjord and had been the same age as her father. They had gone on a few in-service courses together. Edgar Bisjord had worked at the district sheriff's office in Øvre Eiker. He was called out from home because of a traffic accident on the main route 35 south of Vestføssen, but the actual accident was a routine matter. He helped the two parties to fill out the claim report form and left the scene as soon as the damaged vehicles were towed away, but never arrived home. The following day his police car was found at a turning area at the end of a little side road near Eikeren and Edgar Bisjord lay three metres away with three bullet holes in his chest.

Line had been eight years old at the time and frightened that something similar might happen to her father. She screamed when he went to work and, all these years later, could still remember the clammy feeling of anxiety. Her feelings didn't improve when she learned that the perpetrator was from Helgeroa, only ten minutes away. His escape route could have been through Stavern and past the house where Line had been lying asleep.

Ken Ronny Hauge was captured that same evening, and it was sixteen years before he was a free man again. By then he had served more than the legally required two-thirds of his sentence. When Line looked him up she discovered that he had chosen to move back to his hometown, although many people would remember who he was. That surprised her, but almost a generation had gone by since the murder. Moreover, the world had experienced worse and more brutal cases in subsequent years.

When she had phoned him three weeks before, he listened with interest as she explained that the aim of her series was to illuminate the negative aspects of punishment by imprisonment. The often pointless activities and the slow, hard road back into society. She rather hoped that the matter might become an issue in the election campaign that autumn.

Ken Ronny Hauge's had been the last name on her list. Prior to him, seven people had said no thanks, but she had learned how to express herself and what she should emphasise to persuade them. He had agreed to an interview, but made it a condition that he remain anonymous. That was not a problem. Two of the other ex-convicts had supplied names and photographs. It just made the feature more dramatic if she could illustrate it with another kind of picture, something like nicotine-yellow fingers round a coffee cup, a pair of clenched fists, a bowed neck with grey hair, or a close-up of a prison tattoo.

She took a picture of Ken Ronny Hauge from the folder, an old one from *VG*'s picture library. The day after his arrest it had been appeared on the front page beneath the headline POLICE MURDERER. In considerably smaller print, there was another line stating: *Believed to be*, so the editor could defend the label. It was this label that made her doubt whether Ken Ronny would agree to the interview. Several of those who had declined had claimed that the newspaper had condemned them in advance and had a one-sided view of their cases.

The picture looked like a school photograph, probably from his final year at Larvik technical college where he had trained as a car mechanic. She well knew how the newspaper worked. They had probably looked up someone who had been in his class at school and bought the photo for one or two thousand kroner. She didn't see anything unethical about it. Newspapers and news bureaux bought pictures all the time. Nevertheless, she was pleased that she was not the person who had to take responsibility for putting such pictures into print. The justification was nothing other than sensationalist, and caused unnecessary stress for the subject's family.

He was handsome, she decided. That was also perhaps the reason that the picture had been printed on the front page. There was a great contrast between the young man's appearance and the gruesome crime he had committed. His hair was dark, smooth and cut short. He had an intelligent face with dark eyes that suggested he was not completely of Norwegian extraction. From other papers in the folder, Line knew that his mother was called Liv, but his father's name had not been given.

Ken Ronny was the older of two sons. His younger brother was now 35 years old and, as far as Line could discover, had never been involved in any criminal activity. He ran a company that supplied machinery to the stone industry, was married and had two daughters.

Ken Ronny's mother had been found dead in the harbour almost exactly a year after he had been arrested. The death was described as a drowning accident. Line wondered if the journalist who had splashed the picture of Ken Ronny over the front page had been aware of the incident. It was probably a final way out that she had chosen after failing to drink away her sorrow and despair.

There were several aspects of the police murder that made it unusual, the most disquieting being that Ken Ronny Hauge had never admitted guilt or given any explanation about what happened that dark September night in 1991. Not once during the trial had he offered any explanation.

Line was to interview him on Friday and was excited about what he might have to say, but met his gaze from the photograph with a slight sense of dread. She thought of all the evenings she had lain in bed as a little girl without being able to fall asleep, praying to God that the *Police Murderer* would not take her father too. Interviewing him would be like going to meet a danger from the past.

10

Afternoon sunshine trickled through the venetian blinds, throwing stripes of light across the overflowing desk in Wisting's office.

He unscrewed the cap on a container of tablets for which he had paid almost four hundred kroner in the health-food shop, and examined the contents. The expensive pills contained roseroot (rhodiola rosea) and other herbs. According to the product description, the pale capsules would increase his tolerance of stress, stimulate physical and psychological performance, and produce higher levels of energy and vigour. In addition, they would improve concentration and memory, at the same time having a positive effect on mood and motivation.

Everything he needed.

He shook two capsules onto his palm and swallowed them without water while reading through the press release he had written. It was too late to change it. The information had already been sent to a dozen or so editorial offices, and would be disseminated via the news bureaux to all the newspapers in the country.

The text briefly summed up the facts of the case, describing the finding of the three severed feet, giving time and place and confirming that the most likely scenario involved body parts from three different people. In the next paragraph it explained about the four people who had gone missing in the area, and that the discoveries were being checked against these. There was nevertheless still a possibility that the body parts had come from far away. He had

43

also added the stock phrase about the police keeping all possibilities open, but did not exclude the possibility of a criminal act and had initiated appropriate lines of enquiry.

Finally, he had announced a press conference to be held at the police station at eight o'clock that same evening. This meant that the news editors had three hours to reflect. It was St John's Eve and several papers would have only a skeleton staff, but he knew that the press release would set off a landslide. Teams of reporters from Oslo and the news departments of the various television companies were in all likelihood already starting to pack their cars.

Wisting rubbed his eyes with his thumb and forefinger. They would not have a single quiet moment after this.

Audun Vetti had asked that his name be listed as both sender and contact person for the press. Telephone numbers for his mobile and office were also given. It was stipulated that information beyond what was stated in the press release would not be released before the press conference. The Assistant Police Chief's telephone would not remain silent. Wisting was glad that he could avoid answering endless repeats of the same questions, but knew that the most experienced journalists would manage to reach him too.

He reached over for the half-empty coffee cup, gulped the cold liquid and pulled the bundle of case files towards him. It was time to set the ball rolling.

He decided to start with Camilla Thaulow at Stavern nursing home and leafed through the files for her telephone number. She had known two of the missing men well. Described as an especially caring nurse she often took time to have long conversations with her patients. Nevertheless, she had not been interviewed.

He tried to phone her twice in order to make an appointment, without success. Keying in her number once more he was transferred to voicemail but did not leave a request to get in touch.

He felt the beginnings of a headache inside his temple

that he knew would soon spread and explode inside his skull. Taking out the glasses he was not good at remembering to wear he turned towards his computer screen. It could be that Camilla Thaulow had taken a new phone number in the months that had passed since the investigation. Perhaps she had a home phone too, without it being listed in the case files.

His computer opened at the last thing he had been doing, looking up the keywords *low testosterone level* on the internet. Most of the answers contained the same information that he had received from his doctor the day before, and focused on problems with lack of potency, listlessness and depression. Some of the search results had also included the word *tumour* and led him to the home page of *Kreftforeningen*, the national cancer organisation.

He hurriedly clicked it away and looked up Camilla Thaulow in the telephone directory. She lived in Markaveien in Langangen, but had no phone numbers listed other than the one he had already rung.

He clicked further into the net pages of the local newspaper, saved in his favourites section. The press release was already doing its work. The Internet Editor had chosen INVESTIGATING MURDER as the headline. Wisting managed to discover that the newspaper had been in touch with Assistant Chief of Police Audun Vetti, who had confirmed that a murder investigation was under way.

His mobile phone rang. The circus had begun.

Line stretched her arms in the air and yawned, details from the old newspaper reports still running through her head. She had worked with great concentration on the cuttings and made a plan for meeting the police murderer Ken Ronny Hauge. Feeling hungry, she glanced at the clock on the wall. Almost two hours had gone by. Her father should be home by now.

She opened the refrigerator and noted that he had done

his shopping with her in mind. There were new sandwich toppings, cheese, two slices of beef, and a carton of milk. Her father did not drink milk. She had almost stopped as well, but he still thought that she needed a glass every morning and always bought some in when he knew she was coming.

She took a couple of tomatoes from the drawer at the bottom back to the computer. Fresh juice ran out of the corners of her mouth when she bit into them. She sucked it in, dried her mouth with the back of her hand and chewed some more while clicking into *Verdens Gang* on the net. She remained sitting with her mouth half-open as she read the headline: MURDER ALARM SOUNDED IN STAVERN. On the next line, in slightly smaller type, it stated: *Body parts wash ashore on the beaches*.

She put the half-eaten tomato aside and scrolled down through the text, but had not managed to read all of it before the telephone rang. It was Morten Pludowski from the news section. They had worked together on several criminal cases, but had not spoken since Line had been transferred to the features department.

'Have you read about it?' he asked, without introducing himself.

'I'm reading it now.'

'Do you know anything about it?'

'No more than what it says on the net newspaper.'

'Where are you?'

'At home.' She hesitated before adding: 'In Larvik.'

'Wonderful. I'm on my way down.'

'But I'm working on something completely different,' Line protested. 'I have appointments that I can't change. I can't take part in this. I don't want to either. It will make things difficult with Dad.'

'That's ok. We're coming with a team. I just want you to be aware that if you get to know anything I hope you'll phone me.'

46

'Of course. Goes without saying.'

'And I'd like to have a cup of coffee with you when I arrive down there.' He paused for a moment. 'I miss you.'

Line didn't know if it was true or flattery, but realised that she missed Morten P. as well. He had been working on crime stories for over twenty years, but from day one had never had any problem about taking Line with him to accidents and crime scenes. They had good chemistry, and she had learned a great deal from him.

'I miss you too,' she replied. 'Perhaps we can try for lunch tomorrow?'

'I'll phone you if I'm free.' Someone was shouting in the background. 'Now I have to go. Speak later.'

'Good luck!'

The connection was cut, and Line remained sitting with a tingling feeling in her stomach. She would give a lot to take part in the case, but did not have any wish to cover a murder investigation that her father was leading. She had done that only once, and it had been too exhausting for her to want it to happen again. She fiddled with the phone for a while, and then keyed in his number.

'Yes?' answered Wisting abruptly, not bothering to check the display for who was calling.

'Hello, Dad. It's me.'

Some quick thoughts raced through Wisting's head. They had not actually made any arrangement, but he had pre-pared dinner and was looking forward to meeting her later. 'Line,' he said, smiling. 'Where are you?'

'At home. I arrived a couple of hours ago.'

'Yes, I'm sorry about that. I should have phoned you . . .'

'I've seen the headlines,' Line interrupted. 'No need to think about me.'

'There's some food in the fridge . . .'

'I'll manage. Is everything ok with you?'

'Oh yes, of course, we'll manage all right as well,' he confirmed, without entirely believing it. 'You won't be working on this?'

'No, I'm in another department now, you know.'

It went a bit quiet.

'Have you let Buster in?' Wisting enquired, changing the subject. He had taken over the black male cat from Line almost three years previously. Buster had grown big and round, and never ventured very far from home.

'No, I haven't seen him.'

'He'll come if you call him,' Wisting said. 'What will you do this evening?'

'I haven't thought about it yet. Perhaps I'll phone some girlfriends but most will probably be busy. They have husbands and children. Maybe I'll go for a drive to the beaches.'

Wisting's office door opened. Audun Vetti entered, together with the Chief Superintendent. 'Sounds like a good idea.' He waved to the Assistant Chief of Police to invite him to sit in the visitor's chair. 'I've got people in the office now,' he went on. 'We'll talk this evening.'

Vetti sat down, but the Chief Superintendent went to the window and stared out. Wisting concluded the telephone conversation.

'They want pictures,' the Assistant Chief of Police said.

'Pictures?'

'Of the shoes.'

Of course, thought Wisting. Of course they want pictures. He did not say anything, but closed his eyes, reflecting. He had discussed the use of pictures in the newspapers many times with Line, and understood how important they were to the press. The police also might have an interest in ensuring that a case received a higher profile in the news. Dramatic photographs led to increased attention, and a greater possibility that someone out there who held information would make contact.

This case would be at the top of the news regardless, and he was doubtful about publicising anything sensational. At the same time, it was of interest to the investigation. They still did not know who the severed feet belonged to and by making pictures of the shoes public they might prompt a response. And there were pictures in Mortensen's folders of illustrations in which human material was not visible.

'We must have something more to show than we have already described in the press release,' Vetti argued.

'I'll arrange something,' Wisting promised. 'And I'll make a summary of what we know about shoe sizes, manufacture, and so forth.'

The telephone on his desk rang again. He did not recognise the number and waited until Vetti had moved to the door before he lifted the receiver. The Chief Superintendent remained by the window.

'Wait!' Wisting said into the phone before laying his hand over the receiver and glancing enquiringly at him.

The Chief Superintendent waited until Vetti had left the office, then turned to face him. 'I'd like you to show up at the press conference,' he requested. Wisting never felt comfortable in meetings with a massive press corps, but could not find an argument against his attending. His body language expressed his reluctance. 'We need someone there that people depend on.' He threw a glance towards the open door. 'Someone they feel confident can find a way out of all this.'

Wisting knitted his brows.

'That is you, William, as you have demonstrated before. You have the necessary personal authority.' He stepped towards the door. 'Eight o'clock,' he said with a nod and went out.

Wisting looked after him, and then returned his attention to the telephone. 'Yes?'

'I'll make it brief,' the man who had been waiting at the other end began. 'I'm calling from the crime watch section in

49

Grenland.' He cleared his throat and introduced himself: 'Kvastmo, Vetle Kvastmo. I understand that you've got a lot to deal with just now, but that's why I'm phoning.'

'Well then?'

'It probably doesn't have any connection, but we received a report about a missing person this morning.'

'Well then?' Wisting repeated.

We're talking about a lady from Langangen who didn't come home last night. The point is that she works at the care home for the elderly where two men in your case have been reported missing. She did not turn up for the evening shift yesterday either.'

Wisting felt a nerve in his temple start to vibrate, anticipating what was coming. 'Her name?' he asked.

'Thaulow. Her name is Camilla Thaulow.'

11

Wisting sat in the front passenger seat of the police car and leafed through the papers he had received by fax, a short report that had been recorded at 09.23 hours earlier that day. The woman who had been reported missing was the same person that he had tried repeatedly to contact by telephone.

Camilla Thaulow was 58 years of age and lived with her mother in Langangen, a small village of over 500 inhabitants, on the Telemark side, and right on the county border. It seemed that she had left home about two o'clock the previous afternoon to work the afternoon shift at Stavern nursing home. Her mother had gone to bed early and did not discover until the next day that her daughter's bed had not been slept in. She had called her mobile but received no answer. After that she phoned the home for the elderly to learn that her daughter had not turned up for work. Later, the mother had asked advice from a friend and agreed that she should phone the police.

The new missing person case could, of course, simply be an accident. She could have driven off the road and be lying in a ditch, out of sight of the traffic. The old road through Tvedalen and on towards Stavern was winding and narrow, and in a few places there was no safety barrier. However, they were already working on three similar disappearances and, statistically speaking, it was like coming up with a royal flush several times in a row. Wisting did not believe that this disappearance was simply another coincidence in a series, and was anxious to start investigating.

Langangen lay only a quarter of an hour's drive from the police station, but Wisting had not been to the little place for years. Like most people, he drove past at top speed on the motorway bridge that ran between the hillsides.

Torunn Borg was driving, and he was pleased to have her as she had a special empathy with relatives. If it was not established in the course of a few hours that Camilla Thaulow had skipped her job and stayed overnight at a friend's house or that she was the victim of an accident, her 84-year-old mother might not only play a central role in the investigation but also be a media focus. Wisting knew from experience what a great strain that could be for the family of the missing person, and old people often had less strength to resist. Anxiety and insecurity, anger and displacement were common reactions, and it could become more difficult to extract important information. At such times the role of the police also entailed providing care and support.

'Number 23,' Torunn Borg said aloud, stopping the car close to a white picket fence that enclosed a large but simple garden.

The house was half hidden behind a couple of tall elms, and the shadow from the treetops made the white walls dark grey. The iron gate squeaked and there was a crunching sound as they strolled along the gravel path. Somewhere far off, children were laughing.

A thin lady with her hair pulled back in a tight, grey bun peeked out from behind the window curtains before they reached the door. Wisting knocked and heard her move slowly on the inside before a key was turned. A little, wrinkled face appeared at the crack in the door, with small eyes that lay in deep hollows.

'Yes?'

A seam of wrinkles appeared around her narrow lips. Wisting could actually hear that her mouth was dry, she had such difficulty speaking.

In a raised voice he explained who they were and gave the

old woman a grateful nod as she waved them in. She was hunchbacked and supported herself with difficulty on the furniture as she led with small steps into a light and spacious living room with a view over the fjord.

'Coffee?' she asked, supporting herself on the backrest of a chair.

Wisting declined and sat beside the coffee table. The furniture in the house was old and faded, but smelled clean and pleasant. Torunn Borg took out a notebook and sat in a chair beside him.

'We have some questions for you about Camilla,' he said. 'Won't you sit down?'

The woman's blue, bloodless lips trembled as she sat painfully down. 'My body is full of aches and pains,' she explained. 'I'm not young any longer, but there's nothing wrong with my head all the same.'

Wisting smiled.

'She's gone,' the old woman continued. 'That's something I'm not muddled about.'

'She's gone,' Wisting agreed. 'We'll try to find her.'

The old woman mumbled her thanks, smoothing the pleats in her skirt.

'When did you last talk to her?'

'Yesterday,' the woman sighed. 'She was going to work.'

'When did she leave?'

'Just before two o'clock.' She cleared her throat. 'She doesn't usually leave before about half past three. The evening shift doesn't start until four, but there was something she wanted to do. We like to eat together before she leaves, but yesterday we only managed a cup of coffee.'

Wisting glanced over at Torunn Borg. Any irregularity in the daily routine was important to understand. 'What was it she wanted to do?'

The old woman closed her eyes for a short time, thinking carefully. 'She usually tells me everything,' she said, opening her eyes again. 'But not about men.'

Wisting wanted to ask a question, but stayed silent, waiting for her to continue at her own pace.

'Five years ago she had a beau,' the old lady went on. 'Then she became secretive. Didn't say where she was going or what she was doing. But I didn't think it would happen again. She was burned.'

'How was that?'

'I don't know what happened. She loaned him money that never came back. That was all he was after. Money.' She moistened her lips with her tongue. 'She was burned,' she repeated. 'Swindled.'

'How much money?'

The old woman swallowed. 'She never talked about it, but I think it was everything she had.'

Torunn Borg straightened herself up in the chair. 'Do you know his name?' she enquired.

'Gunnar Moland, I think. I have it written down some-where. He said he was a medical intern, but that wasn't true.' She shook her head slowly. 'But that was long ago. She has got over it.'

'Did she have a new man?'

The old woman looked down at her lap and she clasped her wrinkled hands. 'Who knows,' was her mumbled response. 'She used to have a pen pal, but what she has now I don't know.'

'Pen pal?'

'It was a few years ago, when people still wrote letters. A letter with sloping handwriting arrived every other week. Then that came to an end too.'

'You don't know who they were from?'

'No. We didn't talk about such things. I think she met him a few times as well. She drove off early in the morning and was back in the evening. He must live a distance away, but not so far that she had to stay overnight.'

Wisting rose from his seat. 'Can I look around?' he asked.

He got a quick nod in reply and left the room. Torunn

Borg stayed with the old woman to go through the list of routine questions.

Mother and daughter each had their own bedroom on the ground floor, with a bathroom across the corridor. The first floor didn't look as though it had been used for a long time. It consisted of a loft room where white sheets had been draped over the furniture, and three locked rooms where old clothes and cardboard boxes of books were stored.

The daughter's bedroom was the largest. In addition to the single bed with its bedside table, there was just enough room for a writing desk, a small sitting area and a television. Three pictures hung on the walls, all depicting a woman whom Wisting assumed must be Camilla Thaulow. Two were in nurse's uniform, probably taken in her student days, and a more recent one of her sitting in a verdant garden. Like her mother she had friendly, twinkling eyes that looked directly out of the frame.

He sat beside the desk and pulled out drawer after drawer. The contents were tidy. There were household accounts, insurance papers, income tax returns and old photo albums. Nothing seemed particularly interesting, so he put them aside to go through more thoroughly later.

A book lay on the bedside table, a piece of paper sticking out from between the last pages. Wisting lifted it up. *Coincidences* by Charlie Lie. The slip of paper marked page 316. It was a folded post-it note with nothing written on it, a chance bookmark. He sat on the bed and leafed back through to the end. She had 32 pages left. Presumably she had thought to finish it yesterday evening.

The drawer of the bedside table contained a packet of lozenges, paper hankies, a tube of hand cream and a poetry collection. Wisting remained seated, looking around, feeling that, somehow, the direction of the case had shifted.

12

The press conference had begun when Wisting got back to the police station. Through the glass wall and voile curtains of the conference room he saw Audun Vetti holding up two pictures of shoes, one in each hand. The room was full. Journalists sat with laptops on their knees, writing up the first released details. He counted five cameras with red lights.

He walked forward quickly and shut himself into the capacious toilet for the disabled. Turning on the water tap he let it run until it was cold, rinsed his face but felt no better. The mirror above the wash-hand basin showed the face of a tired man and, for the first time, he thought of himself as old. He was 51. His hair had become thinner and lighter, and the corners of his eyes were bracketed by small wrinkles.

This is not a job that keeps you young, he thought, nor is it a job in which you become old.

The team gathered in Wisting's office as soon as the last of the press corps were out of the building. Torunn sat in one of the visitors' chairs while Hammer hoisted himself onto the window ledge. He opened the window and let in some cool evening air and the scent of the pale yellow blossoms from the chestnut tree in the back yard. The sounds of an orchestra playing in the outdoor restaurant at the Grand Hotel stole in towards them. The Chief Superintendent stood beside the wall with his arm leaning on the filing cabinet.

Audun Vetti took the last visitors' chair. 'I wanted you here at eight o'clock,' said the Chief Superintendent.

Wisting disregarded him. 'It's happened again,' he said.

Vetti frowned. 'What do you mean?'

'We have a new disappearance,' Wisting explained, and gave an account of his last few hours. 'She was last seen when she left home yesterday around two o'clock in the afternoon.'

'What do we do?' the Chief Superintendent asked, loosening his tie.

'She drives a red Ford Fiesta,' said Torunn Borg. 'The patrols are looking for it along the roads between Stavern and Langangen.'

'How long should we wait before issuing a public bulletin?'

Wisting shrugged his shoulders. 'Until tomorrow?' he suggested.

Torunn Borg leafed through a bundle of papers on her lap and produced a printout. 'The police response centre at *Telenor* has traced her phone. It is either switched off or out of charge. The last time it gave a signal was yesterday evening about ten o'clock. At that time it was in Helgeroa.'

'In our district,' the Chief Superintendent concluded. 'She's here somewhere.'

'We'll concentrate the search in that area.'

'What about a helicopter?'

'The police helicopter is not in operation just now, but they're coming tomorrow.'

'Who has she spoken to on the phone?' Hammer asked.

Wisting leaned over across the office desk, knowing Camilla Thaulow's network of contacts might provide a decisive clue.

'No one,' Torunn Borg replied.

Wisting glanced at her enquiringly.

'She hardly ever talks on her mobile phone. In the course of the past few weeks she had three outgoing calls. Two home to her mother and one to her work. No ingoing calls.

If she had arranged to meet someone, she didn't make the arrangement by phone.'

They remained sitting for ten minutes more, discussing the case without any new ideas emerging, before they went their different ways to finish off the day's work.

Wisting stared through the window that Hammer had left open. The light summer night was waiting. The longest day of the year was behind him. Around the fjord the Midsummer Eve bonfires were already lit, as a warning of the shorter and darker days to follow.

So far he had not speculated on what might actually have happened. What lay behind the discovery of three amputated feet? Murder and foul play were seldom rational actions, but it was usually possible to find an explanation. In many cases it was easy to form at least an impression of what had taken place, and a theory about the sequence of events. In this case though, he was stuck and couldn't come up with anything logical. It frightened him. One alternative was that a completely sick human mind was behind it all. A human being whose actions were impossible to understand, and therefore also impossible to anticipate.

The telephone drummed against the writing desk and broke his gloomy train of thought. He had turned off the ring tone while they were holding the meeting. It was Suzanne. He should have phoned her earlier but there simply hadn't been time.

'How are things?' she asked.

'I'm just finishing up for the day.' He closed the window.

'I've made some salad with shellfish. It's too much for just me.' Her voice sounded hopeful.

'That sounds good, but I think I'll go straight home and get some sleep. Tomorrow will be another long day. Besides, Line's at home.'

'How are you feeling?'

'So-so.'

'Have you had the results of the blood tests?'

'No, that'll take a few days.'

They made small talk as Wisting closed the office and locked the door. When he reached his car they said good night.

Concentrating more on his own thoughts than the traffic he drove slowly towards Stavern. He couldn't remember so chaotic a case. Everything seemed so meaningless and improbable it was difficult to know where to begin, or how to make best use of their slender resources.

The fjord was filled with small craft. People gathered together on little islands and skerries, the light from their midsummer bonfires reflected on the sea. He sighed heavily, switched on the car radio and drummed his fingers on the steering wheel to an old summertime hit.

At home the courtyard was empty. He parked in such a way that Line would have space to park without blocking him in. Evening darkness was closing in. The cat came creeping out from behind the hedge and stroked his head against Wisting's leg. He bent down and scratched him behind the ear before opening the door, deciding to set his alarm for six o'clock.

The kitchen table was filled with Line's notes, which he glanced at while looking out the cat's dinner. He filled the cat's dish and stood in front of the table reading the old headlines proclaiming brutal murder. Most of the cases he recognised. The police murder at Eikeren being one. He had known that she was working on a series of interviews and had an appointment with a man in Helgeroa. Now he realised she had been talking about Ken Ronny Hauge. It must be almost twenty years. He didn't know that the man had moved back.

There were several other cases, such as the murder of 37-year-old Stine Nymann in 1989, raped and strangled in a park in Mysen. It was not one of the most brutal murders in history, but memorable because it was the first case in Norway in which DNA had been used as evidence.

One of her other interview subjects was obviously Åge Reinholdt, who had killed twice in his life. In 1974, when he was 23 years of age, he murdered his girlfriend with a knife in a drunken quarrel. That got him eleven years behind bars. Ten years after he was freed, he did the same thing again, and a live-in partner the same age as he was, in Romerike, died of eleven knife wounds. It was evidence of an uncontrollable rage.

The darkest aspects of the human psyche were portrayed in the newspaper reports and he didn't like the idea of his daughter empathising with such men or excusing the misery they caused.

When Buster was full he stretched and padded off to the living room. Wisting opened the refrigerator, which was rarely so well filled, and contemplated whether he should fry the slices of beef. Looking at the time, he decided that it was too late. According to the date stamp they would last another couple of days.

There was a noise at the front door and Line called from the hallway. He greeted her with a hug. 'Are you hungry?'

'No,' she answered, taking off her shoes. 'I ate out.'

'I just need to have a sandwich.'

She followed him into the kitchen. 'I didn't mean to leave all this mess,' she apologised, starting to tidy up all her paperwork.

'Let it lie,' Wisting waved her away. 'I'll eat in the living room.'

He buttered himself a couple of slices and put them on a plate. Line filled a glass with milk. 'Are you going to interview all of them?' he asked, nodding towards the kitchen table.

'That's the idea.'

'Most people would give a lot to avoid having anything to do with any of them.'

Line drank from her glass. 'I'm obviously not like most people, then,' she smiled, wiping round her mouth with the back of her hand. 'Do you remember the police murder in 1991?'

Wisting nodded. 'I saw the newspaper cutting. Has he been freed already?'

'He got 21 years, but was released on licence a year and a half ago. Moved back home to Helgeroa. I've an appointment with him on Friday.'

'Are you sure you want to do this?'

Line gave no reply. 'How many murderers have *you* talked to?' she asked.

Wisting took a bite of his sandwich and chewed while he thought.

'Eight,' he answered, swallowing. From some place or other came a thought that there had been more murderers than women in his life.

'Are there any of them who have killed more than once?'

'You know that of course. You've written about some of the cases. A new murder is committed in order to cover up the first one.'

'Yes, but I'm thinking about whether anyone has killed again *after* they have served their sentence?'

Wisting shook his head.

'That's the topic I'm writing about. Whether punishment actually helps.'

Wisting took another bite.

'Have you found any answers?'

'I'd like the readers to find the answer for themselves, but have you not wondered whether there's any point in punishment?'

He had asked himself the question many times. All too many of the people he arrested came back and committed new, worse crimes as soon as they had served their sentences. Prisons functioned as a crime school where new contacts were formed.

'Those who are convicted of murder are an unsuitable statistical group if you want to look at the rate of recidivism,' he replied, trying to avoid the question. 'Most people who become murderers find themselves in some kind of extreme situation that they probably only encounter once in their lives.'

'Under those circumstances punishment doesn't serve any purpose.' Line rinsed her glass and placed it in the dishwasher. 'Then it isn't the fear of punishment that prevents them from committing another crime?'

'Perhaps it doesn't have any individual preventive effect in murder cases,' Wisting conceded, 'but we must certainly have laws and regulations. That someone is punished will hopefully act as a deterrent to others.'

'People who are in such an extreme situation that they commit murder, probably don't think so rationally that they take into account the possibility of punishment before they kill?'

Wisting put down his plate and took a glass out of the cupboard. 'Now you're pestering me with philosophy,' he grunted, filling his glass from the tap. He liked these discussions with his daughter, but at the moment he didn't have the ability to concentrate. 'It depends on the circumstances,' he attempted as a final argument.

Line took out the newspaper article about the man who had first knifed his girlfriend to death 35 years previously, and who had done the same thing again 21 years later. 'A prison sentence didn't help Åge Reinholdt.'

'Perhaps we should have capital punishment?' Wisting suggested, to provoke her in the same way that she had provoked him.

She didn't take the bait. 'I'm going to talk to him on Saturday,' she went on. 'He lives in Gusland. His parents were from Brunlanes, but moved to Oslo before he was born. His mother died when he was little, but his father moved back and took over the farm from his grandparents while he was serving his first prison sentence. Now he has taken it over.'

'Are you going alone?'

She nodded. Wisting did not like the thought, but said nothing. He knew he would not be able to persuade her to change her plans.

'Did you know about it?' she enquired. 'That there were two murderers in your district? Åge Reinholdt and Ken Ronny Hauge.'

Wisting shook his head. Not two, he thought, thinking of the severed feet. Three.

13

He didn't switch on the light, but put on the coffee machine and stood at the window looking down at the square in front of the police station, waiting for the water to run through the filter. He was trying to order his thoughts.

The bulletin about Camilla Thaulow was already prepared and lying on his office desk. The short press release described her, the car in which she had disappeared and the clothes she had been wearing at the time. Dark trousers, white blouse, checked scarf around her neck and a pair of black trainers. A folder of photographs accompanied the report. It had not been easy to find a recent image, as she didn't have a passport and the photo albums at home had not been updated for many years. One of her work colleagues had, however, found a suitably neutral picture that had been taken at the Christmas dinner the previous year. She neither smiled nor showed other emotions. Her hair was styled in the way that her colleagues said it had been while she worked at the nursing home.

The coffee machine rumbled lightly and emitted hot steam. He filled a cup and returned to the window. The new day was going to be a fine one. Buildings in the town centre twinkled with a brownish-red hue in the morning sunshine and the streets were quiet. One of the council's cleansing vehicles moved slowly across the grey asphalt. The cup was slightly too hot to hold. He took a careful gulp, moved his hand and carried it to the table, deciding to go through the cases of the two men missing from the nursing home one more time.

Torkel Lauritzen and Otto Saga were both widowers. He would look for people in the circles around them who could tell more about them. The smallest details could turn out to be crucial, but he didn't find anything that he had over-looked in the files. In the course of the day he would take a trip to the nursing home and look up someone who might know a bit more about the two men.

The morning meeting was short. Most of the time was taken up with a discussion of how the different news-papers had presented the case. All had pictures of training shoes on the front page. *Verdens Gang* had presumably realised that all the editors would go for the same spread, and had sharpened up their coverage with a comment from a well-known television actor who holidayed at a summer cottage in Nevlunghavn. The whole thing was unpleasant.

'Bloody hell,' Hammer complained. 'Not even a murder can be reported without linking it to a celebrity.'

Wisting wound up the meeting and withdrew to his office. Ten minutes went by before he was disturbed by a knock at his door by one of the police guard's summer temps. Wisting looked at the young man in the doorway. His uniform was clean and newly pressed, his hair cut short and his shoes polished. Wisting wondered if he had any idea how much human tragedy and misery he was going to experience in the years that lay ahead.

'Yes?' Wisting said, giving him an obliging smile.

'There's a lady downstairs,' the man said. 'She says she knows who one of the shoes in the newspaper belongs to.'

Wisting got up. 'Which of them?'

'The most recent. The one that was found yesterday.'

Wisting followed the young policeman down to the front desk where a woman in her mid-forties was waiting. She had short, silver-grey hair, was tall and slim and had blue-grey eyes with bags and dark rings beneath them. Wisting shook her hand, but didn't catch her name. 'You know something about the shoe that was pictured in the newspaper?' he began.

'Yes,' she said, searching for something in her handbag. 'I think it belongs to my sister.' She brought out a picture. 'Look at this.'

Wisting took it. It was a colour photograph of a woman in a tracksuit, standing in front of an apple tree that was heavy with fruit and wearing a pair of white trainers. Although the details were tiny, he could make out the three black stripes of Adidas.

'It was taken just before she disappeared,' the woman explained.

Wisting felt that he did not quite understand. 'Your sister?' he asked, hesitantly.

'Hanne Richter,' the woman elaborated. 'She vanished in September last year, at the same time as the old men.'

14

This was a new situation. They had not viewed the case of Hanne Richter as though it had any connection with the three missing old men who had gone. A psychiatric patient, she had no connections to the other three. The fact that one of the feet belonged to her lifted the investigation onto a completely different level of complication.

Hanne Richter had been reported missing on the 10th September the previous year, but had probably disappeared at some point after the seventh, just a few days after Torkel Lauritzen and Otto Saga, who were reported missing on Monday 1st and Thursday 4th respectively. On Monday 8th, Sverre Lund had been reported missing.

Wisting read her case documents again. A paranoid schizophrenic, when she disappeared she had been in a period of what the doctors described as moderate psychotic disturbance. Her treatment was about regaining self-knowledge and consisted mainly of medication.

He jotted down the name of the psychiatrist who had been treating her so that he could make an appointment, but remained sitting, looking at the picture of Hanne Richter in front of the big apple tree. Her disappearance had led neither to any major search nor headlines in the newspapers. She was simply another unfinished case, yet another unknown fate.

Espen Mortensen popped his head round the door.

'Just in time,' Wisting said, grabbing his jacket from the back of his chair. 'I want you to come with me to Hanne Richter's home.'

'I've got the DNA results from forensics,' the crime technician explained, holding up the papers. 'I think we should go over them first.'

Wisting put on his jacket, nodding to indicate that he wanted to hear more.

'Ok,' Mortensen continued. 'The first shoe we found belongs to Torkel Lauritzen. The DNA profile matches the reference sample we got from his son.'

'Good.'

'The third shoe we now think belongs to Hanne Richter, and that probably adds up. We don't have any reference samples, but the gender marker shows that it's a woman's. We'll get that confirmed when the analysis from her sister's sample is ready.'

'What about number two?'

'That has an unknown DNA profile.'

'What do you mean?'

'The profile of the old head teacher we have from the toothbrush we got from his wife.'

'Sverre Lund,' Wisting nodded, glancing at the case file.

'It's not his profile, and neither is there any relationship shown to Otto Saga's daughter.'

Wisting sat down again, unable to keep a tight rein on all these threads. He drew his fingers through his hair and then took the papers from Mortensen, accounts of the methods of analysis and monitoring routines. There were words and expressions he had difficulty understanding, but the conclusion was clear. Only one of the feet they had found belonged to one of the three missing men. 'Could there be a mistake in the analysis?' he suggested.

'I can get them to run the test once more, but I doubt if they'll come up with a different result.'

'Let's do it anyway,' Wisting requested. 'For safety's sake.'

15

Hanne Richter's house was situated at the end of a gravel road. Wisting's car sent dust whirling up that settled on the windscreen as he manoeuvered around the worst of the bumps.

A two-storey wooden house, painted white, sitting on a paved foundation, its decay was evident. Surrounded by a large garden with old fruit trees, with grass grown high and old leaves gathered in small piles, the paint was flaking off its walls, the roof tiles cracked and moss covered. Wisting recognised the tree in front of which Hanne Richter had been photographed. The apples had been harvested long ago, the leaves had fallen and new ones sprouted. Now it stood with new, white apple blossoms.

Her sister stood on the steps, twisting her fingers round a key. Wisting stepped out, greeted her with a nod and stepped towards her. Espen Mortensen followed. 'Did the police come here when she was reported missing?' Wisting asked.

'Yes indeed.' She turned the key in the lock. 'They went through all the rooms, the cellar and the sheds. They also went up into the crawl space in the loft. It was as if they thought she'd hidden there.'

The house met them with a warm, close smell. The sister of the woman who had lived here remained standing, allowing Wisting to take the first step over the threshold.

'Sorry it's so untidy,' she called after him. 'My sister was a bit special. She had a lot of strange whims and ideas. She's been admitted to hospital, but of course you know that.'

Shoes were lying out on the floor in the little hallway. A coat and two jackets were hanging on a coat stand. Wisting entered further. The hollow sound of his footsteps on the parquet flooring testified to the room's emptiness.

'It's just as it was when she vanished,' her sister explained, following him in. 'We haven't done anything, just taken out the rubbish and food waste that had begun to smell.'

Wisting studied several photographs of two little girls that were hanging in the corridor. They were posed photographs taken by a professional photographer, first in a nursery and later at school as the girls eventually became older. 'They're my daughters,' the woman behind him explained. 'Hanne didn't have children.'

'So the house has remained empty since she disappeared?' Mortensen asked.

'We have sort of . . . just waited. But now we'll need to pack everything up and tidy it all away. The rental agreement comes to an end in August.'

'Was she renting?' Wisting asked.

'What shall I say? We haven't done anything about it. I mean, she just completely vanished. Her benefit payments have gone into her bank account every month, and she had a direct debit for her rent. Things have taken their course, so to speak.'

In the living room Wisting stopped and looked around. Sparsely furnished, it had a dining table at one end and a group of seats round a low table in front of a television at the other. A large plant that resembled a palm, with brown, withered leaves stood in front of the patio doors. Despite the simple furnishings, chaos reigned within the four walls. It looked as if whoever lived here was about to redecorate, or preparing to spring clean.

A previously well-filled bookcase had been emptied of books, which were stacked in huge piles on the floor, on the table and on the chairs. The bookcase had been pulled from the wall. Wall panelling had been broken off and lay scattered across the frayed, worn carpet. A couple of wall lamps had been unscrewed and taken to pieces. All the electric plugs had been pulled from the walls and a portable radio taken apart.

'That's the illness,' Hanne Richter's sister explained. 'Persecution mania; she thought that someone was watching her and controlling her life through radio waves. She took everything apart.'

'Who was it she thought was after her?'

'Some mafia organisation or other. They got into the house when she was sleeping or away from home. Moved things or took them away. Knocked her out with drugs and carried her off.'

'Carried her off?'

'It's a part of the delusions. She thought the mafia abducted her and surgically inserted a radio transmitter in her body, so they could control her by satellite. At regular intervals, they collected her to change the batteries.'

Wisting picked up a mobile phone that had been taken to pieces. 'It can't have been easy,' he commented.

'Not for any of us,' the sister admitted, looking around the room. 'The doctor thought that she must have deteriorated before she disappeared.'

'Did she have any visitors here?' Wisting asked.

He put down the phone, went over to the row of windows and looked out over the orchard. Dead flies were lying on the window ledge. The curtains were faded by sunlight. He drew them aside. Behind the garden there was a dense forest of spruce trees.

'No.' Her sister came up beside him. 'The community nurse came here, of course, but her old friends and work colleagues broke off contact. That applied to us in the family as well. She became too tiresome and unpleasant to deal with.' Wisting let go the curtain again. 'They searched through the forest with dogs,' the sister went on, nodding towards the window. 'They were afraid she might have hanged herself or something in there.'

71

'Was she suicidal?'

'No, but you could well understand it if she just couldn't take any more.'

Wisting nodded. That had been the police's theory too. 'She didn't have a boyfriend or anything like that?'

The woman shook her head. 'Not that I know of. Of course, she made new friends while she was an in-patient.'

'Did they visit her?'

She shrugged her shoulders.

'How long has she stayed here?'

'Four years. The man who owned the house moved into a care home for the elderly.'

Surmising a line of connection Wisting felt a shiver run through his body, almost pinning him to the floor. It was thin, but could be followed up. 'Care home for the elderly?' he repeated.

'Yes, but he's dead now. He died just before Hanne disappeared. The whole thing has become so problematic. The house rental goes into the estate of the deceased person, but it can't be settled as long as the tenancy isn't clarified. I think the heirs want to sell the house.'

'Which care home?'

The woman stared at him. The expression on her face changed, and he realised that she was following his thoughts. 'In Stavern,' she replied. 'At Stavern nursing home.'

16

The house owner was called Christian Hauge, and he had died, aged 80, on Sunday 10th August, three weeks before the first disappearance. The death had not been reported to the police, so Wisting would probably have to talk to the staff at the care home to find out about the circumstances.

Wisting leaned back in his office chair, staring at the computer screen. Although there was no reason to believe that there was anything unnatural about the death, he had discovered something he did not like.

Christian Hauge had only one child, a daughter who had died in 1992. Two grandchildren were left behind as lawful heirs. One was Ken Ronny Hauge, who had been found guilty of killing a policeman.

He had never believed in coincidences. There were always explanations, patterns, threads and logical connections. He grabbed his coffee cup and drank down a gulp. A question Line had asked him yesterday evening had made him uneasy: whether a murderer would be able to kill again, in the same way burglars or other criminals fell back into their old bad habits.

The telephone rang. It was Line. 'Hello,' she said happily. 'I just wanted to say that I won't be home tonight. I'm staying at Tommy's.'

'Is he home?'

'He's landing in a couple of hours.'

Wisting had not quite understood the relationship between Line and her Danish friend, and was not quite sure whether he liked it. 'Tell him I was asking for him,' he managed to say.

They chatted a little before they finished their conversation. Wisting became thoughtful, and sipped at his coffee again. Perhaps Ken Ronny Hauge's name had only popped up in the case in the same way that Line by chance had phoned him when he was thinking about her?

Ken Ronny Hauge had been born and brought up in the area, as both his mother and grandfather had been. It was not a coincidence that his grandfather should have spent his last days at the nursing home in Stavern. Rather, it was the way of the world. The coincidence was that his picture had been lying among Line's notes on the kitchen table at his own home less than twenty-four hours before. He rubbed his eyes and pushed the thought away. Perhaps he had to accept nevertheless that there was a place for coincidences in life, beyond the set of rules that nature brought into being, and that science described.

The coffee in his cup had gone cold. He took it with him into the conference room, rinsed it in the sink, and refilled the cup. His stomach protested against the first mouthful. He went to the window and looked out. An outside broadcast vehicle from TV2, complete with roof aerials, was sitting outside the police station. A camera lamp was directed towards Audun Vetti, who was standing stiffly in his uniform with a microphone passing back and forwards between him and a reporter.

Wisting fumbled, turned on the office TV by remote and scrolled to the news channel. The Assistant Chief of Police filled the television screen. '. . . we have also appointed an oceanographer from the Meteorological Institute who will report how the feet may have drifted with the tides,' he explained.

'What will you achieve with that?' the reported asked.

'We hope to work out a possible point of origin.'

Wisting alternated between looking out the window and

at the screen, shaking his head. The television journalist ended by thanking Audun Vetti for the interview and returned to the studio with a promise to report on developments.

He switched off and threw the remote control onto the table, hitting a half-empty paper cup that someone had left behind after the meeting earlier. Wisting swore and cleared away the nearest papers before fetching a cloth to soak up the spill. Small things had begun to irritate him, he noticed.

The Assistant Chief of Police was walking along the corridor as Wisting went back to his office. The serious expression he had worn in front of the television camera was transformed into a broad grin. 'How's it going?' he asked. 'Anything new?'

'Why did you tell them about the oceanographer?' Wisting questioned.

'I had to give them something,' Vetti explained, 'to show that we're making progress.'

'We could surely keep some cards close to our chest?'

'It doesn't make any difference to the investigation, does it? What are you afraid of? That the perpetrator will turn the tide to hide his traces?'

Wisting shook his head, feeling no need to respond to biased arguments. A large part of his work as an investigation leader was to have an overview of what details were issued to the media. If someone or other were to make a confession they could be dependent on holding information only a guilty person would know. The history of crime was full of false confessions.

'Since you haven't managed to come up with any results I have to give them something,' the Assistant Chief of Police continued. 'Or have you some progress to report at last?'

Wisting felt his face redden, but managed to bottle up his irritation and temper. 'The poor man won't get a moment's peace to work,' he pointed out. 'He'll be overwhelmed by phone calls from journalists.'

'I didn't mention who he was,' Vetti said dismissively.

'How many oceanographers do you think they have at the Meteorological Institute?'

The Assistant Chief of Police was spared having to answer by Nils Hammer running from his office at the end of the corridor. 'They've found Camilla Thaulow's car!'

17

The police helicopter was still hovering above the discovery site, the downdraught from its rotors twisting and fluttering the crime scene warning tape.

Hellerød was situated west of the 302 main road between Larvik and Helgeroa, just before Tveidalskrysset and the old connecting road to Telemark. An uneven road penetrated the forest for five hundred metres. It was a long time since any cars had used it and it was lined with overhanging deciduous trees. At its end there was an open space in front of a small lake.

Wisting manoeuvred his car right up to the dense edge of the forest to make room for the recovery vehicle and fire service divers. The car was not visible in the dark, still water. The crew of the helicopter had spotted its red roof through the surface.

'One thing is sure,' Hammer said, closing the door of their car. 'This is no accident.'

'If it's the correct car, true enough,' Wisting commented. He looked around and called to a uniformed police officer: 'When will the divers be here?'

'Soon.'

Hammer picked up a straw and put it in his mouth. 'It's her car,' he said. 'Who else's could it be?'

Wisting nodded. Whoever had driven the car here had done so to hide it. He glanced at the helicopter, which had increased its height and was flying in wide circles. Obviously the pond was shallower than the perpetrator had expected, or the car might have remained here for years without being found. This spot was hidden away and people seldom came, as the overgrowing trees and bushes showed. That probably meant that the culprit was familiar with the area. He might, of course, have found the dumping ground by chance, but it was more likely that he was a local.

The ground sloped gently down towards the water's edge with enough of an incline for the car to be pushed and gain sufficient momentum to disappear into the water, or the accelerator and clutch pedals could have been be fixed up with sticks or stones. Wisting had seen that before in insurance fraud cases.

They walked over to the lake. Very little sunlight reached between the trees, but out in the middle of the water it reflected enough to dazzle. Wisting screwed up his eyes but could not see anything of what they knew was lying down there.

'There are a couple of tyre tracks here,' explained the police constable on guard. Pointing, he said, 'Someone has tried to cover those marks over, but they're obvious tracks.'

Wisting looked at the two rows of compressed grass leading down into the water. A few dry branches had been laid over them, not enough to hide them.

Another car came jolting down the road, Espen Mortensen in the crime scene vehicle. Wisting glanced again at the branches. There could be some crucial traces on them. Every time someone takes a grip of an object he leaves behind small, invisible skin cells. The introduction of new DNA legislation the previous autumn had given the police wider powers to obtain reference samples from suspects, and to record convicted criminals in the DNA register. It had been explained how everyone loses a certain number of skin cells each day and how, in the course of a month, we each renew our entire epidermis. Human debris is worth its weight in gold to the police.

They waited half an hour for the divers' car, and another half hour for Mortensen to finish his work along the edge of the lake. A tow truck reversed along the forest track, and the recovery crew got the winch ready.

Wisting followed the air bubbles from the two divers across the water until they stopped six or seven metres from the edge. The beams from their powerful lights were thrown backwards and forwards underneath the water until, several minutes later, one of the divers broke the surface, pushed his mask onto his forehead and pulled out his mouthpiece.

'It's about two or three metres out,' he shouted, moving towards land. 'It's starting to get buried in the mud. It's difficult to see, but it doesn't look as though there's anyone inside.'

Hammer pulled the straw from the side of his mouth. 'Empty?'

The diver had reached land and was stretching for the towing hook the man from the recovery vehicle was holding out. 'Looks like it.' He pulled at the cable so that it loosened. 'But you'll soon be able to see for yourselves,' he said, disappearing beneath the water again.

Two minutes later he was back and gave the signal to go. The cable straightened slowly as the tow began its pull and the rear end of a red Ford Fiesta rose from the water.

'That's it,' Wisting confirmed, reading the registration number out loud.

When the car was at last dragged onto dry land dirty, brown water streamed out of the driver's door, which was hanging from its hinges. Wisting and Mortensen approached from their different sides and looked in. It was empty.

Hammer picked up a work glove that one of the men from the recovery vehicle had dropped. He put it on and opened the car boot, looked down into the small luggage compartment and shook his head. 'Empty,' he stated, closing the lid again.

'Perhaps she's still lying in the lake?' Mortensen suggested.

Wisting turned towards the water, nodding. 'Do you have search equipment?' he asked the diver who was wading ashore. 'Dredgers and hooks?'

'They're in the car.'

'How long will it take to cover it all?'

The diver turned round and studied the lake. It was about forty metres from one end to the other, a bit narrower across.

'A rough search shouldn't take more than two or three hours.'

'Good. I want it done before midnight.'

18

Line let herself into Tommy Kvanter's flat in the centre of town while he was preparing dinner. A light whirring from the kitchen fan and the sound of pots and pans combined in the hallway with blues, rock music and a tempting smell of spices and hot food. She took off her shoes, calling to him. He didn't hear, and she had to go all the way into the kitchen before he saw her. His face lit up with a broad smile.

He was standing wearing a black apron with the request *Kiss the Cook* written across the chest. She acceded with a quick peck on his cheek, but Tommy held her tight, pulled her towards him and found her lips. Pressing her against the kitchen worktop he ran his fingers through her hair. She breathed in his scent, thinking how good it was to have his strong arms around her.

'Good to see you,' he whispered into her ear. His voice and breath tickled so that she involuntarily tried to wriggle out of his grip. He held on to her with one hand, while pushing the saucepans off the hotplates on the cooker with the other. The apron and their clothes were left lying on the kitchen floor.

Wisting put his glass on the patio table. Daylight was disappearing. The evening was warm and without a breath of air; grasshoppers were chirping and night swarms played in the candlelight. Suzanne smiled across the table, and could see that he was much more concerned about his work than their surroundings.

The trees at the far edge of the garden had grown close

together and blocked some of the view over the town and the fjord, but between the spreading branches he could see the continuous stream of car headlights and house lights being switched on. He picked at the salad.

The case would be a topic of conversation in many of the houses and he wondered what people's thoughts and opinions were. The public required more and more of the police, demanded answers and were quick to point the finger. Police work was exposed by modern media as never before, and they were more vulnerable when mistakes were made. Scrutinised closely by both press and public they were pushed into a greater focus on quality and ethics. Nor could they risk a situation where the population harboured mistrust of them. Confidence in the police was closely connected to the authority they needed to carry out their work, and they had to take seriously the fact that respect no longer went along automatically with the uniform.

His mobile phone lay on the table in front of him, its display showing that just over two and a half hours had passed since he left the dark lake among the trees near Tveidalskrysset. The divers would still be at work in the water. Floodlights and generators had been set up. Mortensen was probably still going about in his white overalls and overshoes, gloves and cap. Dog patrols would be searching through the woods for some clue or another that would take them further. He had to concentrate hard to think about anything else.

He stuck his fork into a lobster tail and put it into his mouth, chewing well and smiling back at Suzanne to let her know what he thought about the food, leftovers from the day before. 'Sorry that I'm such bad company,' he said. 'There's just so much going on at the moment.'

He had expected her to be understanding and brush away his apologies. 'I bought some dietary supplements for you,' she said instead. 'Something called *Enaxin*.'

Wisting nodded, although he was not really interested.

They were certainly creative when it came to thinking up names for their products.

Suzanne reached for the wine bottle. 'Are you sure you won't have any?'

'Yes, it's okay,' Wisting confirmed, drinking from his glass of *Farris* mineral water.

Suzanne poured some for herself. 'You can stay overnight,' she suggested, flirting.

Wisting hesitated. Tired and worn out, he had no desire.

Line drew invisible circles with her index finger on Tommy's naked chest. The skin surrounding the hard nipples was completely smooth. Making love was like going on a voyage of discovery with him; each time she discovered some new aspect of them both. It was also a bit frightening, as if she never really got to know him properly and was afraid there might be a dark side that she would not like.

'What was it like to be in prison?' she asked suddenly.

He turned his head and looked at her. 'Why are you wondering about that?'

She pulled the duvet over her to cover her bare breasts. 'Tomorrow I'm going to interview someone who spent sixteen years in prison.'

'What did he do wrong?'

'He killed a policeman.'

Tommy sat bolt upright. 'Why are you going to interview him? That must surely be old news.'

'It's for an article I'm writing for the weekend magazine,' Line said. 'I'm going to profile six murderers. Get them to talk about what the sentence did to them and what their lives are like now.'

Tommy got up and remained standing in the nude, looking down at her seriously. 'Do you think up these interviews for yourself, or is it the editorial team that gives them to you?'

'It was my own idea.'

He laughed. 'You are strange,' he said, and leaned over to kiss her before vanishing into the kitchen.

Line smiled after him and stayed in bed a while longer before going to the bathroom. She had a quick shower, dried herself and went naked to him. Tommy had heated up the cooker again and laid her clothes on a chair, pretending to watch her surreptitiously while she dressed. Taking out two glasses he uncorked a bottle of wine, filled hers and took his own to the cooker. Line sat at the table. He stirred one of the pots, turned to her and drank from his glass.

'It was bloody awful,' he said. 'Lonely and isolated, with no chance to keep in touch with family or friends. You've got only a gang of key-rattlers around you, who decide all the time what you can or can't do. Your life is put on hold, you don't have a life of your own any longer and even your inmost thoughts and feelings are controlled by others.' He took another drink. 'I was in with the roughest, but you can't get me to believe they didn't snivel in their cells at night like the rest of us.'

Line sat holding her glass in her hand. 'All the same, you ended up in jail a second time?'

Tommy sighed heavily. 'It was crazy. I promised myself, the first time I got out, that I would never go in there again. Never in my life, but it didn't work out that way.'

She looked at him for a long time. 'Perhaps you can comfort yourself with the knowledge that you're not the only one. Eight out of ten who are released end up back in prison. And that's exactly what is a bit of a paradox, given that the intention is that prisoners should come out as better and more law-abiding people.'

Tommy gave her a serious look. 'No, it brings out the worst in you. I became unbelievably unravelled inside. When I got out the second time, I practically couldn't relate to other people. I became anxious about going out the door.'

'That's precisely what I want to shed light on. What being

inside does to people, and whether it serves any purpose – beyond keeping them off the streets for a while. It costs a huge amount of money. One prisoner costs society 2,000 kroner a day – that's over 700,000 kroner a year. You could get a lot of rehabilitation for that money.'

'That's my girl.' He smiled warmly and turned back to the pots, gave them a stir and turned to face her again. 'I'll never go back there, if that's what you're wondering.'

She got up and placed her hand on his shoulder. She was about to say something about how fond she had become of him, but he beat her to it: 'Dinner's ready!'

She had not checked to see what he was preparing, but now leaned across to the cooker. Chicken breasts were simmering in a cream sauce in the frying pan, and stewed mushrooms with onion and bacon in the pot beside it.

'There's salad in the fridge,' he said. She took it out and carried it through to the living room where Tommy had already set the table.

'What have the other criminals done?' he asked when they sat down.

'No, we don't need to talk about work now,' was Line's opinion. 'Let's relax.'

'I'm serious,' Tommy said. 'Who have they killed?'

Line was not sure if he was really interested, or if he was asking because it absorbed her so. 'I've interviewed someone who murdered a thirteen-year-old boy, and on Saturday . . .'

'What did he get for that?' Tommy interrupted.

'Eighteen years, and served fifteen of them. On Saturday I'm going to talk to someone who first served eleven years for killing his girlfriend . . .'

'So a policeman's life is worth more than that of a thirteen-year-old boy?' Tommy broke in once more.

'What do you mean?'

'The one who killed the policeman was inside for sixteen years, but the one who murdered the young boy served fifteen years. And for his girlfriend the third one got only eleven years?'

'Each case is dealt with individually when it comes to measuring the length of sentence.'

Tommy became thoughtful. 'You're right,' he said eventually. 'Now we'll relax and enjoy ourselves.'

19

Wisting went home to Herman Wildenveysgate and stayed the night. Later he regretted it. The dawn was breaking when he finally fell asleep. Staggering out of bed when the alarm sounded, he got through his regular morning rituals and to the office, still not feeling fully awake.

They held a short morning meeting, surveying the previous day. The divers had finished searching the lake around midnight. It had been more than empty, without even the usual empty bottles and wrecked bicycles. The only thing that caused a certain degree of interest was an animal carcass they thought was a roe deer that had died at the waterside and slid down into the depths.

Wisting made a list of what he intended to do that day. The first thing would be to go out to Stavern nursing home: it had been on his notepad for a while, and he wanted to make the trip that morning to ensure that nothing else got in the way.

At twelve o'clock he had an appointment with the psychiatrist. He had told Nils Hammer, who had looked at him sceptically until he realised that it was Hanne Richter's psychiatrist he was talking about. He also considered initiating new interviews with the family members of the missing men, but doubted that he would be able to make a start on that today. In this particular phase of the investigation it was usual for unexpected things to happen, and it was difficult to hold to plans for an entire working day.

He signed out a service vehicle and went down to the

garage. Camilla Thaulow's red Fiesta was in the inspection area. Espen Mortensen stood there, noting something on a writing pad. 'Found anything?' he asked.

The crime scene technician pointed to a transparent bag containing a multi-coloured scarf with a checked pattern. 'That's about all. The water has washed away all traces.'

'It matches her mother's description,' Wisting nodded, picking up the evidence bag. 'Anything else?'

'Nothing really. The keys are in the ignition, the gearstick in first. It was driven into the water at a relatively high speed.' He pointed towards the car with his ballpoint pen. 'No rigging of the pedals. The driver's door was open, of course, so a piece of wood across the accelerator pedal could have fallen out, but it's also possible that the driver sat behind the wheel, then crawled out and swam to land.'

'Risky.'

'Not really. You have to keep your nerve, but it would've been the surest way to get the car out into the water.'

'Not exactly a job for a lady.'

'Do you think she might have staged it herself?' Mortensen asked.

Wisting shrugged. The idea had just fallen from his lips, a thought that had not been fully fleshed out. 'It's a possibility. This case is so incomprehensible I don't know what to think.'

Mortensen told him that a report would be ready for him that afternoon. He asked him to continue and left.

The sun quickly warmed the cramped saloon car. Wisting adjusted the ventilators on the air conditioning so they were blowing directly at him, and looked thoughtfully through the windscreen. It was covered in the flattened remains of dead insects.

The fjord was milky-blue and calm. Today the beaches and rocky shores would fill up once more with volunteers searching for dead bodies.

Stavern nursing home was a two-storied brown-stained

building with a flat roof and extensions coming off at various angles. It was an option for elderly people who, for health reasons, could no longer live at home. Wisting had visited the place one Christmas almost twenty years before, when Line sang in a children's gospel choir in the foyer. An old building, it looked well maintained, but rather like a barracks. It was not a place he would choose to spend his old age. The staff had received good references in all the interviews and that was probably the deciding factor for residents to thrive.

Inga Svendsen, the departmental manager, greeted him, offering him coffee in her cramped, basement office. Folders, books and ring binders filled the shelves along the wall and the day's newspapers lay open on the desk. Wisting sat on the only visitor's chair. She glanced inquisitively over at him, but at the same time appeared resigned. Wisting thought he recognised that look. It was holiday time, the place was certain to be understaffed and would be unbearably warm.

'Can we talk about Camilla Thaulow first of all?' he enquired.

'She works in my department,' Inga Svendsen confirmed. 'This disappearance is very unlike her. She's conscientious and has hardly ever been off sick.' She gestured towards the computer screen. 'She took a few days off when her mother had a hip operation two years ago, and since then hasn't missed a single day.'

'So, where can she be?'

'I don't know. Nobody here knows.' She cleared away the newspapers in which the discovery of the red Fiesta was reported. 'But I understand that it's now a criminal investigation? This too.'

She was thinking of the missing men. Wisting avoided a reply by putting the cup to his lips. 'What did her work involve?' he asked.

'She was a care worker, participating in occupational

therapy and rehabilitation initiatives, helping the residents with practical assistance and taking care of daily tasks. Personal hygiene, morning and evening care and feeding for those who need help.'

'Was there anyone here she had more contact with than others?'

'Those who worked permanently on the same shift, of course,' the departmental manager nodded, rattling off a few names. 'She was well liked by everyone, both staff and patients.'

Wisting posed a few different questions in the hope of discovering some possible trigger for her disappearance, or something that could be connected to the two other disappearances, but made no progress. Nor did he find out anything more about Otto Saga and Torkel Lauritzen.

'Torkel had almost become too healthy to stay here,' she explained. 'He didn't have the same need for care and support as when he was admitted. The nursing home was not the right place for Otto either. He had more of a social disability and should have been in a dementia wing.'

Wisting leafed through his notepad to a page with the heading *Christian Hauge*. 'There was another man staying here: Christian Hauge. He died on the 10th August last year.'

'That's right.'

'Do you know what he died of?'

'Does that have anything to do with the missing persons cases?' the departmental manager asked.

'It might have,' Wisting did not want to explain that he was the man who owned the house from which Hanne Richter had vanished, or that he was the grandfather of a police murderer who had returned home.

'That information is normally confidential,' Inga Svendsen elaborated.

Wisting remained silent, waiting for her to tell him all the same.

'It's not exactly a secret though. He came here after a major heart attack four or five years ago when he was in need of care. After the doctors had to amputate his other leg as well, he became extremely weakened and seemed to lose the spark of life. With a prosthesis he was able to move about freely of course, but with two amputations he was forced to use a wheelchair.'

'Amputate?'

Inga Svendsen nodded. 'A lower leg amputation. He got a blood clot in a vein in his leg. The disturbance to his circulation led to gangrene and the doctors had to remove the leg bone to prevent it spreading.'

'But that was the second amputation, you said?'

'Yes, he had lost his other foot many years ago.'

'Why did that happen?'

'I don't know.'

Wisting bit his lower lip. 'Which foot are we talking about?' he asked.

The departmental manager thought carefully before she answered: 'The last time now, they removed the right foot.'

'But the actual death was of natural causes?'

Inga Svendsen nodded. 'Heart attack.'

'Do you know anything about the relatives?'

'He had two grown up grandchildren who visited. The younger one was a regular visitor, and brought the great-grandchildren.' She smiled. 'Otherwise, I don't think he had any family. Camilla Thaulow went to the funeral. One of us always does that and Camilla wanted to, even though the announcement stated that the ceremony would be private.'

She glanced at the clock as if to make the point that she had other things to do. Wisting did not see any reason to remain longer. He too had other tasks. He got up and was accompanied out.

The walls in the corridor were decorated with framed black-and-white photographs. Wisting recognised the old Brestrup farm, Lysheim school, the old BP-station at the harbour and the restaurant at the beach beside the Kronprins gap site. When he smiled the departmental manager followed his eye.

'These are mementos of Stavern,' she explained. 'From Petter Norli's book. Pictures he found in his father's photograph archive. They were put up on the wall here last summer. There's a picture of Torkel and Otto here as well.'

She took a few steps and stopped at a picture of five young men on a stone stairway with wrought iron railings. It was summertime and they were sitting in short-sleeved shirts. The man who sat at the front was holding a pipe in his hand. 'Lund, the head teacher, is with them too,' she said, pointing to the man furthest back on the right. 'He's gone also, of course.'

Wisting leaned forwards. Sverre Lund was sitting with the top of his shirt buttoned and wearing a pleasant smile. He studied the other faces. The picture had to be about sixty years old, but all the same he recognised the distinctive facial features of Torkel Lauritzen on the left at the middle step on the stairway. He pointed to him with his finger and looked at the departmental manager to check if he was correct.

She nodded. 'And there's Otto Saga,' she said, pointing to the man beside him.

'Who is this one, the man with the pipe?'

'I don't know,' she said, 'but the one beside Sverre Lund is Christian Hauge, the man you were just asking me about.'

Wisting's eyes became narrow lines in his face. He squinted at the man on the top step while he felt his heart beat faster. 'So they knew each other from the old days?'

'Certainly. They were all from Stavern. They were very pleased when the picture was put up. They called themselves the five-man group.'

'Why was that?'

'Well, I suppose it was just because there were five of them. Five pals.'

'The five-man group?' Wisting repeated, without taking his eyes off the men in the picture. Four of them were dead, or at least it had to be supposed so. He would have liked to know who the fifth man with the pipe was.

20

The road was closed off by a gate and a sign that forbade entrance. Line thought at first that she had driven the wrong way but, when she crested the brow of a hill, saw that the road led to a little property down by the sea. The sunshine sparkled on a byre with a corrugated iron roof. The actual farmhouse was white, and was situated in the middle of the property. It appeared run down and badly maintained, and the surrounding fields, which had once been arable, were gradually reverting to wilderness. The garden was overgrown and full of rusty car parts, an old lorry grown through with grass and spotted with rusty holes. The shell of a burned down washhouse lay on the fringes and climbing plants twined round an old chimneystack in the midst of the ruins.

Down by the water's edge was a boathouse with a *sjekte*, a traditional clinker-built vessel, tied to the jetty and a dilapidated fishing boat sittting in a homemade dock. Half of its wooden hull was gone and it resembled the skeleton of a prehistoric animal. A dog ran barking towards her, but kept its distance when she got out of the car. A man in denim jeans and a white singlet came out of the barn, drying his hands on an oily rag. Line immediately saw it as a picture she wanted to print, a pair of working hands in a dirty rag.

'Ken Ronny Hauge?' she asked, putting on a smile.

'Just Ken,' the man nodded. He scrutinised her, allowing his eyes to rest on her breasts long enough for her to be aware. Then he smiled too. Line extended her hand to greet him. The man's glance moved to his own dirty hand before returning the gesture.

'I'm grateful that you showed up,' she said, gazing into the building behind him. A heavy miasma of motor oil and sawdust hung in the air. In the middle of the room there was an American car with its bonnet up. Car parts, welding lights and cutting equipment were scattered around, and the walls were covered in shelves of tools smeared oily black. A radio was on.

'We can sit down in the shade,' Ken suggested, pointing towards a seating area beneath an oak tree.

The dog shuffled behind them and lay underneath the table while Ken Ronny Hauge went inside for something to drink. It was obvious to Line that he, like so many others, had used his prison time to exercise. His singlet was close fitting, and the muscles in his back were visible beneath the thin material. His arms were strong and sinewy, and he had already managed to acquire a summer tan. He returned with two bottles of cola and a glass for her.

She had wondered for a long time about how she should start the conversation, but had not thought of a good introduction. 'How does it feel?' she asked spontaneously. Only then realising that he did not understand, she added, 'To be free?'

The former prisoner drank from the cola bottle. Remaining seated he picked at the label. 'To begin with it felt strange,' he said. 'Everything looked different. Larvik was a different town, with a hotel on the beach promenade and a park in the harbour where before there had been only queues of traffic for the ferry. It was uncomfortable to see how life outside had gone its own way while my own stayed still. To see how pals from that time had become grown men, that the girl I had been in love with had married and had children. Their confirmation pictures were in the newspaper.'

He threw out his arms.

'But right here, this place, time has also stood still. I was here a great deal when I was younger. My great-great-grandparents came from here. My grandfather owned the place with his brothers, but my brother took it over fifteen years ago. He could have sold it for millions to rich folk from Oslo who wanted a place in the country, but I think he held on to it for my sake. He doesn't need the money either. Rune has always been smarter than me, and is doing well, with his own company and all that. The house has decayed, but it has stood here waiting for me.'

'Sixteen years is a long time,' Line commented.

'You can't take it in,' Ken Ronny Hauge nodded, 'night after night when you're lying in your bunk listening to the warden locking the cell doors, and his footsteps disappearing down the corridor. You've got a lot of time to think in sixteen years.'

'What did you think about?'

He shrugged his shoulders. 'I didn't let myself think about the future, tried to take it one day at a time. Nowadays I'm not so bothered when I think back. In many ways I got on well. The boys were nice. The staff was all right. Sometimes I almost wish I was back. After sixteen years, prison becomes somewhere safe, regular and familiar, a community where everyone accepts each other and there's room to be a failure.'

Line made notes, pleased with the comprehensiveness of the former prisoner's answers.

'It's not serving the sentence that's difficult,' Ken Ronny Hauge continued, 'but being released. It's almost like you have to teach yourself how to live all over again.'

'How did the transition go?'

'The prison arranges for a gradual return to society. You get more frequent leaves of absence and move to an open prison, so that you get a taste of freedom. But when you're released, you're released to nothing.'

'Nothing?'

'No job, no social circle, nowhere to live. As a former prisoner you don't just fall outside society, but drop right to the bottom. You become the dregs of society.'

'You're getting on well here?'

'I'm lucky. I live here free of charge. Repair old cars for people.' He nodded in the direction of the barn. 'The Yank car is owned by a well-heeled guy in Tønsberg. He doesn't know a thing about cars, other than it's fun to have one sitting there. I qualified as a car mechanic in prison, and I guess I'm well paid, considering. It's a bit unfamiliar, earning several hundred kroner in hourly rate, to somebody who was used to fifty kroner a day.'

'What did prison do to you?'

He thought carefully. 'It wore me down. It took away my sense of belonging and personal identity. I think I managed to keep myself going by looking on myself as a student rather than a prisoner.'

'You studied?'

'I got a bachelor's degree in criminology and sociology, and learned Spanish. Hablo Espanõl.'

'Spanish?'

'My brother has a house in Albir on the Costa Blanca coast. I can use it as much as I like, as soon as I'm finished with parole.'

'Parole?'

'The parole period. Although you're released, you're not completely free. If I do something wrong in the course of the first two years, then I'll have to go back inside and serve the rest of my time. I'm not allowed to travel abroad until January.'

'What did you do with your time apart from studying?'

'Most of my time was spent dreaming about a normal life.' He scratched the dog behind the ear. 'A good, quiet life with a wife, children, an estate car, a job as a mechanic and a salary. Boat trips out to sea. Pull up a cod or stand far out on a rock and feel the sea spray on my face. I dreamed of ending up with too little time, of being able to fill my time with so many activities that I didn't have time for them all.'

The conversation flowed easily. Ken Ronny Hauge talked about his feelings of sorrow, loss and pleasures behind bars, coming out with little stories and anecdotes of daily life. Two hours later, Line's reporter's notepad was filled with keywords and quotes. Ken Ronny Hauge had such a colourful way of speaking she looked forward to stitching his story together into a thrilling character portrait. She could feel within herself that it was going to be a good account. Folding up her notepad she placed it inside her bag.

'It felt good to talk about it,' the man facing her said unexpectedly. 'Nice to talk to you. I don't talk to so many people, and prison is not really a subject that anyone brings up.'

Line smiled. It was good when interview subjects had a comfortable experience and were not simply left feeling empty. 'You've never spoken about what really happened,' she ventured. She had decided to let that aspect of the case lie until a natural opening appeared.

'What is there to talk about?' Ken Ronny Hauge sat down again, shrugging his shoulders. 'I can't do it over again or change anything.'

'Many people must ask themselves why you did it?' She paused before playing a new card. 'The wife and children of the man who died have got answers about who and how, but never why.'

'It's not so easy to answer. An event with little planning that had consequences which I didn't foresee.'

'But what were you doing there? Why did you carry a gun with you? There are lots of unanswered questions.'

Ken Ronny Hauge opened and closed his mouth and, for a moment, it looked as though he might tell her the whole story. 'That wasn't what this interview was supposed to be about,' he said. 'I've served my sentence, and told you what it was like.'

Line nodded as a sign that she respected the fact that he did not want to talk about the murder. 'Has it helped?' she asked instead. 'Are you a better person now than before you went to prison?'

Ken Ronny Hauge stared at her while he thought and suddenly there was something in his eyes that made her uncomfortable. It was almost like staring back at something dark and unfathomable. 'No,' he finally answered. 'On the contrary.'

21

The name of the psychiatrist was engraved on a nameplate on his office door, Jon Terkelsen.

Wisting had been waiting in the corridor for ten minutes when the door opened and a tall, thin man of around sixty, with a receding hairline and short hair, emerged. As Wisting was about to introduce himself he noticed a man in a white coat inside the room. There was something familiar about him, but the crossover points between psychiatry and the police were many. He waited until the patient had left.

'Sorry for the delay,' the psychiatrist apologised, ushering Wisting inside.

The room was small and functional, with four bookcases filled with medical literature and a filing cabinet in which the top drawer did not quite shut. Various medical references and diplomas hung on the grey walls, and there was a photograph in a pewter frame on the desk, facing the doctor.

It felt strange to sit on the visitor's side of the desk, in a chair in which countless people of unsound mind had sat before him. Psychologists, psychiatrists and clergymen were people Wisting never felt completely comfortable with. He had a feeling that they could see right through him and read his innermost thoughts.

'Hanne Richter, yes,' the psychiatrist said, opening a thick folder. 'I've cleared the issue of patient confidentiality with the Chief County Medical Officer. We can speak openly, but I'm afraid I have little to contribute.'

'A little is better than nothing,' Wisting smiled. He

crossed one leg over the other and placed his notepad on his lap. 'Why was she admitted?'

'Hanne Richter had an increasing paranoia since 2005. Without admission and treatment she would have lost all prospects of real improvement and recovery.' Wisting waited for him to continue. 'In the autumn of 2007, she was sectioned and admitted to a locked ward in Tønsberg. A few weeks later, she was transferred here. To begin with, she wouldn't permit herself to be corrected, but after a while she adapted to the department's routines. She was happy to co-operate, but lacked any insight into her illness.'

'What kind of treatment did she receive?'

'An important part of the treatment is dependent on the patient acknowledging that he or she is unwell,' explained the doctor. 'Hanne Richter participated in a psycho-educational programme predicated on her learning about the symptoms of schizophrenia and being trained in social skills.'

'What about medicines?'

'Anti-psychotic medication was crucial in bringing her out of the psychosis, and the paranoid delusions eventually went into remission. She was discharged after six months, but kept in touch with the department through weekly interviews and medication.'

'What kind of delusions did she have?'

'She reported fairly classic delusional symptoms.' The psychiatrist leafed through his papers. 'She thought she was the victim of a conspiracy between the Russian intelligence services and the Italian mafia who had apparently operated on her to insert a radio transmitter into her head that allowed them to observe her via satellite.'

'I visited her home,' Wisting said. 'She had taken apart almost all of the electrical equipment.'

'In the most recent consultations I noticed something of a deterioration,' the psychiatrist admitted. 'A kind of shift in the state of her illness.'

101

'In what way?'

'The delusions changed in character.'

'Is that usual?'

'Most often you can observe a clear continuity and a conspicuous pattern in a patient's delusions, but sometimes new ones crop up.'

'What did you talk about the last time she was here?'

'She was certain that strangers entered her house when she was away or while she slept. She said that furniture had been moved. The milk in the fridge had been adulterated with a sleeping draught so that she didn't waken when they were working in her house during the night.'

Wisting drew a hand through his hair, wondering where the distinction between imagination and reality lay in a psychiatric patient. 'What about these abductions?' he asked. 'Did she talk about those too?'

The psychiatrist nodded.

'That was a part of her perception of the world. She had notions that this mafia organisation had doped her, carried her off and operated on her to insert the radio transmitter. At regular intervals, they repeated this to exchange the transmitter for a new, more up-to-date version with a greater operating distance.'

Wisting squirmed in his seat, not knowing how to shape a stray thought he had. 'You're sure these abductions were delusions?' he eventually enquired. 'That nothing might actually have taken place, but in a different manner and with a different purpose than she described?'

The psychiatrist indulged in a smile. 'I have been practising for more than thirty years,' he said. 'Believe me, Hanne Richter was diagnosed correctly.'

Wisting's eyes narrowed. Cocksure certainty was a quality he disliked. 'She's away now, of course,' he pointed out.

22

Two unanswered calls were shown on his mobile when he came out of the psychiatrist's – both from his father. Now 79 years old he had been a widower for 22 of them. He was independent and wanted to be as little bother as possible, but recently he had been asking his only son for help more often. The clock on the phone showed 13.23. He had forgotten that he had promised to drive the old man to a two o'clock appointment at his eye specialist. He still just had time but was exasperated to be held up.

His father had been complaining that he couldn't see clearly, his vision foggy and sometimes double. He had made the cataract diagnosis himself. It was simply part of being old, he knew, almost as common as grey hair, but it tormented him. He had to read newspapers with one eye closed, and couldn't manage with books. Wisting phoned him, to reassure him that he had not forgotten.

'Let me take a taxi,' his father said. 'You've got a lot to do.'

'I'm already on my way,' Wisting said dismissively and a quarter of an hour later, his father was sitting beside him in the car, wearing a large pair of sunglasses that fitted tightly on his head.

'Has it got worse?' Wisting enquired.

'A little,' his father conceded. 'Line's home,' he continued quickly, as if he wanted to talk about something else. 'She called in yesterday. I could've got her to drive me.'

'It's fine,' Wisting assured him.

'How's the case going?' Wisting admitted that they were groping in the dark. 'Oh, I know all about that,' his father commented, removing his sunglasses. The pupil of his left eye was covered by a greyish haze.

'Did you know them?' Wisting asked abruptly, suddenly realising that his father was about the same age as the men who had disappeared.

'Not well, but more than some others.'

'But you knew them?'

'Many years ago,' his father nodded. 'Sverre Lund was probably the one I had most contact with.'

'The head teacher?'

'Your mother was at school with his wife. I've forgotten her name.'

'Greta.'

'Yes, that's right. Is he one of the ones you've found . . . remains of?'

'We don't know for certain, yet.' Wisting reached for a bag on the back seat. 'I've got something I'd like you to look at,' he said. He took out the photograph he had borrowed from the nursing home and handed it to his father while he drove. His father held it up to one eye and screwed up his face. 'Do you know any of them?' Wisting asked.

'That's Sverre,' his father replied, pointing to the man furthest back on the stairs. 'Is that Torkel?' he asked, pointing to the person who sat diagonally below the old head teacher.

Wisting nodded. 'And then that's Otto Saga and Christian Hauge,' he explained, pointing.

'Christian Hauge, yes,' his father mumbled. 'He's dead now, poor man.'

'Poor man?'

'He was widowed early, and had a daughter who got mixed up with a drunkard. There were two grandchildren. You know about it of course? The police murder?'

'Yes indeed,' Wisting admitted. 'He's out now and living in Helgeroa.' He neglected to tell him that Line was going to meet him. 'What about the one with the pipe?'

His father held the picture up so that the reflection of the sun on the glass didn't get in the way. 'There's something familiar about him, but I can't think what.' He laid the picture on his lap. 'Is it important?'

'It might be,' Wisting answered. 'The four others are probably dead.'

They had reached the eye specialist's when the phone rang. It was Nils Hammer. 'Where are you?'

'In town.'

'You need to come out to Blokkebukta cove. There's a severed foot lying there.'

Wisting glanced over at his father, who held up his hand to prevent his son from saying anything. 'I'll manage,' he said. 'I'll take a taxi home.'

23

Blokkebukta cove was situated in the lee of the Skaggerak, behind a large spit of land covered in pebbles that had been left behind after the ice age, a moraine spine extending from Finland through Sweden to enter the sea at Mølen. A pleasant spot, the area had been used as an overnight stop for bathing tourists for almost a century. The caravans were sitting on flat areas extending to the encircling grove of trees. Three sandy beaches stretched out one after the other, separated by steep hillocks and sections of dense, shady oak forest.

Part of the most northerly beach was closed off. Wisting drove as close as he could before leaving the car. Journalists stood like a wall in front of the red and white crime scene tape, but quickly gathered round him, bombarding him with questions. Wisting ignored them and crouched under the tape.

Nils Hammer was standing with Espen Mortensen on the pebbles. The beach was a bit rougher at the discovery site, consisting of small stones and broken shells, and waves rushed backwards and forwards, almost in rhythm with Wisting's own breath.

The foot was a left limb, exactly like the three others, but this find was different. The shoe did not have the same faded appearance from having been in water for a long time. The pleats of skin and flesh protruding from a thick, yellow sock had taken on a grey colouring, but the rotting process had not set in completely.

'Camilla Thaulow?' Hammer suggested.

Wisting squatted down, studying the foot in the sharp sunlight. 'The type of shoe matches, at least,' he said. 'Black Nike.'

All the same, there was something different, Wisting thought, examining the shoe with the curved logo of one of the world's biggest sports equipment manufacturers. The other feet had drifted to land several nautical miles from here. This had to have been dumped somewhere else to have washed ashore at this place. Since it was only three days since Camilla Thaulow disappeared the dumping spot had to be somewhere in the vicinity.

Wisting turned and peered at the barrier. In a huddle beside the journalists were the amateur spectators, seaside visitors, tourists from the campsite, and summer cottage folk. He scanned them – it was a habit he had adopted. It wasn't unusual for the perpetrator to appear among the spectators. Pyromaniacs were especially known for it – returning to the scene to watch what they had set off. However, it could also apply to other criminals. The fact that the guilty party dared to show himself could even, in a way, serve as an alibi.

He scrutinised the faces: women with children in their arms, men with bare chests and large bellies, a couple of young boys on bicycles. There was nothing in particular to notice. Neither was there anything to suggest that whoever was behind all this could know the fourth foot would be washed up exactly here, exactly now.

'What the hell is happening?' Hammer groaned, bringing Wisting back. 'What are we talking about? Someone who kills and dismembers, and who throws the left feet into the sea?' Wisting did not reply, but acknowledged that it was beyond his comprehension. 'Why are we not finding the remainder of these people?' Hammer continued. 'We've had people searching the beaches and rocky shores for days, but nothing has turned up.'

'If this is her foot . . .' Wisting began. Loud voices from

the press corps fifty metres behind them interrupted him. The journalists were drowning each other out and the photographers pressing their triggers.

Audun Vetti forced his way through, presented himself inside the barrier and raised his hands. 'I shall have a discussion with my investigators, and then return with a statement,' Wisting heard him announce.

'*My* investigators,' Hammer chuckled.

The Assistant Chief of Police descended with purposeful steps. He stopped to stare at the foot on the powdery shells. 'A left foot,' he declared. Wisting saw no reason to disagree. 'It appears . . . fresh,' Vetti continued.

'That was our impression too,' Wisting conceded.

'Is it hers? The missing nurse?'

'It's too early to say.'

The Assistant Chief of Police peered over his shoulder. 'But what shall I say to that bunch up there?'

'As I said, it's too early to say anything at all.'

'We must confirm the discovery at least?'

'Must we?'

Vetti remained standing. 'Do we know anything more?' he asked. 'Is there anything more we can talk about?'

'The less we say, the less there is to retract if it turns out to be wrong.'

Vetti nodded, smoothed his hair over the bald crown, turned and approached the waiting crowd.

'What if it is hers?' Mortensen asked, preparing to remove the foot. 'You were about to say something when Vetti arrived. Some kind of deduction.'

'Nothing, really, but Vetti is right, naturally. If it is Camilla Thaulow's foot, it confirms that there is a connection.' He turned round, staring across the shining sea. 'It means that we are only three days behind the culprit. We are about to catch up with him.'

24

William Wisting parked at one of the visitors' spaces at the Rødberggrenda housing co-operative, and looked around.

He should have come here earlier. As soon as it became clear they were facing something more than a straightforward missing persons case he should have sent investigators for new interviews with the relatives. It was several years since he had realised that his greatest weakness as a leader was that he couldn't bear to entrust important investigation tasks to others. It was both a wish and necessity for him to have a close involvement with the assignments he thought most essential. It was not enough to read a report, a statement or a record of an interview since he could not reach through reading the sort of intuitive impression that might emerge in a conversation, and that might expand into a chink in the mystery.

Looked at this way, his worst enemy as an investigator was time. Not that he considered it a growing advantage for the perpetrator, whom he knew he would catch eventually, but it was a challenge to get time for everything. He had taught himself to be sure to have time enough for the most important things. As a rule it didn't involve making a choice, only approaching tasks in the correct order. He didn't like any sense of losing control. At the same time, he had to take time to allocate tasks to others when it was often just as easy to do the job himself. Nevertheless, it demanded that he prioritise his different duties and this was very challenging in itself.

The car door slammed behind him. At one time, in the

1970s, the Rødberggrenda housing co-operative had represented the new way of thinking about housing. With its playgrounds and common outdoor areas the intention was that the residents should feel as if they were living in a village. Now the decline was obvious. Vandals had put their various signatures in a row on the garages. The grass on the small lawn between the parking area and the row of houses was scorched and filled with clover and withered dandelions. The fence around the playground had fallen in places, rubbish bins were overflowing, and children of varying ages played around a rusty climbing frame. Both the game and the conversation were conducted in a foreign language.

Kristin and Mathias Lauritzen lived in the middle of a row of seven flats. They were both in their mid-fifties. She was Otto Saga's daughter, and he was the youngest son of Torkel Lauritzen, who had disappeared from the nursing home within three days of each other. It was this 'coincidence' that had placed their names high on the list of people he wanted to speak to.

A background check on them had already been carried out. Mathias Lauritzen had been receiving disability benefit, and his wife Kristin worked as a cleaner in a children's nursery. A number of payment defaults had been noted in their credit records, enough to check their alibis against the possibility that something criminal had taken place. Money was always a possible motive for a criminal act. Since they didn't have an exact time of day for when the old men had vanished, it was difficult to come to any conclusion. Their alibis were not watertight for all the hours involved, but appeared credible.

Before he entered, Wisting had already formed an impression of the married couple that he could not have obtained from simply reading about them. A lawnmower was standing in the middle of the little lawn in front of the house after someone had left the job half-finished. On the staircase, there were three tied plastic bags filled with

110

stinking rubbish. An overflowing ashtray was balanced on the banister. The nameplate on the door also displayed the names of the sons who had left home long before. All this spoke of the people who lived here.

It was Kristin Lauritzen who opened the door. She was plump and her face was puffy. Her curly hair was dishevelled, as though she had been lying sleeping.

'I phoned earlier today,' Wisting said after introducing himself.

The woman responded with a nod, showing him in. The air was stuffy and warm. The architects for the housing co-operative had laid out the flat in traditional fashion with the kitchen and bathroom to the left of the entrance door, a corridor that led to an L-shaped living room with tall windows on to a small balcony and flimsy doors that divided two adjacent bedrooms from the living room. Most of the internal furnishings looked as if they had been there since the flat was new.

Mathias Lauritzen was sitting in a deep armchair. He was a large, stocky man, and stared at Wisting with blue, watery eyes. He did not get up, but moved a weekly magazine from his lap as the policeman entered.

'Is there any news?' he asked.

Wisting sat down. 'We've received answers from the tests that the forensic experts have carried out on the feet,' he began. 'They confirm that the first shoe that was found belongs to your father.'

Mathias Lauritzen said nothing. It didn't seem as though the information affected him at all.

'What about the others?' his wife asked.

Wisting shook his head. 'We haven't had it confirmed that any of them belongs to your father.'

'What do you mean?'

'No DNA relationship has been established between yourself and any of the finds,' Wisting elaborated. 'The forensics experts are carrying out another analysis of the samples, but there is nothing to suggest that the result will be different.'

Mathias Lauritzen got up, flinging the magazine onto the coffee table. 'Fuck,' he swore, taking several steps out of the room before turning, coming back and sitting down again. 'I'd hoped we could soon be finished with all this.'

'We won't be finished until we know what happened,' said his wife cautiously. 'It's not certain that we'll ever be finished with it.'

'But it would've helped if we could get them declared dead, so that we could move on and put it all behind us.'

Wisting took out his notepad. Until just a few days before, they had all thought that the disappearance cases involved their fathers having an accident of some kind. The discovery of the severed feet suggested something more. 'What do you think has happened?' he asked. Neither of them could give an answer. Wisting straightened up, asking the direct question: 'Do you know of anyone who might wish for this to happen?'

'Are you asking if the old man had any enemies?' Mathias Lauritzen enquired.

'Did he?'

'Enemies . . .' The man in the deep leather chair seemed to relish the word. 'Not any longer. For the past forty years, the enemies have existed only in his own head.'

'What do you mean?'

'Soviet invaders,' Mathias Lauritzen explained. 'The communists were his enemies. They were Kristin's father's enemies too,' he went on, nodding in the direction of his wife, 'Our fathers were members of a military group sitting in readiness for an occupation.'

Wisting raised one eyebrow. 'Readiness for an occupation?'

'The cold war,' Mathias Lauritzen explained. 'They were afraid that Stalin would invade Norway and were active in the intelligence network.' He held up his hand. 'You mustn't

112

ask because I don't know much more. The whole network was exposed in the media at the end of the 1970s, I don't know any more than that. The old man never talked about it, at least not to me who's never been in the military.'

Wisting had difficulty shaping his thoughts, but it was as though something had opened up. He felt he might be close to something important, something they had previously overlooked.

'Otto was the leader,' Mathias Lauritzen continued, referring to his father-in-law. 'Of course he worked in the Air Force, and got to study a lot of things in the newspapers. I think he was the one who recruited the others.'

'Who were the others in this group?'

'Head teacher Lund was involved in any case,' Mathias Lauritzen said. The expression on his face changed as soon as he had said this, as though he had made a discovery. 'But for fuck's sake,' he exclaimed, getting up once more. 'He's away too of course. What's happening, really?'

'That's what we're trying to find out.'

'Have you found a foot belonging to him?' Kristin Lauritzen asked tentatively. 'Head teacher Lund's?'

Wisting shook his head. 'How many were in this group?' he asked.

Mathias Lauritzen shrugged his shoulders. 'A couple more, at least,' he replied. 'Four or five altogether, I think.'

'A group of five?' Wisting suggested. The man did not react to the suggestion. 'Was Christian Hauge a member of the group?' he went on.

'Liv's father? I don't know, but it could well be. Dad and he had a lot of contact, but I don't think they had much to say to each other after what his grandson did. He shot a policeman. You know about it?'

Wisting nodded and rose abruptly from his chair. 'I've got something I want to show you,' he said. 'I'll just nip out to the car.'

He walked towards the door, without either of the two residents bothering to accompany him. He went over to his car, got out the old photograph and returned directly to the living room.

'Do you know anyone in this picture?' he asked, placing it in front of them.

They both leaned over. 'That's Dad,' Kristin Lauritzen said, pointing to the man on the right of the middle step on the stairway. 'That's Mathias' father sitting beside him. Where did you get this?'

'I got it at the nursing home,' Wisting said. 'Do you recognise anybody else?'

Kristin Lauritzen frowned, concentrating on the picture. 'Is that Lund, the head teacher?' she asked, pointing to the man at the very back on the right. 'We had him at school, though he wasn't head teacher then.'

Wisting confirmed this. 'Do you know who this might be?' he asked, indicating the man with the pipe on the front step.

They both scrutinised the picture, but finally shook their heads.

25

Wisting studied the photo of the shoe and foot that had washed ashore at Blokkebukta cove. The wing-shaped Nike-logo was blurred by dried salt water. The picture made him think of Gary Gilmore. On the 19th July 1976, he had robbed a petrol station on the west coast of the USA and killed the man behind the counter. The next day, he did the same thing again at a motel. He was sentenced to death and, six months later, shot by a firing squad in the American state of Utah. With that he became the first person to be executed after the reintroduction of the death penalty in the United States by the Supreme Court earlier that year.

Gary Gilmore asked to die. He refrained from all opportunities to appeal, and attempted to kill himself before the authorities did it. Since that time, over a thousand people had been shot, gassed, hanged, poisoned or killed in the electric chair in the USA. In the course of the same period, more than a hundred innocent people condemned to death had been released from death row. Among other things, new DNA evidence had demonstrated their innocence and rescued them from execution. How many innocent people were in their graves no one knew.

Wisting saw before him the headlines that were spread out over the kitchen table at home where Line was working. A thousand executed criminals in just over thirty years was around the same number of people who had been sentenced for murder in Norway in the same period. History had taught them that, in Norway too, people had been wrongly convicted of murder. The difference was that in Norway

115

none of the criminals convicted of murder had been executed. Eventually they were released into society again.

A few years before, he had read a book about Gary Gilmore. For his last meal, he had eaten a hamburger, hard boiled eggs and baked potato. He ended the meal with coffee and three glasses of whisky. Then he got up, saying, *'Let's do it!'*

Wisting traced the line of the curved Nike-logo on the picture with his finger. It was part of the Gary Gilmore legend that his last words had led to the advertising people at Nike coming up with the advertising campaign *Just Do It*. The three syllables became a slogan that not only persuaded people all over the world to exercise more and become healthier, but also women to leave their rotten husbands, and young boys to pluck up the courage to ask girls out on a date.

Just do it. Wisting leaned back, rubbing his eyes. It was not so easy. He was confused, and unsure of the way forward.

'It's false,' Espen Mortensen said behind him. Wisting turned round towards the doorway, staring uncomprehendingly at the crime technician. 'The foot,' Mortensen continued explaining, pointing at the picture Wisting was holding in his hand. 'It's not real.'

'What do you mean?'

'The foot doesn't belong to anybody.'

Nils Hammer popped his head round the door behind Mortensen. Wisting glanced at the photograph he had in his hand, in which fibres of flesh were sticking out of the shoe, and then back at the two investigators. He didn't know how to form the thoughts that were racing through his head and turn them into a question.

'What do you mean?' Hammer asked.

Espen Mortensen entered the room.

'I made further tests on the shoe in the lab and thought there was something strange,' he said, sitting down on the

116

visitor's chair. 'The skin was so sort of thick. On the inside, it was mostly fat and gristle, so I removed that.'

'And?'

'It was a pig's trotter and knuckle.'

'A pig's trotter?'

'They sell them in the shops. They call it *syltelabb* – it's a delicacy in Southern Norway. People eat it at Christmas time down there. They even have a world championship in eating *syltelabb*. I saw it on TV. Kristopher Schau took part, but came last.'

Wisting held up his hand to call him to a halt. 'I know what a *syltelabb* is,' he said.

'Has somebody played a joke on us?' Hammer asked.

Mortensen shrugged. 'A practical joke. Quite a good one, obviously.'

Hammer swore, pulling himself up onto the windowsill. 'People are sick in the head. Here we have amputated feet getting washed ashore, the newspapers implying there could be a serial murderer on the loose, and somebody plays a trick on us?'

The door out to the corridor was still open. Audun Vetti walked by, but stopped and came back into the doorway. 'Any news?' he enquired, studying their faces.

'Apparently not,' Wisting replied. 'The foot from Blok-kebukta is a dead end.'

'What do you mean?'

Espen Mortensen explained: 'Someone's been having some fun with us. The shoe contained a pig's trotter.'

'It was false,' Hammer added, with the Assistant Chief of Police looking as though he did not quite understand. 'It's got nothing to do with the case.'

Vetti sat down on the empty chair in front of the desk. His tongue went in and out of his mouth. 'But I've already confirmed it to the media,' he said, smacking his lips. The chirruping of birds in the tree outside reached them when silence descended on the room.

'You had to say something,' Hammer commented drily, but it didn't look as though Vetti understood the irony.

'I require, in fact, that the information I issue to the press is quality assured,' he said, getting up.

Wisting opened his mouth to say something, but shut it again, biting his tongue until the Assistant Chief of Police had left the room.

26

Wisting let himself into the house in Herman Wildenveys-gate and went inside to the kitchen. Line's papers were still lying across the kitchen table, sorted into piles so that they didn't take up the entire space. He ought to talk to her about Gary Gilmore, he thought. The dilemmas surrounding the American death penalty could put Norwegian sentencing practices into perspective. Show how the price Norwegian prisoners paid for the people's feeling of security and sense of justice was, despite everything, small.

He put his own notes on the kitchen worktop and opened the refrigerator. Line had been there too, filling it with fruit, yogurt cartons, several bottles of *Farris* mineral water, and various cheese spreads. He took out an apple and entered the living room, opening the doors to the verandah. The evening air was full of the sound of insects. A neighbour had visitors, and he heard laughter and talk.

He breathed in the scent of flowers, grass and the warm walls of the house on which the sun had been shining throughout the long summer day. Leaning on the railings he gazed over the town. The sultry, still heat dampened all sound. On the sea, the boats had lit their lanterns and were either on their way back to harbour or had dropped anchor.

Something about sailing boats fascinated him, how they slide forward majestically. Whether the fjord lay like a sheet of beaten copper in the sunset, or frothing in protest against the whiplashes of an angry gale, the sailing boats maintained their course and their dignity. Straightening up he took a bite of the apple. It struck him that the most important aspect of a sailing ship was what could not be seen. The secret of its steadiness lay in the heavy keel, and that was what he lacked in this investigation – a staunch and stabilising keel. The investigation was being tossed hither and thither, without them knowing what lay at the bottom of it all.

In his neighbour's house, someone brought out a guitar and several of the guests sang along. Wisting ate the rest of his apple, throwing the core over the grass to bounce over the cliff and down towards the town.

The cat came dashing out from the bushes in the back garden. It gave out a few painful whimpers, ran across the lawn on speedy paws and jumped on the verandah.

'Hello there, Buster,' Wisting smiled, bending down. 'Are you hungry?'

The cat miaowed its response, rubbing its head against his leg. It followed him closely into the kitchen, purring when Wisting opened the cupboard door and brought out a tin of cat food. He tipped the contents into a bowl on the floor. Buster butted his head against Wisting's hand, starting to eat before he had finished serving.

He threw the can in the rubbish, sat down at the kitchen table and brought out the working notes he had taken home with him. They were mainly printouts from the internet. In 1948, the Defence Department had established an operation to carry out evacuation, sabotage and surveillance on Norwegian soil in the event of an invasion. Based on the experiences of the Second World War it would be organised in networks with key personnel within the various areas.

He recalled the case being raised in the media in the autumn of 1977, the same year that Wisting had started at the police training college. When the police took action against an illegal distillery on a holiday property at Langesundsfjorden they discovered a bunker filled with weapons, equipment and ammunition enough for more than a hundred men. The ship owner who owned the property claimed that he was storing the weapons as a member of a secret organisation under the control of the Defence Department's intelligence services. As Mathias Lauritzen recalled, there had been a tremendous uproar in the media. In the Norwegian parliament, the *Storting*, the Minister of Defence at first denied that the ship owner had any connection to the intelligence services. He later had to correct this reply and confirm that there was talk of a weapons store belonging to a paramilitary network going under the name *Stay Behind*, and subject to the Defence Department's intelligence services. Their assignment meant staying behind in the occupied area and taking action behind enemy lines.

The revelations about the secret network had been more than thirty years previously. Wisting was unsure whether this had any link to the investigation, or if it was the sort of thing that simply comes to the surface when they started to dig.

Buster was full up. He stretched out his long cat body and shuffled off into the living room. Wisting glanced at the clock on the kitchen wall. It was after eleven o'clock and it was Friday night – he did not expect Line to come home.

He got up, wondering what Suzanne was doing. She had entered his life less than a year before and filled a void. Ingrid would always be the most important woman in his life. That could never be changed, but he had discovered that a new love could be something completely different.

He wanted to phone her, but decided to call his father first. It was really too late, but he knew that the old man liked to sit up watching television. He keyed in the number, and his father answered almost immediately – he could hear dull voices from the television in the background.

'How are you?' he asked.

'Fine, thanks. It was just as I thought – a cataract.'

'Oh yes.'

'They're arranging an operation for me. Apparently it's a simple matter.' Wisting heard the TV being turned down at

121

the other end. 'The whole thing is over in twenty minutes and, next day, your sight is back.'

'That's great, of course. When is it to take place?'

'They'll send an appointment letter, but it won't be until after the summer.'

'How did you get home?'

'I got a taxi requisition. I could have got that to get there too, but it was good that you drove me.'

Wisting went to the fridge, studied the contents and chose a yogurt.

'Have you managed to do your shopping?'

'No, but Line dropped by. She phoned first and bought me a few things. I've been enjoying some fishcakes.'

Wisting opened the fridge once more, checking whether she had left some fishcakes for him too, but found none.

'How's the investigation going?' his father wanted to know. 'It was on the news. A foot was found out at Blokkebukta cove too, I understand. I just saw a picture of you as well, but it didn't look as though there was anything much that was new.'

Wisting explained that the last foot had been a counterfeit.

'It might of course be that it was the culprit you're looking for who put it there all the same,' his father suggested. 'As a diversionary tactic.'

'It's more likely to be a crude joke. What else would it be good for?'

'To spoil your calculations. I understood that this oceanographer could calculate the place where the feet come from. If he had included that foot in the calculation, the answer would be wrong.'

'You've got that right, but I think all the same that there would have had to be two calculations. The other feet had been in the water longer. Time is a factor he uses in the calculations.'

'Perhaps it's easier to calculate where the false foot came

from. It certainly can't have been in the water for many days.'

Wisting agreed. The difference between the two calculations, however, was that as far as the false foot was concerned, they would probably not find anything at the other end. As far as the other three were concerned, the calculation could lead them to three corpses.

'By the way, I thought of who the man in the photograph is,' his father said abruptly. 'Him on the step with the pipe.'

Wisting tightened his grip on the phone and breathed in, letting the breath remain in his chest.

'Who?' he asked.

'Carsten Meyer. He's a few years older than me. A really intelligent chap. Got a job at the Defence Department's research institute at Karljohansvern in Horten after his national service here in Stavern, but later he began working at the weapons factory in Kongsberg. He was involved in making the Penguin rockets, I know that.'

'Do you know where he is now?'

'I haven't seen him for several decades. He moved to Kongsberg, of course. It could well be that he still lives there, if he's still living.'

Wisting finished the conversation with his father and remained with the phone in his hand, wondering what he should do with this new information. Then he keyed in Suzanne's number.

'Have you gone to bed?' he asked.

'Almost,' she replied in a hoarse voice.

'Is it okay if I come over?'

'That would be fine.'

27

Wisting was one of the first at the police station on Saturday morning, but someone had already managed to leave a package wrapped in grey paper on his desk. Delivered by messenger, it had been accepted down at the desk and carried up to his office. He knew what it contained, but pushed it to one side, deciding to wait to open it up. Other tasks had higher priority.

On the desk in front of him were several phone messages the girls in the criminal proceedings office had taken the previous day. Most of them were from journalists who wanted him to phone, but among them was a message from Doctor Hardberg who wanted to talk to him. Wisting thought back to the doctor's surgery four days earlier and all the tests he had carried out. Some of the results might have arrived. Probably it was not important, as then he would have phoned him on his mobile. In any case, today the surgery was closed. He placed the message in front of his desk calendar, threw all the other notes down into the box for paper recycling beneath his desk and switched on the computer.

He found Carsten Meyer in the data from the national register. 79 years old he had lived in Kongsberg for the last 35. The screen showed that he was a widower, had one son now living in Horten, and two grandchildren, one of whom lived in Kongsberg while the other lived in Stavern.

Meyer was the last surviving member of the five-man group. Wisting had no idea what he might have to say, but a drive to Kongsberg would take no more than an hour and a half, and he would be back in town by twelve o'clock.

The main road wound its way northwards along the Lågen river, which ran quiet and shallow beside him. The morning dew still lay like a veil of grey over the undulating agricultural landscape. He passed potato fields, spruce forests, small farms and enclosures of frightened pigs that ran round in circles.

He pulled out the map printout when he drove into the old mining town where many of the country's high tech industries were located.

Carsten Meyer lived in the old area of workers' houses on the west side of the river. The house looked as though it had been newly renovated and extended.

Wisting parked on the street. The entranceway opened directly on to the narrow pavement. He rang the bell, then stood and waited.

The door opened almost immediately. A man in his thirties stood scrutinising him. He was of middle height with light brown hair parted in the middle and falling into his eyes. He looked tired and had dark rings under his eyes. There was something familiar about his face, but Wisting couldn't remember where he had seen it before.

'Is this Carsten Meyer's?' he asked.

The man facing him nodded.

'He's in the living room,' he explained, taking a couple of steps back to let Wisting enter.

'Is it about the feet?' he asked when Wisting was inside. 'How . . .?'

'I know who you are,' the man continued, leading Wisting in. 'I'm from Stavern.' He turned round and held out his hand. 'Daniel Meyer,' he introduced himself. 'Carsten is my grandfather. I'm visiting him for a couple of days. He's been waiting for you.'

Carsten Meyer was sitting in a winged armchair by the window. The chair was upholstered in green, with carved arms and legs. The old man lifted his eyes and tightened his grip on the armrest as they entered. Age had left its obvious mark on him. His veins were like blue lines beneath his parchment thin skin.

'A visitor for you,' his grandson explained in a loud voice.

The old man leaned his head against the back of the chair, squinted at Wisting and nodded.

'Did you ask him to come?' he asked his grandson.

Daniel Meyer shook his head.

'He found his way on his own.'

A glass of water was sitting on a side table with, beside it, a newspaper opened at the crossword, a bowl with an old pipe and a brown tobacco pouch. Carsten Meyer leaned forward slowly and reached for the glass of water, his hand shaking a little as he lifted it to his mouth. His larynx moved up and down beneath the loose old man's skin while he drank and some of the water ran down his chin. He put down the glass, drying his face with the back of his hand.

Wisting sat down, placing the picture of the five-man group on top of the newspaper on the table.

The old man bent forward, studying the photograph without picking it up.

'There you have us,' he said with a smile.

'You're the only one left,' Wisting said.

The man in front of him became serious again, leaning backwards in his chair.

'We've almost been waiting for you to get in touch,' he said, nodding in the direction of his grandson, his ally. 'But I'm afraid you've come a long way to no purpose.'

'Can you tell me about the five-man group?' Wisting enquired.

'How much do you know?'

'That you were members of a force that was preparing for an invasion.'

The old man reached for his pipe, putting it in his left hand as he helped himself to a pinch of tobacco from the pouch.

'The assignment was to stay behind as agents and saboteurs in the event of a Soviet invasion,' he explained. 'Initially, personnel with experience from World War II were recruited, but we were too young to have taken part in that. After the war, we enlisted and became members of the Norwegian occupation forces in Germany.'

His hand fumbled at his breast pocket, returning with a matchbox. He put the pipe in his mouth and opened the small box. His hands were steadier now, as though these were customary and practised gestures. His face shone behind the lit match.

'Otto returned home as a lieutenant,' Carsten Meyer continued, sucking life into his pipe. 'We others began our civilian life.'

The sweet smell from the pipe tobacco spread through the room. The old man put the spent match into the bowl, coughed and remained sitting with his pipe on his lap.

'I of course became a semi-civilian and got to take part in the development of new weapons,' he went on. 'But Otto became a trusted officer. He had a military background that gave him a key role in the organisation. He was the one who brought us others in. The nationwide alert force required Norwegian citizens with a variety of professional and environmental backgrounds. It involved finding reliable people with morality, motivation and integrity.'

The pipe found its way to his mouth again.

'It was a serious undertaking, but in those days we still had a spirit of adventure and accepted when we were invited.'

The old man's eyes became evasive, as though they were filled with old memories.

'The network consisted of small action groups spread over the whole country,' he continued. 'No one knew about each other. We were given lessons in sabotage campaigns with explosives, conducted shooting training, and were given responsibility for storing weapons, ammunition and other equipment. Eventually we got other assignments.

127

Sverre Lund was appointed to the education department, and Torkel Lauritzen became head of personnel at *Treschow-Fritzøe*. These were posts that enabled them to pinpoint communist sympathisers and those who might be suspected of that. Daniel can probably tell you a lot more.' He pointed with the mouthpiece of his pipe towards his grandson. 'He's writing a book about it.'

Wisting glanced towards his grandson on the settee. Only now did he notice that the low coffee table was covered in notes.

'There are still many stories that haven't been told,' Daniel Meyer said. 'I'm a war historian. It's mostly a hobby, but I've written several articles for *Vi Menn* magazine and the newspaper supplement *A-magasinet*. I'm interested in crimes that were committed during the war and in the post-war years.'

'War crimes?'

'No, but crimes that were committed under cover of being part of the war. How the home front carried out almost accidental liquidations, for example.'

'Did the alert force commit such crimes?'

'No, but it's an exciting part of the post-war period that interests me.'

'Is the organisation active nowadays?'

'Of course,' Daniel Meyer nodded. 'Not in the same form as when grandfather was active, but if Norway should be occupied once more, we have a system that would gather information and intelligence from the occupation force for the Norwegian authorities. It's integral to the operation that the organisation should and must be secret.'

'Daniel interviewed them before they disappeared,' Carsten Meyer continued. 'But I think you have to look in other places than the alert organisation to find any connection with the disappearances.'

'You talked to them?' Wisting asked, turning to the young writer.

'Several times with all of them – Torkel Lauritzen, Otto Saga, Sverre Lund and Christian Hauge. They were a tight-knit team, even though it's many years since they operated together.'

'When was the last time you were in touch with them?'

Daniel Meyer considered carefully.

'Last summer. The last time was a few weeks before Christian Hauge died. We talked about the old days. There was nothing in what they said to suggest that they knew that something might happen to them. I've got sound recordings. Naturally, you can have access to both them and my notes, but I don't think you'll find anything.'

Wisting didn't reply. He wanted to accept the offer, but although the solution might have its roots in the past, the actual answer had to lie in the present.

He turned to the old man again: 'Did you have any contact with them?'

The pipe had gone out. Carsten Meyer took out his matches and lit it again before he responded.

'Fellowship was important to us,' he nodded. 'We were a tight-knit bunch. Although I moved away, we kept in touch, but we haven't seen so much of each other for the past twenty years. Something was broken by the police murder.'

The police murder again, thought Wisting.

'Maybe you remember that?' Daniel Meyer asked. 'It was Christian Hauge's grandson who shot him. He used his grandfather's gun.'

'Are you writing about that too?' Wisting enquired, nodding towards the piles of paper on the table.

'No. That had nothing to do with the organisation.'

'Do you know Ken Ronny Hauge?'

'We're the same age and from the same place.' He leafed through his papers. 'Grandfather commuted backwards and forwards between Stavern and the research institute in Horten, but moved here to Kongsberg together with grand-mother when he got a job at the weapons factory in 1974. I was only two years old then. My parents lived in the same street as Ken Ronny's mother.'

'Were you as tightly knit as your grandparents?'

Daniel Meyer shook his head.

'What happened with the policeman was as much of a surprise to me as to everyone else.'

'You know he's moved back?'

Daniel Meyer didn't seem surprised, but replied in the negative: 'Actually, I didn't know that. I didn't even know that he'd been released. I see his brother occasionally. He's done quite well, but I haven't spoken to Ken Ronny since that day the police came for him.'

28

Line flicked through the photographs of Ken Ronny Hauge stored on her computer. He was a different man from the one she had seen in the archive pictures.

She had photographed him in segments. A hand clapping the dog. His dirty fists in a rag. An index finger placed thoughtfully at the far corner of an eye. Pictures that could not identify him, but that told a great deal about who he was. She had taken other photographs as well, whole portraits in high definition from which she could pick out elements to make good illustrations.

He somehow looked different when she thought of him as Ken, instead of Ken Ronny. In fact, he resembled the doll she had played with as a child. It was difficult to imagine him as a murderer.

In a couple of the pictures that could have gone straight into an advertising campaign, he was raising a cola bottle to his mouth with a tanned and sinewy arm.

There was something about him that roused her curiosity. Thinking how his story could become a report in itself, she realised that she was looking for an excuse to visit him again, to find new, unanswered questions for her report.

Hearing Tommy come out of the bathroom she clicked the photographs away. He came in to her wearing jeans, but with a bare chest and a bath towel over his shoulders.

'Any news?' he asked, nodding in the direction of the computer.

Line shook her head as she updated the browser. There were no developments in the case of the amputated feet. Her own newspaper had a spread with an actor who was well known from a soap series on TV. He had a summer cottage in Ula, and expressed the opinion that what had happened was both terrifying and sinister, according to the introduction.

Tommy threw the towel down, pulling a T-shirt over his head.

'When will you be finished today?' he wanted to know.

She was to meet the double murderer that day, Åge Reinholdt, who had settled on his grandparents' smallholding near Gusland after his last sentence.

'I don't know, but I need to write out a lot while it's still fresh in my mind.' She folded the laptop closed and glanced at him with a look of guilt in her eyes. 'I'd thought I would travel directly home afterwards. Sit there and get on with my work.'

'That's fine with me,' Tommy smiled. 'I was thinking of having a couple of beers with some pals this afternoon. We could meet up this evening if you manage to get finished.'

She sent him a grateful smile.

'Phone me when you're finished with that bloke,' Tommy added. 'So I know that you've survived the experience.'

29

Wisting received the phone message as he swung out from the Esso station in Kvelde. He had filled the tank, bought a hot-dog and was caught up in thoughts about Carsten Meyer and his grandson. Had it led to something? He had gained insight into the lives of the men who had disappeared, but nothing more. Like most things in this investigation – everything they did brought them one step further into what appeared to be a closed book. The disappearances of Hanne Richter and Camilla Thaulow did not seem to fit with any theory about a mysterious something that might have happened in the post-war era.

It was Nils Hammer calling. It was a short message – they had found another new foot.

Twenty-five minutes later, Wisting was standing once more with fine-grained sand in his shoes, shading his eyes from the sun with his hand.

This shoe had not been washed ashore like the others, but was found out in the water beside a floating pontoon outside Solplassen campsite. No one had wanted to touch it, but eventually the warden of the site had waded out and caught it with a net borrowed from some children who were fishing for crabs.

By the time the warden returned ashore an enormous crowd of spectators had gathered on the beach. Wisting reckoned that they were well over a hundred. Several people from the press had also arrived, but the editors of the major newspapers had probably received MMS-photographs that were already on the internet.

The shoe had been placed in a white plastic box. Wisting bent over it – a left shoe.

He peered up at Mortensen.

'Is it real?'

The crime technician nodded.

'It's been in the water a long time,' he said, hunkering down beside Wisting. 'Exactly like the others.'

Wisting nodded. It was a leisure shoe from Nike, but appeared to be the cheaper type. It was white with an orange insert on each side, the material bleached by seawater and the enamel round the lace holes rusted. Parchment-like skin, tanned by its time in the water, was hanging out in loose fibres. The torn up network of tissue inside had clotted together and looked tough and slimy.

'Sverre Lund?' Hammer suggested.

Wisting agreed. They had most likely found the left foot belonging to the old head teacher.

'It does at least match the description his wife gave of the shoes,' he said. 'She bought them for him.'

'We should have the results of a DNA test at the beginning of the week,' Mortensen said.

Someone in the group of journalists shouted down to them. The first television camera had also appeared. Two policemen, standing with their hands at their backs, marked how close they were permitted to approach. Wisting didn't catch what was being shouted, but chose not to do anything about it. Audun Vetti had still not corrected the information about the discovery of the previous day, and would probably not turn up today.

'Let's pack up,' he proposed, shifting his gaze to the holidaymakers. He saw a couple of video cameras among them too, and had to accept being captured on their holiday footage. Several men had lifted their children up on their shoulders so that they had a better view. A light-haired boy eating an ice cream said something that caused the others to laugh.

Wisting bowed his head, thinking of the telephone conversation he had ahead of him with Mrs. Lund, and started to walk to his car, but didn't manage to leave the beach without answering questions from the reporters. He stood facing them and nodded to indicate that he was ready. A few of the photographers circled him to avoid shooting too directly into the sun. The light on the television camera glowed red.

'Can you confirm that yet another foot has been found?'

'Yes,' he replied, expressing himself formally. 'The police received a report just before twelve o'clock that a shoe had been found floating in the sea outside Solplassen. It contains probable human remains. We have taken charge of it and will be conducting further investigations.'

'This is the fifth,' one of the reporters ascertained. 'Are they from five different people?'

Wisting swallowed. He would need to take upon himself the task of correcting the misapprehension.

'This is the fourth shoe,' he explained, listening to how his voice remained steady and calm. 'There was an announcement of a similar find at Blokkebukta cove yesterday, but closer examination of that shoe has confirmed that the contents were not human.'

The group in front of him drowned each other out with their voices. He didn't catch any questions, but understood that he must elaborate further. The simplest way was be to completely open.

'The shoe contained slaughtered pig,' he stated. 'We think that it is a crude joke.'

'What's your opinion of it?'

'It is blameworthy and lacking in respect.'

'Has it ruined the investigation?'

'It has hindered us, and that is unfortunate, but it has not exactly wrecked the investigation.'

'Are you any closer to a solution?'

'We are working in our customary fashion with a number of different theories.'

Wisting saw that the journalists were going to form a critical follow-up question about the lack of results from the work of the police, so he moved his eye to the female journalist who was standing beside the man with the television camera.

'How can you know that the foot you have now found today is a real one?' she asked.

Wisting noticed that some children were jumping up and down behind him, trying to get into the recording. The cameraman moved to avoid them.

'Both the shoe and contents show signs of being in the water for a long time,' Wisting elaborated, turning towards the camera. 'The find appears to be all too real.'

'But can you confirm whether it involves a fourth victim, or if it is a body part that can be connected with the earlier discoveries?'

'It is a fourth victim,' Wisting confirmed, deciding that that would be enough. 'There will be a written statement in the course of the afternoon.'

There were a few more questions, but Wisting excused himself with a quick nod of the head. He glanced over to the shore before returning to his car. Then he stopped abruptly and turned to the people who were still standing in small groups chatting about the discovery and suddenly remembered where he had seen the war historian Daniel Meyer earlier: he had been one of the spectators when the counterfeit foot had been found out by Blokkebukta cove.

30

Ebbe Slettaker had connected his computer to the projector that was suspended from the ceiling in the conference room, but had not yet switched the projector on. The oceanographer alternated between glancing over his thick glasses at the computer screen, and at the investigators who gathered round the table. The Chief Superintendent and Assistant Chief of Police were present also.

Wisting made use of the time while the oceanographer was getting his presentation ready. Four feet in total had been found. One of them had been confirmed as belonging to Torkel Lauritzen who disappeared from Stavern nursing home on 1st September the previous year. Another could be said, with a strong degree of certainty, to belong to the psychiatric patient, Hanne Richter, who had been reported missing on 10th September, but who had probably disappeared several days prior to that. It was reasonable to suppose that the foot found less than two hours earlier belonged to the retired head teacher Sverre Lund, who had failed to return home on Monday 8th September. The fourth foot was a mystery. The DNA profile had excluded the possibility that it belonged to the fourth missing person, Otto Saga, and no other people had been reported missing in the surrounding area.

'Why are we finding only feet?' Hammer asked, reaching for the coffeepot.

The oceanographer stole a glance at them over his spectacles.

'Different body parts float in different ways,' he said. 'Wind and tide divide them up.'

'Are you ready yet?' Wisting asked, looking at his computer screen. It showed rows and columns with numbers in different coloured areas.

'Shortly.'

Wisting continued to give an account of the missing men's membership of the five-man group and the secret alert force. The investigators leaned forwards and began to take a deeper interest. All the same, there was little they could get to grips with or take direction from.

'Perhaps we ought to bring in one of those profilers?' the Chief Superintendent suggested, using an American accent to pronounce a word that did not have a good Norwegian equivalent. 'An expert who can say something about the personal characteristics of the person we're looking for.'

Wisting thought he could see the Assistant Chief of Police light up at the thought of releasing such novel news at the next press conference.

'Surely we're not as desperate as that?' Hammer said.

'Would it not give us a pointer about whether we're searching for a man or a woman, how old he is, what kind of background he has? Education, profession, family, motive? Whatever?'

'All we have is four feet.' Mortensen reminded them. 'We haven't got a crime scene or a murder weapon. That's not much of a basis on which to build a profile. It would be simply interpretation and guesswork. All we would end up with would be a conclusion based on theories without any proof, a hypothesis. We can't base an investigation on that.'

'I can tell you what kind of person we're looking for,' Hammer interjected, drinking from his coffee cup. 'A madman.'

No one had any objections to that.

'I believe,' Torunn Borg said, speaking for the first time, 'that the solution might lie far back in time. That someone has dug up something or other in their mutual past, such as these secret military operations, for example.'

'Hanne Richter breaks that pattern,' the Chief Super-intendent protested. 'The same applies to Camilla Thaulow, who disappeared on Tuesday.'

'But there is a connection,' Torunn Borg continued. 'Hanne Richter was living in Christian Hauge's house.'

'Besides, she was mad,' Hammer went one, 'and most likely knew a lot of other mad people.'

'Christian Hauge died of natural causes,' Audun Vetti reminded them. 'He is not a part of the investigation.'

'He was a part of the five-man group,' Torunn Borg said. 'If nothing else, that puts him in a peripheral role.'

Wisting nodded. He thought they had got an interesting discussion going – that was the way that most thoughts and ideas emerged.

'What about Camilla Thaulow?' he asked. 'How does she fit in?'

'She worked at the nursing home where Christian Hauge, Otto Saga and Torkel Lauritzen all lived. She might have come across the same secret that cost the others their lives.'

The Assistant Chief of Police clearly did not think that this discussion was going to be productive.

'What kind of secret would that be?' he asked, shaking his head.

No one could give him an answer.

'Something or other must have happened in September of last year,' Hammer said. 'That was when they disappeared.'

The discussion round the table went on to deal with what had dominated the news nine months previously, the pre-sidential election in the USA and various consequences of the international financial crisis.

Wisting closed his eyes, feeling how tired he was as the others talked. Probably they were looking for an event that had never reached the newspaper pages. When he thought of all the documents he had read in the past few days, there was all the same some kind of September connection. Seventeen years earlier, Ken Ronny Hauge for unknown reasons had shot and killed a police officer, an event that had cracked open the close solidarity within the five-man group. In August of last year, Christian Hauge was the first member of the group to die. Shortly afterwards three others disappeared.

He thought he could just about make out the contours of something, that he might be close to something he would soon be able to grasp, but for the moment he chose to keep it to himself. It was too flimsy – just a fleeting thought.

He opened his eyes again, jotting down a keyword.

Following the discussion among the investigators the oceanographer leaned back. Although his assignment was confined to calculating possible trajectories of drift for the feet he had signed a declaration of confidentiality and been granted full access to the investigation material. That meant they didn't need to take care when they were discussing the case in his presence.

'Are you ready?' Wisting asked again.

Ebbe Slettaker nodded, starting up the projector with the remote. A map of the archipelago outside Stavern came up on screen.

'I have taken a long time to program in data about tides, wind and the topographical formation of the shore area,' he explained. 'I have constructed a model of the actual sea area covering 400 square kilometers and containing about 25 billion cubic centimetres of water by volume.'

Wisting peered at the map. It stretched from Malmøya island, east of Larviksfjorden, down to Langesundsbukta in the west. To the south it disappeared in the Skagerrak with Tvistein lighthouse as the most outlying landmark.

'The strongest tides in the inner part of the Skagerrak consist of tidal water that raises and lowers the water surface by 0.24 centimetres in a period of six hours,' expanded the hired expert. 'That means a flow of around 3 billion cc of water. On the bottom and at depths of more than 90-100 metres, the speed of the flow of tidal water will

140

be relatively little, while on the surface it will be greater.'

The listeners nodded. Although the amount of background knowledge they had was insignificant it was the result that was important.

'The last foot that was found today, confirms and strengthens my theory,' Ebbe Slettaker continued.

Wisting leaned back in his chair. The man with the thick glasses spoke with a professional gravity – he liked what he was hearing.

'I would nevertheless remind you that we are discussing the forces of nature,' the oceanographer went on. 'I give no guarantees about these results, the middle value of a mathematical calculation.'

Ebbe Slettaker finished his introduction and bent over his computer. He pressed a key and a blue cross appeared as a marker for the first discovery on the southern peninsula of Stavernsøya island.

'The first shoe was found at 58 degrees, 59 minutes, 12.24 seconds north and 10 degrees, 3 minutes and 9.58 seconds east.'

Wisting could feel the beginnings of impatience.

'I have calculated the following trajectory of drift,' Slettaker elaborated, pressing on the keyboard.

The map on the wall came to life, almost like an animated weather warning on the internet. A clock up in the right corner gave the time. Minutes and seconds moved backwards at the same time as a blue line grew. It was drawn in a faint arc towards Svenner before it stretched towards Rakkebåene, passed Tvistein lighthouse and disappeared out into the Skagerrak.

'Illustrative,' Espen Mortensen commented in recognition of the work Ebbe Slettaker had undertaken.

'The next foot was found here,' continued the oceanographer as a red cross appeared up in Corntinbukta outside the shipyard area. He refrained from giving the longitude and latitude degrees and set the animation going instead. A

141

red line drew itself from the little cove, moving outside Rakkebåene and touching the blue line before going off the map.

Wisting leaned forwards. The picture that was, literally speaking, drawing itself in front of them, was interesting.

A green cross marked the discovery site in Skråvika. The line drawn from the third find stretched out in the same direction as the others, crossed the red line and disappeared out in Langesundsfjorden.

The discovery of the fourth foot was marked in a deep yellow. All of the crosses lay within a kilometre of each other.

The yellow line stretched from the beach at Solplassen, and followed the same arc as the others towards Svenner before it passed the area with deep banks and shoals outside Rakke and travelled south of the lighthouse at Tvistein. Right at the outer edge of the map it crossed the three other lines.

'A tangent point,' Nils Hammer remarked pertinently.

'Do you mean that the rest of the bodies are lying out there?' the Assistant Chief of Police wanted to know.

The oceanographer got up, walking across to the screen.

'The newspapers are writing that the bodies have possibly been butchered after being murdered,' he said, looking round at their faces. 'I have understood that that is a theory you have, too. That the bodies have been cut up and dumped in the sea, but that the feet have escaped from their packaging, while larger body parts may still be on the bottom of the sea.'

Wisting nodded. Ebbe Slettaker had put into words what they had each thought but not properly formulated.

'The estimated drift trajectories can point to this area,' he pointed to where all four lines joined, 'being the probable starting point for an undersea search. It's here that you will possibly find the dregs.'

He walked back to his computer and remained standing, leaning over it.

'Moreover,' he expanded, looking at them over his glasses, 'we can combine the calculations with logic and healthy common sense.'

He clicked on the keyboard once more, and a row of small numbers appeared on the screen.

'This area is the deepest part of the actual waters,' he elaborated, pointing to an area southeast of Tvistein lighthouse. One of the numbers he rested his finger on showed a depth of 357 metres. 'If I wanted to drop something in the sea in the hope that it would never come to the surface again, that is where I would do it.'

31

Wisting stood at the office window watching a fully rigged ship as it sailed out over the fjord with the sun shining on its sails. His neck and shoulders were stiff, and his muscles were tense.

Assistant Chief of Police Audun Vetti and Chief Superintendent Eskild Anvik were sitting in the visitors' chairs behind him. Nils Hammer leaned against the filing cabinet.

Wisting had never had problems with motivation. An internal engine drove his work forward. Not particularly concerned about praise, social status or the avoidance of criticism, seeking out answers was motivation enough. The pursuit of a solution drove him on, the search for justice, the feeling of righting a wrong, creating balance, and in the end the satisfaction of achieving the goal. And of course, the more distant the goal seemed to be, the more motivated he became.

He heard the others eagerly discussing the case among themselves, but all he could feel was a sense of emptiness, an emptiness that held him back and made it impossible to get started properly.

He knew that motivation was a fundamental wellspring for all good police work. If he could not manage to keep up the motivation of the investigation group, then they would lose their power to act.

At the point they had reached in the investigation he would normally be in the kind of mental state where he was deeply focused and filled with a sense of being on top of things. He was not there at the moment. Instead he felt exhausted, and found himself thinking about how good it would be to go to bed that night.

'Although we have some crosses on a map, it will be like looking for a needle in a haystack,' he heard the Chief Superintendent say. 'How many billion cubic metres of water was it the oceanographer was talking about? It's nine months since the corpses were dumped. What can we expect to find out there?'

Wisting turned to face them. Although he did not feel up to it he had decided that he would not show that to the others. He had to avoid them focusing on the obstacles they might encounter. To motivate his team he would have to look for reasons that they would be successful, not point out all the pitfalls.

He was about to speak when Espen Mortensen appeared with a pad full of notes.

'They have a remote controlled mini submarine at the diving centre in Stavern,' the crime technician explained. 'It has an operative depth of 700 metres.'

Wisting walked round the table and sat down. Technological developments had made undersea searching far more practical than only a few years previously.

'Great,' he commented, moving the large package wrapped in grey paper that had been delivered by messenger earlier that day, and prepared to take notes.

'It's equipped with two video cameras, a still camera, a grabber, floodlights and sonar.'

'When can they be ready to operate?' Wisting wanted to know.

'They're in more or less constant readiness for search and rescue, and can be there in an hour.'

The Chief Superintendent held up his hand.

'What does it cost?'

'There's an hourly charge of 3,450 kroner. That includes someone to drive it and a boat with a skipper. The pictures

145

can be relayed over the internet so that we can sit here and watch.'

'Good lord . . . a search like this can go on for days, weeks, without any guarantee of a result.'

Mortensen checked the notes on his pad.

'The mini submarine has a breadth of field of 4-8 metres, depending on the visibility conditions in the water, and must have an overlap of 1-2 metres in order to retain a high percentage of certainty for the area being searched. It travels at a speed of 2.5 knots maximum. The area that Ebbe Slettaker has marked on the map is about one square kilometre. It will take one week to search through it all.'

'A week?'

'Forty hours.'

Wisting did a mental calculation and saw that the Chief Superintendent, who was responsible for the budget, did the same.

'We are talking about five possible murders altogether,' he said before the Chief Superintendent reached his answer. 'We have budget entries for extraordinary expenses. I want them to get cracking in an hour's time.'

32

Line raised the camera, capturing Åge Reinholdt's workman's hands in her lens. He was sitting with a crab pot between his legs, working on the ropes at the opening. His movements were quick and experienced, his hands firm and tanned. Hands that had taken the lives of two women.

She had bought a used digital *Hasselblad* a year before. Although it had one previous owner, she had paid over a hundred thousand kroner for it, and thirty thousand more for two lenses. She had always wanted a camera like this. No other camera could capture natural colours and nuances in the same way, not least when it came to skin and skin tones. It had been a *Hasselblad* camera that photographed the first men on the moon. The pictures had gone around the world, so immediate and real they made people feel that something had changed forever.

She would not have been able to afford it if it hadn't been for the fact that, four years earlier, she had ended up in a situation in which she took a series of photographs during the arrest of one of the world's most wanted terrorists. The hateful face of the defeated man had been splashed on front pages all over the world. The moment was preserved for posterity in 1/250 of a second, but still it notched up royalties every time it was printed. That infinitesimal fraction of time had paid for the deposit on her flat in Oslo, and was also most certainly, when all was said and done, the reason that she now worked for the biggest newspaper in the country. Afterwards, she had thought of it as an example of synchronicity, a number of accidental occurrences that added up to a meaningful coincidence. Perhaps it had been the same for the man sitting in front of her. That the mysterious game of chance had turned him into a double murderer.

She pushed the thought away. Whatever random events could lead to, life still meant making the right choices. Although everything that happened had a connection to something else, people had free will and the ability to affect both their own life and the lives of others.

The first impression she had formed was that Åge Reinholdt was a reserved man who lacked self-confidence. His handshake limp and lethargic, the accompanying facial expression vapid. No smile or friendly nod.

He had got up when she arrived, but sat quickly back down on the straight-backed chair beside the faded wall of the house without inviting her to sit.

She had read somewhere that people are biologically programmed to make lightning decisions. The brain does not take unnecessary time to think through what has to be done in a critical situation and the same function comes into force when meeting new people. It takes only seconds to make up your mind about the person to whom you are saying hello. In meetings with interview subjects, Line regarded it as a moment of truth.

Åge Reinholdt seemed almost uninterested in her presence. He looked down at his work, or fixed his eyes on a point over on the edge of the woods. She had difficulty in deciding whether it was shyness or arrogance that made him like that.

He finished working on the pot, got up, placed a stone sinker inside it and put it in the back of a pickup truck together with a pile of others. The table in front of them was used as a workbench. Battens of suitable length lay ready together with lengths of cord to fit.

'Do you sell them, or do you fish yourself?' Line asked.

'I fish myself,' Åge Reinholdt explained, beginning on a new pot. 'I'm up and pulling them at four o'clock every morning. The first pan is on the boil at half past seven. When the shop down at Søndersrød opens, I've got between 100 and 150 crabs for them.'

'As many as that?'

'It varies, of course, but the secret lies in the bait.'

'What do you use?'

'That's what the secret is.' He put his work down and smiled at her with a row of teeth that spoke well of the dentistry service in Norwegian prisons. 'Crabs can smell underneath the water,' he claimed.

Line returned his smile and remembered how she had fished for shore crabs when she was little. It never took many minutes from the time she had fastened a mussel onto the line and cast it out until the first crabs appeared. She had never thought about it, but it had almost been as though they could smell the bait.

'They smell with their antennae,' he explained, wiggling with his fingers on his forehead. 'They can smell a tasty morsel up to a kilometre away.'

'What kind of tasty morsels do you lure them with?'

The man facing her had taken on a different energy now, a kind of involvement.

'I get out of date meat products down in the shop,' he said, 'packets of sandwich toppings, chops, tenderloin, and juicy steaks. The more perished and bloody, the better.'

'Do you make a living from it?'

Åge Reinholdt shook his head.

'I've received disability benefit from the day I was released. The money from the crabs is more like holiday money.' He leaned back, staring straight ahead. 'That was the life I dreamed about. My grandfather fished with pots, and that was the way I always thought my life would be. It took a few wrong turnings, but now I'm here.'

'Where did you go wrong?' Line asked, feeling her way with words so as not to cross him in any way. 'What was it that led to the wrong turning?'

149

Åge Reinholdt remained sitting, not uttering a word.

'My mother died when I was eight,' he said finally. 'I've never understood what she died of. It was as though she just withered away. One Sunday morning she didn't get up. In the evening they came and carried her away.'

Åge Reinholdt took hold of the tobacco pouch that lay on the deal table in front of them. Line nodded, as an encouragement for him to continue.

'Afterwards I sometimes thought that it might have been best that way. She escaped.'

'What do you mean?'

'He hit her,' he said by way of explanation, dividing the tobacco in the paper. 'Hurt and tormented her. I don't remember much of it, just that I crawled onto Mum's lap when his eyes darkened. I thought that he wouldn't strike out while I was sitting with her. I remember the smell of her and the fast heartbeats before she lifted me down and told me to go into the living room and turn on the radio.'

He put the rolled cigarette into his mouth and lit it with a lighter. Then he took a deep breath, took out the cigarette and spat.

'That's a part of the story, but I don't know if it has anything to do with what happened later. With what I did.'

Line held on to the eye contact she had with him and cocked her head to the side.

'We lived in a flat in Sagene. Dad worked in different workshops along the Akerselva river. In the evenings he and his pals sat at our house drinking. Maybe I was unmanageable. He did everything to make me pay attention, hit me, burned me with cigarette butts, shut me in or threw me out. It was all the same. I began to drink to escape.'

The dry tobacco crackled when he inhaled.

'I've had plenty of time to think about these things,' he continued. 'Talked to people who are experts. Psychologists and that. They think I'm transferring and repeating the

150

violence on to others, but I don't believe that keeping me locked up has made me less violent.'

Line leaned forwards. The conversation was going in the right direction.

'Yes? What effect has prison had on you?' she asked.

Åge Reinholdt leaned across the table, pulled an overflowing ashtray towards him and tapped the ash off his cigarette.

'It's made me mad,' he said, spitting once more. 'You need to go mad when you are left to your own devices and to your thoughts, confined in a space of six square metres for most of the hours of the day. I remember the anxiety that got hold of me when I had scratched five lines on the edge of the table and realised that this was the way I was going to spend the next ten years. It sat like a lump in my belly. Do you know how many lines there's room for along the edge of a table that measures one and a half metres?'

Line shook her head.

'757. Two years and 27 days. I continued on the ends, and turned the table round a year later. Then I still had another 2000 lines to go, but there was no room for any more. It didn't matter anyway. By then I had lost any overview a long time before. The days and weeks ran into each other. The only way I could register that a week had gone past, was that the food was served at different times at the weekends. It was something you looked forward to. That dinner was at three o'clock instead of five.'

'All the same you ended up in jail again,' Line said cautiously. 'Ten years after you had been released.'

'Madness,' Åge Reinholdt asserted with a nod. 'It won't happen again.'

'What did you do for all these days? All those hours?'

'When I served the first sentence, in the seventies, there was no TV in the cells, so the solution for me was books. The prison had a good library, and I tried to escape reality

151

by immersing myself in books. I didn't read a single other book after I was released.'

He stubbed out his cigarette and let his hand rest around an empty coffee cup.

'The second sentence was actually worse, although there was cable TV in the cells and various leisure options. In the course of the first six months I realised that I might as well not exist at all. I meant nothing to anyone. I had no one to use my phone time on, and no visitors. I was just there, exactly like a potted plant. I became depressed and self-destructive and began to slash myself with knives, if for no other reason than to prove to myself that I really existed.'

Line scrutinised his arms and saw the scars she hadn't noticed before. Some of them ran lengthwise and were deeper than what would be called slashes. She wanted to take photos of them, but considered that it would be inappropriate to lift her camera while the man in front of her was still talking. Instead she jotted down some keywords: depression, psychological difficulties, suicide attempts. Åge Reinholdt shed light on aspects of imprisonment that other interview subjects had not opened up on.

'I still have the same thoughts,' Åge Reinholdt went on. 'Being deprived of contact with other people has serious consequences. The only people I talked to were prison staff, overworked leaders of leisure activities, health personnel and other inmates, other madmen. I accept that I must be punished for what I did, but isolating someone because they have done something crazy, that's inhuman. It does irreparable harm, and is not the best thing for anyone.'

He got up, threw away a splash of cold coffee, and stared out to sea.

'That's why I live here,' he said. 'Some people might think that this is also living in isolation, but I've got freedom. Everything is open in front of me, as far as the eye can see.'

Line turned to look. Thickets on every side enclosed the overgrown agricultural landscape, but facing them was the

152

sea. It was so blue that the sky seemed paler. The coast was steep, but without an edge of foam. Against the grey-blue silhouette she saw the lighthouse at Tvistein, and behind that a cargo ship bound for Langesundsbukta.

'Coffee?' asked Åge Reinholdt suddenly.

Line glanced at the stained cup he was holding.

'Yes, please,' she responded, mainly to be polite.

She got up while Åge Reinholdt disappeared into the old main house, and picked out another lens from her bag. She took a few photographs of the view before walking several metres from the house, and hunkered down to focus on a rusty harrow that was lying dug into the earth, slowly becoming choked with nettles and dandelions. It was an image that contrasted strikingly with the blue background.

'I had to heat the kettle up,' said Åge Reinholdt behind her. 'It'll be ready in a minute. I'm not used to visitors.'

During her preparations for this interview, Line had decided to ask Åge Reinholdt if he had met a new woman. As far as she knew, he had only had two girlfriends in his life, and he had murdered them both.

'You haven't found anybody that you want to share the rest of your life with, then?' she asked, just as she had planned.

He smiled, and it looked as if he was wondering how to answer, before he ended up with a short, 'No.'

'Do you miss that?'

'We humans are not created to live alone,' he admitted. 'But I think it's too soon. Or else it's already too late.'

He stuffed his hands into the pockets of his baggy work trousers, seemingly bothered by the topic.

'It's not so easy for someone like me,' he continued. 'The years in jail have made me antisocial. I keep myself to myself. The only place I go is Furubakken, for interviews with my psychiatrist, and then into the shop with my crabs. They're not exactly pick-up places.'

153

He kicked a tuft of grass, grabbing at the tobacco pouch in his breast pocket.

'It was actually easier when I was inside,' he elaborated. 'I thought it was me who was mad, but letters with proposals of marriage turned up all the time from women I had never met or had any idea about. Can you imagine it? I had killed the girlfriend I was living with, and then I get letters from women who want me?'

'Have you met any of them?'

'One of them drove 300 kilometres to visit me every Sunday.'

'Have you any contact with her now?'

A different expression came over Åge Reinholdt's face and he shook his head.

'No,' he said, turning and walking towards the house. 'I think the coffee will be hot now.'

He stopped in the doorway, put the newly rolled cigarette into his mouth, lit it and turned to face her.

'You'd better not write about any of that,' he said, and disappeared into the house.

154

33

The sun was setting over a flat calm sea, with the cry of seagulls in the air. The air had turned slightly cooler.

Wisting had eaten his fill of the seafood that Line had brought from the fishmonger's shop by the steamship harbour and served with herb bread and garlic mayonnaise.

They were sitting across from each other at the table on the verandah. Sounds from the town rose and sank like breakers in the air, mixed with the buzzing of wasps and bumblebees working amongst the rosebushes that were growing wild beside the wall of the house.

'That was good,' Wisting thanked her, 'a nice surprise. I had actually thought I would heat myself some frozen food.'

Line smiled back at him.

'Did you know that crabs can smell?' she enquired, holding up a crab shell.

'Yes,' he nodded. 'Especially if they're left lying for a while.'

She laughed.

'They use their sense of smell to find food on the bottom of the sea,' she explained.

'I'd prefer not to think about what crabs or other sea creatures eat before they become delicacies for us,' Wisting remarked, bending over the table to study the shell. 'Where's its nose?'

She laughed, throwing the shell into a bowl of scraps before she got up to clear the table.

'Were you not supposed to be with Suzanne tonight?' she asked. 'We could have invited her.'

'I'm not good company,' Wisting said dismissively. He got up and gathered the plates and cutlery. 'I need to do some work. Reading reports,' he went on by way of explanation, but understanding that he would miss having her near. 'What about you?' he asked, following behind her into the kitchen. 'Shouldn't you have been with Tommy?'

'I've got to work as well,' she explained, nodding towards the kitchen table.

Wisting rinsed the plates before placing them in the dishwasher. He glanced at the space his daughter had turned into a work area – her computer was switched on and a series of summer images changed on the screen, operating as a screen saver. An abandoned agricultural implement in a meadow filled with flowers. A beautiful summer bird on a yellow flower growing through a rusty iron pipe. Brilliant colours and striking contrasts. She was a competent photographer. Suddenly the face of a stocky man appeared. His eyes were searching, a little to the side and past the photographer.

The photograph gave him a sense of déja-vu. The same experience he had when Daniel Meyer appeared at the door of his grandfather's house in Kongsberg earlier that day, before he managed to place him as one of the crowd of spectators out at Blokkebukta cove.

'Who's that?' he asked, nodding towards the screen as the picture changed to one of the man pressing a cigarette tightly between his lips and lighting up.

Line turned round, peering over at the screen.

'That's Åge Reinholdt,' she explained. 'The double murderer I told you about. I interviewed him earlier today.'

Pieces of a jigsaw picture in his memory fell into place for Wisting.

'That was strange,' he commented. 'I saw him yesterday. At a psychiatrist's at Furubakken.'

'It's not so strange,' Line smiled. 'He's gone mad, he says. Goes to the psychiatrist's three times a week.'

Wisting smiled back.

'It's strange all the same,' he thought, 'that I saw him yesterday, and then you speak to him today. Neither of us has ever met him before.'

'Synchronicity,' Line explained.

'Hm?'

'Coincidence without connection. If you think about it, it happens quite a lot. For example, when a car drives out from a full parking place so that you get an empty spot just as you drive in.'

'That never happens to me.'

'Or if you think about a person,' Line went on. 'Then that person suddenly calls you on the phone. Two chance occurrences.'

Wisting understood what she meant.

'It's exactly like the fact that I interviewed Ken Ronny Hauge yesterday.'

'The police murderer?'

Line nodded, continuing: 'And today there's an interview with his brother in the *Østlands-Posten* newspaper.'

'Is there?'

Line went over to the box of discarded newspapers behind the door and took out the paper.

'It's on the Saturday pages,' she elaborated, leafing back through the pages before laying the newspaper on the worktop in front of him.

Sharp Sales was the inventive title on an article describing the success story of a local company that supplied automatic cutting and grinding tools to the stone industry. *Made gold out of granite*, the text proclaimed beneath a photograph of the founder, Rune E. Hauge. Large new contracts had been entered into with a slate quarry in Oppdal, a new granite quarry in Gudbrandsdal and three big stone quarries in Finland. The success lay in the development of a unique laser-based cutting technology.

'That's his little brother,' Line explained. 'A chance co-incidence.'

In his work, Wisting had seen how coincidences could play against each other. He had often thought of how coincidences became decisive, but also understood that what might be regarded as a chance coincidence, might just as well be seen as an unavoidable interaction of events.

'It could at any rate seem like a coincidence,' he said.

'What do you mean?'

'How many events does a person actually experience in the course of a day, do you think?'

He went on before she had an opportunity to reply: 'What is an event, actually? Blinking is an event, going to the toilet is an event, sitting in a café is an event, thinking a thought is an event too. All the things we do and all the things that happen, are events.'

Line nodded, but looked as if she did not fully comprehend.

'So how many events do you experience in the course of a day?'

'A thousand?' she suggested.

'That doesn't sound unreasonable. Probably there are more. It depends on how detailed you want to be. Eating dinner can be considered as one event, but the actual dinner consists again of many minor events, such as, for example, putting the fork into the food or lifting a glass. Chewing, swallowing and belching. I think that, in the course of a week, you have taken part in 50,000 small and large events.'

He glanced over to see if she agreed. She nodded.

'Is it probable then that, in the course of a week, during one of these events, a situation crops up that can appear to be a coincidence decreed by fate?'

She understood where he was going now, and simply smiled in response.

'Statistically speaking, it's almost remarkable if an event like that doesn't take place,' he concluded.

'So coincidences are not coincidental?' she asked teasingly.

'Well yes, that's exactly what they are,' he expanded further. 'Nothing else, but I think that we humans have a particular ability to suppress and forget the neutral and meaningless things. We remember the time we thought about someone just before they phoned us, but we forget about the times we thought of the same person after which they didn't phone.'

Line folded up the newspaper.

'Some things in life are random all the same,' she felt. 'Eighteen years ago, Rune Hauge started as an apprentice in the stone quarry at Tvedalen, at the same time as his brother was sentenced for murder. The little brother has become a millionaire several times over. The big brother has nothing. No one could see that in them at that time, that life would work out so differently for them.' She turned to the computer, on which one of the photographs of Åge Reinholdt remained on the screen. 'In the case of Åge Reinholdt, you can in a way understand what turned him into a man of violence. He was thrashed and punched from when he was a little child, but Ken Ronny Hauge had no such external influences. He ended up behind the walls of a prison while his brother became a great success.'

Wisting smiled at her.

'By chance?' he asked.

'It seems to be, anyhow.'

34

Wisting sat beneath the outdoor wall light, placing the package wrapped in grey paper on his lap. It was one of those rare evenings with no chill in the air, which was soft and soothing.

He tore off the paper and threw it down at his side, glanced at the formal dispatch communication from the police in Søndre Buskerud prior to leafing through the yellowing documents.

The file of criminal proceedings against Ken Ronny Hauge was not thick. He estimated that he would take a couple of hours to read through the papers concerning the case.

The file was organised with contents lists of the police reports, witnesses, technical investigations and a separate list of documents for everything connected with the defendant.

He began with the report that had been written by the first patrol to arrive on the scene where Constable Edgar Bisjord was found shot dead on that September night in 1991. It did not contain much more than cold factual information about time and place: who had raised the alarm about the discovery and how the crime scene had been secured.

The reports from the crime technicians at *Kripos,* the national criminal investigation department, were more interesting and revealed how the investigators had got on the track of the perpetrator within a few hours.

The introductory report was divided into three parts. It

described the victim, the police car and the surrounding area. The crime scene investigation gave a good impression of what had happened. There was a description of two sets of tyre tracks leading on to a side road. One set belonged to the police car, and the other was from an unknown vehicle that had turned at the end of the road and left behind deep marks on the gravel after accelerating out again.

Edgar Bisjord must have come across a suspicious car, indicated for it to stop, and then followed it along the short side road until it came to a halt. Subsequently, the young policeman had got out of the police car and approached the vehicle.

It was something that all policemen on patrol do countless times while on duty. Vehicle registration document and driver's licence were checked. A missing backlight or speed was commented on before the driver was sent on his way, sometimes with a fine or a checklist.

However, on the night of 23rd September in 1991, it had developed into something completely different from a routine inspection. A weapon was pulled out and seconds later, the policeman was lying dead on the ground.

Wisting leafed through the folder of illustrations. The uniform cap was lying one metre away from his dead colleague. The coloured pictures of the policeman lying on his back made an impression. The blood had spread into the grey, dry gravel underneath him. His eyes were wide open and fixed in what looked like panic. Round his mouth there were thick crusts of congealed mucus and froth.

He closed the folder of photographs and went back to the text. The most important find that the crime scene investigators came up with was on the passenger seat of the police car. Edgar Bisjord had written down a car number on a writing pad: LS10424. A yellow Opel Ascona registered to Ken Ronny Hauge from Helgeroa. As a final duty, Edgar Bisjord had jotted down the number of the car he was stopping.

Ken Ronny Hauge was arrested at 7.45 pm, less than twenty-four hours after the murder. The police in Larvik assisted in the arrest and Wisting recognised the names of some of his retired colleagues.

A moth was dancing round the light above him, casting flickering shadows on the pages of the report. Wisting made a note of some keywords on the notepad lying on the armrest and leafed through the pages.

The crucial piece of evidence was the residue that was taken from Ken Ronny Hauge's hands. Tiny percussion cap particles indicated that he had handled a weapon during the hours leading up to his arrest.

Ballistic tests on the bullets established that Edgar Bisjord had been killed with a Colt M1914. The murder weapon was never found, but from the investigation material it appeared that the accused's grandfather, Christian Hauge, was listed in the weapons register as possessing a similar weapon that had been reported missing several years earlier. At the trial it was concluded that Ken Ronny Hauge had stolen it from his grandfather at some earlier time.

The evidence was actually overwhelming. The amazing thing about the case was that Ken Ronny Hauge never offered any kind of admission. At the trial he had declared himself not guilty but did not come out with any explanation about what he had done or not done on that fateful night.

Wisting grew thoughtful. He had never known a case that had been so open and shut, but in which the perpetrator nevertheless chose not to explain himself, if for no other reason than to come out with his own version of events, or to co-operate in exchange for a lighter sentence. It only happened in cases in which the truth was worse than the facts the police had already presented.

Buster came creeping through the open verandah door. He had eaten well and was full of scraps; he sat down in front of Wisting and started licking his paws.

'Will you sit there much longer?' Line asked from the doorway.

Wisting glanced at the clock. It was already past midnight.

'No,' he said, packing up the case files. 'I'll stop now. What about you?'

'I'm going out for a drive, just to think about something else.'

Wisting got up and followed her into the house. She threw on a jacket, kissed him on the cheek, and disappeared outside.

Thoughts about what had really happened at Eikeren that time eighteen years previously accompanied him into the bathroom and while he got himself ready for bed. Ken Ronny Hauge had fired a shot to escape, but he found nothing in the case files about why he had done it. The only logical explanation was that he had been in possession of something in the car that he had to hide. Could his silence indicate that he was not alone? That he had an accomplice he wanted to protect?

Wisting read through his notes one more time before putting them on the bedside table, switching off the light and turning to face the wall.

Dawn was breaking when he fell asleep.

35

Erling Tunberg was ten years old. He had spent every single summer in the caravan at Lydhusstranda beach together with his parents and sister, who was four years older.

He had wakened early, before everyone else in the entire place, and he knew why. It was Sunday, and today Even would arrive.

It had always been like that. Even came down one week later than he did. It was a long week in which he just waited and thought about all the things they would do together, swimming, diving, cycle trips, crab fishing, late nights. His mother called them summer friends.

It was just as though there were only the two of them. They met other boys too, but it wasn't the same.

He lay for a long time, listening to the unfamiliar silence. Usually there were lots of sounds outside, footsteps on the road, people talking round a table or a radio that was left switched on.

After ten minutes he got up. The others were still sleeping. He put on his tracksuit trousers and a T-shirt, took a packet of biscuits with him, and went out under the awning.

He looked out through the plastic window as he chewed on a biscuit.

The sun had scarcely risen – the first rays came projecting across the Naver fjord. He stuck his feet into a pair of sandals, zipped up his jumper and went out. The grass was wet with morning dew. A slight breeze touched his skin. A car passed up on the road. Apart from the sound of the waves it was completely silent.

He walked to the shore, right down to the water, and took a few quick steps backwards before the waves erased his footprints again. He liked waves. They kind of belonged with everything that had to do with the sea. At home in Gjøvik they had Lake Mjøsa, but that was not the same. There was so much to look at here. Stones and shells in different colours and sizes. A bird's feather. He bent down, picked up a stone and wiped the grains of sand off it. A variety of patterns emerged. It was rubbed completely smooth and round by the movements of the water. He skimmed it across the surface and saw how it shot high up in the air in a curve before being swallowed by the waiting sea.

He lifted up a stick that had been washed ashore, using it as a walking stick when he clambered up the hill that separated Lydhusstranda from the beach known as Fristranda. Teenagers gathered here in the evenings. They sat round a bonfire, sang songs and drank beer without disturbing anyone. During the daytime there were hardly ever any people. The green grassy hills and the gradual slope down to the sea were full of large stone blocks, and the bottom of the sea was covered in shells and seaweed. His father had told him that it was the Germans who had strewn the cove with the stones during the war to prevent the English from landing there.

Erling squinted up at the sun that was glittering on the water, screwing up his eyes so that he could see better. Something was lying down there between the stones, a couple of metres from land. An object lay jostling with the pebbles to the rhythm of the rushing waves.

He crawled down from the hillside and came closer. It was a black bin-bag filled with – something or other. The waves pulled at it, but couldn't manage to bring it further in.

A man with a white Labrador appeared on the path at the other end of the beach. The dog was running free, jumping at the water. The owner called to it when he noticed Erling, but the dog did not obey. It came right over to greet him

Erling hunkered down and clapped it on the head. The dog wriggled away, stood with its nose towards the water, and gave a couple of penetrating barks. His ears lay flat while its tail went down and wagged stiffly. Erling took a couple of steps away.

The man approached them, scolded the dog and fastened the lead onto its collar. 'It won't do any harm,' he smiled, pulling the dog towards him.

Erling didn't say anything, but stood watching until they disappeared into the woods at the back of the beach area.

He could see that the side of the bin-bag was torn and that something wrapped in a white plastic bag was inside it.

He kicked his sandals off, pulled his trousers up to his knees and began to wade out. The water was cool. The round stones at the bottom made it painful to walk and he held his arms out at each side to keep his balance. He knew that it most probably was rubbish that somebody had thrown overboard from a boat, but it could just as easily be something else. He had heard of smugglers who dropped drugs from boats. Even if it was only rubbish, the bag couldn't be left lying in the water. He should drag it out and put it in the container over at the shop.

He poked the stick tentatively into the tear on the bag. It came into contact with something soft. He bent down and folded the plastic to one side. There were four bags tied together in there. He lifted one of them out and placed it on a flat stone. The knot was tight, and he couldn't manage to untie it. Instead he got hold of it with both hands and tore up the bag. The sight caused him to take an automatic step back. The first thing he thought was that he had to show this to Even.

166

36

William Wisting and Nils Hammer stood behind Espen Mortensen, each with a cup of coffee, gazing at his computer screen.

'The mini submarine took to the water an hour ago,' Mortensen explained. 'They had a bit of a problem with the cable winch, but now they're on the move.'

The floodlight from the mini submarine cast its light far ahead. Visibility would be about ten metres. The video pictures had a blue-green tinge to them, but they were good and clear.

The bottom of the sea was surprisingly flat, a grey carpet of fine-grained sludge. Several colonies of stem-like coral protruded from the soft seabed, resembling feathers standing waving with the movement of the water. The currents had created furrows in the underwater landscape, and in some places the seabed was pierced by a variety of bottom-dwelling creatures to form small dimples and holes.

A couple of fish swam past without showing any apparent interest in the large vessel that had invaded their realm, their blank, black eyes searching for food. The floodlights made their slender bodies shine as though they were oiled with a silvery lustre before they suddenly took off and disappeared.

The display on the lower edge of the computer screen showed the time as 08.35, that the mini submarine was moving forward at a speed of 1.8 knots, and that it was at a depth of 364 metres. Other figures gave the current amplification factor and the position.

'Can they use the sonar?' Hammer enquired.

'Yes, but they can't locate a corpse or smaller objects with it.'

Wisting drank from his cup. He was impressed by the technology and the possibilities it opened up, but he was sceptical as to whether they would manage to find anything even with this advanced equipment. No matter what, it was like looking for a needle in a haystack.

He brought his cup with him back to his office, took out the container from the health-food shop and picked out two capsules that he gulped down with his coffee. The herbal tablets actually were making him feel a bit better.

A pile of new reports and interview records had been placed on his desk. The one on the top had been written by Torunn Borg and was a summary of interviews she had conducted with the staff at Stavern nursing home. The conclusion was that none of Camilla Thaulow's colleagues could shed any light on her disappearance, or steer them towards the fate of the two missing residents.

Camilla Thaulow was described as a shy and reserved woman whom it took a while to get to know, and even those who had worked with her for a long time knew little about who she really was.

Torunn Borg appeared at the door to sum up what he had already realised from his reading. There was nothing new.

She sat in the chair facing him, smoothing her hair back from her forehead with a resigned movement. Her brown eyes were tired and had dark circles round them.

'I've been thinking about something,' she said by way of commentary on the fruitless work she had carried out. 'Perhaps we should have talked with the patients instead? I've a feeling that she almost talked more to them than to her colleagues.'

Wisting had to admit that he hadn't thought of that, but she was of course correct. They needed to go round all the residents as well.

'Aren't many of them senile?' he asked.

'They have a protected wing for those with senile dementia, but Camilla Thaulow didn't work there.'

'How many people are we talking about?'

'Fifteen, so it'll take time to talk to them. They *are* old people, you know.'

'Can you take someone along with you?'

She got up.

'Who should I take?'

Wisting shook his head. Torunn Borg smiled back at him.

'I'll drive over there and make a start this morning,' she said. 'They're sure to be up early.'

She went to the door, but stopped and turned to face him.

'I didn't put it in the report, but I asked them a little about Christian Hauge too.'

'Yes?'

'It was one of the nurses who expressed it well: there was a bond between them.'

'Otto Saga, Torkel Lauritzen and Christian Hauge,' Wisting suggested.

Torunn Borg took a couple of steps back into the room.

'But then something happened. They were in the habit of eating together and sitting together in the common room, discussing things far into the evenings, but Hauge withdrew from that. Isolated himself, in a way.'

'Do they know why?'

Torunn Borg shrugged her shoulders.

'No, but I think it might have something to do with the grandson.'

'The police murderer?'

'It started after he was released. He visited a few times. I think his grandfather was ashamed.'

169

She turned and disappeared out of the room before Wisting had a chance to enquire more closely about what she meant.

He spent an hour reading through the remainder of the reports. Most of them were concerned with tips about possible sightings of Camilla Thaulow and her car. Those pieces of information that seemed interesting at the outset were checked out, without leading to anything.

Then he made up his mind. It was a sidetrack, but he couldn't get round it. He got up from his seat, went down to the basement and took out a service vehicle.

The gate at the end of the dusty gravel track was open. Wisting drove through, up a final hump and down a hill.

Ken Ronny Hauge lived in an old skipper's house beside the water. The place was situated on the inside of a cove where it was less windy. A bare-chested man stood bent over the bonnet of an old American car, but glanced up when Wisting swung into the yard. A dog ran barking towards him from the barn before running back to lie in front of his master's feet.

Wisting slammed the car door shut and approached the man.

'This is the first time,' Ken Ronny Hauge said, greeting him with an outstretched hand.

'What is?' Wisting asked, shaking his hand.

'That I've had a visit from the police.' He reached out for a white T-shirt and put it on. 'I had expected to be pestered long before now.'

'I hadn't thought to pester you,' Wisting said, attempting a disarming smile.

'I know who you are,' the other man smiled back, directing Wisting to a seat in front of the main house. 'Your daughter was here on Friday, but that's probably not why you've come.'

Wisting shook his head. He didn't have any questions ready and had to feel his way forward.

'We're conducting an investigation,' he commenced.

'I've noticed that,' the other man said, nodding in the direction of the previous day's newspapers on the table. 'But hadn't expected to be part of it.'

'And you're not, but your grandfather has a peripheral role.'

They sat down. The dog came shuffling over to them and lay down in the shade beneath the table.

'Grandfather died almost a year ago.'

Wisting nodded.

'Three men whom we presume to be murdered disappeared just after that,' he explained. 'Three friends of your grandfather; Otto Saga, Torkel Lauritzen and Sverre Lund.'

'I remember Lund,' Ken Ronny Hauge said, looking past Wisting with thoughtful eyes. 'He was the head teacher at the school. I know who the others were too.'

'I understand that you visited your grandfather several times before he died?'

'It was a kind of repayment,' Ken Ronny Hauge nodded. 'He was the only one who visited me in prison. Once a fortnight for as long as his health held out.'

Wisting turned the other man's choice of word over in his mind. Repayment.

'But he wasn't lonely in the nursing home,' he objected. 'Two of his pals from the old times also stayed there.'

'Yes of course, and I didn't see it as a heavy duty either. It was enjoyable.'

'What did you talk about?'

'Everything and nothing. This and that. What about it?'

'Did he ever talk about the other three?'

Ken Ronny Hauge understood where Wisting was going. 'Not about anything that would explain what happened to them. They were a closely-knit bunch. It was their common background that created the strong solidarity.' He came to a halt, glancing over at Wisting. 'You know about it?'

'The group that was in readiness for an occupation?'

'No matter. It was a kind of solidarity that was passed on as an inheritance. We grandchildren became friends as well, although we probably didn't stick up for each other in the same way as the old men.'

Wisting wondered what he actually meant by this, but didn't ask. He thought he could detect a kind of bitterness in his voice, disappointment of some kind about how his old friends had betrayed him.

'We never talked about that,' Ken Ronny Hauge went on. 'That grandfather had been a member of a military network was almost an open secret. It was in the newspapers of course and was something that everybody knew about, but all the same it was never talked about. Not then.'

'Do you have any contact with the others?' Wisting asked, naming Daniel Meyer as an example.

'No,' Ken Ronny Hauge responded. 'I know Daniel and my brother has some contact with him. He's apparently writing a book about the secret services. Grandfather told me that he had interviewed him about it, but I haven't spoken to him. Daniel and his brother grew up in the same street as Rune and me, you know. His brother lives in Kongsberg, I think. Other than that, there aren't so many others. I think Trond's a boozer in Oslo.'

'Trond?'

'Trond Lauritzen. He's Kristin and Mathias' son, so he's the grandson of both Otto and Torkel, of course. We went to school together, but I haven't spoken to him for ages. Not to his sister either. She's called Trine and she's married with children in Bergen, I know that. Knut Lauritzen lives in Stavanger. Torkel Lauritzen is his grandfather too. His parents live in Stavern.'

Wisting nodded. He had written down all the names on his notepad and placed them in boxes with lines of connection between. Oddmund Lauritzen and his wife Marie were two names that were left on his list of relatives and the bereaved that he should talk to.

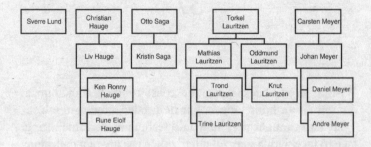

'Head teacher Lund had no children,' Ken Ronny Hauge rounded off.

He remained sitting, staring into space before he added: 'I don't really talk to anybody. The first person I've talked to properly since my release was your daughter.'

'Do you have any contact with your brother?'

'Rune?' he asked, as he bent down to pet the dog. 'How should I put it? He has of course been a kind of benefactor to me. I couldn't have stayed here if it hadn't been for him.' He flung out his arms. 'He's the one who owns the place.'

Wisting posed a few more questions while he tried to read the man. Body language would often say more than words. He attempted to capture signals about whether Ken Ronny Hauge was deliberately keeping something back. He searched for hesitations in his responses, looked for physical uneasiness, evasive eye movements, or other signs of discomfort, but Ken Ronny Hauge appeared simply indifferent. There was nothing he managed to draw out, neither from his voice nor his eyes. His face was completely expressionless.

37

Wisting drove back along the coast road. It took him a quarter of an hour longer, but he needed time to think.

He had thought that he would feel uncomfortable sitting face to face with a man who had taken the life of a colleague and left a mother on her own with two small children. However, he didn't feel any kind of grudge, just a sort of emptiness. His years as a policeman had left their mark. At the beginning of his career it often happened that he became uneasy or unwell when meeting really brutal criminals. Now that felt like an infinitely long time ago. He wondered whether he should have asked about the police murder, but it would have been inappropriate, and he probably wouldn't have received any proper answer. Many had tried before him. Line too, most likely, when she had visited him on Friday.

The air quivered over the outstretched rocky shore alongside the road. Circling seabirds flew by. White-painted wooden houses huddled beside stout pine trees in small coves.

Long breakers, the vestiges of a storm on the other side of the Skagerrak, caused the sea to swell and fall. A cargo ship was balanced on the horizon. There was not a cloud in sight.

This investigation was like the waves out there, he thought, impossible to catch hold of. It was like something that lay amongst the pebbles, washed in to land and then dragged back out again.

He left the coast and drove through the agricultural landscape tightly packed with farms, past roadside stalls offering strawberries, potatoes and other vegetables. He parked in front of one of these on an impulse and approached a young girl with a long, red plait reading a magazine behind a deal table. She put it down and smiled.

The punnets of strawberries in front of her bulged with enormous, ripe berries. He bought two punnets to pop in and surprise Suzanne with during the day.

He put one strawberry in his mouth before placing the bag on the floor in front of the passenger seat, glancing at the clock and deciding to call on Rune E. Hauge before driving back to the police station.

The successful businessman lived in Rekkevik, on the eastern side of the Larvik fjord in a modern house built in a style and materials that suited the location, a large, sunny property with its own jetty.

In the cove at the other side Colin Archer had built the polar ship Fram, which almost a hundred years before had carried his own great-grandfather, Oscar Wisting, together with Roald Amundsen, to the South Pole.

Wisting parked outside the house, went up to the door and rang the bell. A slightly built woman with a fizz of blonde curls opened up. Wisting introduced himself and enquired after Rune Hauge.

'He's sitting at the front of the house,' she explained, making a sweeping arch with her arm along the wall of the house. 'Just go round.'

Wisting walked along the path to the other side of the house. He heard voices from the spacious outdoor sitting area beside the water. When he approached, he saw two familiar faces. Rune Hauge, whom he had seen in the newspaper article Line had shown him, and Daniel Meyer, whom he had met in Kongsberg the previous day. They were sitting in deep garden chairs with a glass each on the table in front of them. Both fell silent when they saw Wisting.

'Am I disturbing you?' he asked.

'Of course not,' Daniel Meyer assured him. He got up and

stretched out his hand. 'It was nice to meet you,' he said, introducing Wisting to his companion. 'I was just going.'

He finished what was left in his glass and put it back down.

'We'll talk later,' he said, nodding to Rune Hauge before walking along the same path on which Wisting had arrived.

'You know each other?' Wisting declared, sitting down.

'We grew up together,' Rune Hauge nodded in agreement. 'Can I offer you anything?'

'No thanks,' Wisting responded, taking out his notepad.

He began in the same way he had with his brother, telling about how three of their grandfather's old friends had disappeared and that it was presumed that they had been victims of a crime.

'Daniel and I were just talking about it,' Rune Hauge explained, becoming serious. 'And about what could be the motive for such a thing.'

'Did you come to any conclusion?'

He shook his head.

'Nothing other than that it could have a connection to what the old men got up to during the post war years.' He leaned over the table. 'What kind of theory do you have?'

'In the meantime, we've conducted the investigation on a broad front,' Wisting explained. He had no wish to give an account of the police's operational theories to the man sitting across from him at the table.

'But since you've come here talking about grandfather that means, of course, that you're also looking at the past?'

Wisting nodded.

'There's something else that's bloody strange,' Rune Hauge said, leaning over the table. 'Have you looked at the connection with Hanne Richter?'

'What do you mean?' Wisting asked, not giving a direct answer. They hadn't gone public with the information that one of the feet that had been found belonged to the mentally ill woman.

176

'She disappeared at the same time as Otto Saga, Torkel Lauritzen and Sverre Lund, you see,' Rune Hauge elaborated, putting his elbows on the table. 'And she was staying at grandfather's house.'

'We're looking at that,' Wisting confirmed.

'There must be a pattern, to be sure,' the other man thought. 'Some kind of network or other that they're entangled in. A connection.'

'They all disappeared several weeks after your grandfather died,' Wisting asserted. 'Did anything in particular happen during those days?'

It looked as though Rune Hauge was thinking carefully. 'I was away when he had the last attack,' he explained. 'I was attending contract meetings in Finland, but managed to arrive home before he died. I can't think of anything special.'

'Do you know Camilla Thaulow?' Wisting continued to question him.

'Yes, bloody hell,' Rune Hauge replied, snapping his fingers, as though he had suddenly thought of something important. 'She's gone too, of course.'

'You know her?'

Rune Hauge got up and walked backwards and forwards on the terrace.

'I don't know her,' he explained. 'But she was certainly one of the nurses who looked after grandfather. She was even at his funeral.'

As brothers, Ken Ronny and Rune Hauge didn't resemble each other, Wisting thought. Where Ken Ronny seemed indifferent, his brother appeared enthusiastic. The muscles in his face contracted, he gesticulated with his hands, and his eyes narrowed or opened wide as he spoke.

Rune Hauge sat down again, and remained talking for half an hour. When Wisting got up to go, he had an impression that he had answered far more questions than he had asked. The successful businessman answered questions by asking counter questions. There was actually only one thing he had said that Wisting had latched on to: all those who had disappeared were entangled in a network. It was a summary of Wisting's own thoughts.

38

Even arrived at four o'clock. Erling Tunberg had spent the last few hours lying on his back on the grass above the beach with a long straw of dried grass in his mouth, gazing at the twisted branches on the huge pine tree over his head.

He watched every car that drove down the road from the barrier at the top of the hill until the large Chevrolet belonging to Even's father finally arrived. The sound of the powerful engine was so loud he heard it before he saw the car.

At the roadside he stood waving, and then followed the car over to the campsite.

Even had grown taller, almost a head taller than Erling, and leaner. They remained standing, looking uncertainly at each other.

'Is the water good, eh?' Even asked, nodding towards the beach.

'Brilliant,' Erling confirmed. '24 degrees. Want to go in for a swim?'

Even turned to his mother: 'Can I go for a swim?'

She laughed, knowing it would be impossible to suggest anything else, and took his bathing trunks from a bag. Even disappeared into the caravan and changed.

The slight hesitation and uncertainty after not seeing each other for nearly a year, was suddenly gone. They bounded towards the waves and ran out, the water splashing around them, going under as soon as it was knee-deep. They swam below the water until their eyes were tingling and they had to come up for air. Then they dived under again and swam

179

out to the raft that was anchored out at the deepest point. They heaved themselves up onto the deck, lay down on their backs and caught their breath. A couple of older boys plunged in, and so they were alone.

'There's something I have to show you,' Erling said.

Even sat up.

'What is it?'

'I can't tell you. I'm not really sure what it is exactly. You'll need to see it for yourself. Something I found this morning.'

'What is it?' Even repeated, getting up.

'I've hidden it up by the stone wall.'

Even turned round and peered towards the land. In the woods behind Fristranda beach, an old stone wall wound its way, dividing the properties from one other. A few summers previously, Erling's father had told them a story about Gjest Baardsen, who had broken in to the Manor House in Larvik almost 200 years before and stolen silverware, pocket watches, gold and silver jewellery, powder flasks, knives and several hundred *speciedaler* coins from the county. He had hidden the stolen goods beneath the stones in the wall before he was arrested. When he fled, he had gone to Arendal, without taking time to bring the booty with him. The valuable objects must still lie some place or other among the moss-grown stone walls. That summer Even and Erling had turned every single stone, but the only thing they had found was a squirrel's lair and a bag of old porno magazines that were lying hidden in a cavity. A cavity big enough to hold Gjest Baardsen's booty, except that others had found it before them.

'Anything valuable?' Even asked tentatively.

Erling just smiled slyly before getting up, diving in and swimming towards land.

They each put a towel over their shoulders, put on their sandals and walked over to Fristranda.

The path along one side of the stone wall was quiet and

speckled with sunlight that reached through the branches. Some large oak trees had found fertile soil between the stones and sprung up. Twisted tree roots were protruding and intertwining like a knotted net.

After fifty metres, they reached an open area where an enormous old rose briar covered the stones. They clambered over to the other side of the wall and walked a few more metres before Erling began to remove some.

'Where did you find it?' Even asked.

'On the beach,' Erling replied, lifting away the last stone.

Even leaned forward and peered into the secret cavity. A black bin-bag was lying there. Erling let him lift it out. It smelled a bit, like the mounds of slippery, rotten seaweed that had been lying a long time on the foreshore.

Even found the opening and pulled out one of the white plastic bags inside. He glanced over at Erling before untying the knot and peeping in, but it took some time for him to realise what it was he was looking at.

It was money. Heaps of money.

He picked out one of the banknotes and studied it. It was still damp after lying in the water. He had not seen banknotes like these before. It was green and strangely designed, almost completely square. He turned it over. On one side there was a picture of a man with thick, white hair and sideburns. On the reverse there was a picture of someone working in a field. *Norges Bank* was written on both sides. *Femti kroner* – fifty kroner.

'Money,' was all he said.

'They're old,' Erling explained, pointing to the date. *1952*.

'How much is there?' Even pulled out the other bags. 'Have you counted them?'

'There's 250,000 in that one.' Erling nodded to the bag Even had opened. 'There must be more than a million altogether.'

Even opened a bag and peeped inside.

'Are there only 50-kroner notes?' he asked.

Erling nodded.

'But they're not all so old.'

He picked up a banknote from one of the other bags. This one had a picture of a man with a big, thick beard. *Noregs Bank*, it said, in *nynorsk*, the New Norwegian language. *Femti kroner*.

'Where do they come from?' Even asked in wonder.

Erling shrugged his shoulders. He had been wondering the same thing all day.

39

Wisting's reading had given him a different impression of Oddmund and Marie Lauritzen than he had of the younger brother who had married Otto Saga's daughter. While the brother and his wife lived in a deprived housing co-operative, Oddmund and Marie Lauritzen lived in an area west of Stavern where the houses were surrounded by high railings and large gardens. Oddmund Lauritzen worked in the council administration, while Marie was the manager of a children's nursery they owned in partnership.

The address belonged to a quiet side street with large properties where old fruit trees afforded shade from the afternoon sun. A wrought iron gate on to the street stood open, and a gravel path led to an entrance with white pillars. A newly clipped royal poodle greeted him with a piercing bark, and stood pawing at the door until it was opened.

Wisting saw the family resemblance, but Oddmund Lauritzen was taller and heavier built than his younger brother. His face was long and sharp with blue-grey eyes, his hair thick and grey. He greeted him with a nod and led him through the house and out to a paved terrace at the back where Marie Lauritzen was sitting at a garden table.

'There isn't any news,' Wisting hastened to say.

Oddmund Lauritzen pulled a chair over to the table and invited Wisting to sit down.

'We were wondering a little about what was happening,' Marie Lauritzen said carefully.

'I'm afraid I don't have any answers,' Wisting explained.

'I had hoped that you could tell me something that would shed new light on the investigation.'

The married couple sat silent for a short time before the husband started to speak: 'There is one thing,' he began. 'I haven't yet told to my brother.'

Wisting nodded for the other man to continue.

'I don't know if it'll make you any wiser, but it's something you ought to know. Perhaps it'll be useful when you look at it in connection with something else.'

Wisting straightened up. He had experienced this before, with people sitting on important information, reluctant to go to the police with what they knew, exactly because they didn't understand its importance.

'I've just finished the first week of my holidays,' Oddmund Lauritzen expanded, 'and have had some time to go through some of my father's papers. All of his post is forwarded to me, and I look after all the practical details. We agreed on that, Mathias and I.'

'Mathias isn't so smart with paperwork,' Marie Lauritzen said.

'There will of course be a distribution of the estate from all this, but that takes time,' her husband went on. 'As long as he's just missing, we can't have the estate wound up. Only after a year can we go to the district court and have him declared dead.'

Wisting nodded. It was called a 'presumption of death judgement'.

'Father was always meticulous with his papers. I do his income tax returns, and know what he has by way of income and assets and all that. I haven't bothered to look in his folder of receipts, but thought I should go through it now to make everything easier later.'

'It was Mathias who asked you to do it,' his wife reminded him. 'He wanted to know how much there was in the estate.'

'That's right,' the man agreed, nodding. 'I knew from the

tax assessment that he was left with a lot when he sold the house and moved into the nursing home. There could be a few hundred thousand for each of us.'

'You have to get to the point,' his wife said.

'Yes, it concerns his bank statement for August last year. The statement shows a cash deposit of 2.4 million.'

Wisting tried to gather his thoughts.

'2.4 million?' he reiterated.

Oddmund Lauritzen nodded.

'Altogether. There are seven deposits in seven different banks in Oslo. Wednesday 27th August. Paid in over the counter.'

'In Oslo? Do you know where the money comes from?'

'No, and it has gone again.'

Wisting sat back in the chair, as though he needed space to take in this new information.

'Two days later, he goes round to banks in Sandefjord and Tønsberg and takes the money out again.'

'Somebody must have driven him around,' Marie Lauritzen said.

'Do you have the bank statement?' Wisting asked.

Oddmund Lauritzen got up and returned with two sheets of paper. Wisting studied the summary of the large sums that in the course of a few days had gone in and out of Torkel Lauritzen's account. He had seen it before, how money could be the motive for the most gruesome crimes people could commit against one other. He stared at the numbers and thought that he could sense it. The case was finding its bearings.

40

Most things were about money, Wisting thought. *Follow the money*, that was what the anonymous source had said to the Washington Post journalist when the Watergate scandal was on the go in 1972 and Nixon had to resign as president.

Money always left a trail. *Follow the money* had become a basic rule for all investigations after the Al Capone case in the 1930s. The American authorities never managed to catch the infamous Mafia boss for the murders he had in all probability committed. Instead it was an accountant who had him imprisoned for tax evasion.

He wondered why this financial evidence had not turned up before. It was purely routine to check the movements within bank accounts when people were reported missing, but this, of course, concerned movements after the person had disappeared. Nevertheless, they had work to do when the banks opened in the morning.

He was hungry and lifted a strawberry from one of the punnets he had bought earlier in the day. He put it in his mouth and felt the sweet flavour spread. He ate one more berry before swinging into a petrol station to buy a hot-dog and a carton of cream. He put it on the floor beside the berries and drove home to Suzanne.

There had always been a kind of conflict between work and family when Ingrid was alive, especially when the children were little. He had a bad conscience when he couldn't manage to get everything done in his working day and his wife and children had to take second place.

His relationship with Suzanne was completely non-committal. The little they had talked about the future, contained a common understanding that neither of them had any need to make long-term plans. They were both busy with their own lives and were willing to give each other space for that. At the same time, he understood that she wanted them to spend more time together. He wanted that, too, but his work held him back. It gave him a sense of uneasiness and the old feeling of bad conscience.

She was not at home. Her little red car was in the driveway, but she didn't open the door when he rang the bell. He walked round the house to the terrace, but it too was empty. He approached the large windows, put his hand up to the glass and peered inside without really knowing what it was he was looking for. Then he carried the strawberries and cream back to the car.

It was actually for the best. Dropping in on her in this way felt like a duty. He refrained from phoning her and instead drove to the police station. He could try to call in again when he finished work.

Torunn Borg drove into the basement garage in front of him. She got out of the car before him, and stood waiting by the door to the stairwell.

'Finished with the old folk?' he asked.

Torunn Borg nodded.

'I don't think anything came of it.'

'Think?'

'There was no one who knew anything, but there's one of them who perhaps knows more than he was willing to say to me.'

'Oh?'

'Alf Storeggen.'

'The lawyer?'

'He's lived there for two and a half years,' Torunn Borg explained while Wisting opened up the metal door at the foot of the stairs. It divided the basement of the police station, where the cells were situated, from the rest of the building. 'He has Parkinson's.'

Alf Storeggen's name had been listed for many years as the first of several partners in one of the town's largest firms of solicitors. He had conducted a number of criminal cases, but was first and foremost a commercial lawyer. He was highly respected and had a string of directorships in companies and organisations.

'I don't know if he was just making himself look important or if he really knows something,' Torunn Borg continued. 'But he had to think through a problem first, then he would possibly contact you.'

'Me?'

'He wanted to talk to the boss. The person who had responsibility.'

Wisting didn't believe that Alf Storeggen had any need to make himself look important. The lawyer had a long professional life behind him. His file of clients must be large and would probably contain many secrets.

'What about you?' Torunn enquired. 'Has your day been productive?'

He smiled at her.

'I have found a money trail,' he explained. 'We can talk about it with the others.'

They found Nils Hammer in Espen Mortensen's spacious office, sitting with his feet on the desk eating peanuts from a bag while he watched the underwater pictures beamed from the archipelago and a depth of more than 300 metres. Mortensen was sitting in front of his computer writing a report.

'Seen anything?' Wisting asked, nodding towards the living images. A grey, carpeted landscape spread out across the screen.

'A helluva lot of empty bottles,' Hammer explained, pointing at the screen where the neck of a bottle was sticking out of the sludge. 'We could get rich if we picked them all up.'

Wisting smiled and started to leaf through a bundle of screen printouts that lay on the desk beside Hammer. There was scrap iron, chains and twisted metal.

'There's quite an enormous rubbish dump on the seabed there,' Hammer gave as his opinion, pulling out a picture of a completely rusted and buckled pram that was covered in algae. 'People throw away all sorts of things.'

Wisting stopped at the picture of a shipwreck. The mini submarine must have been manouevred around it several times and had taken photographs from various angles. A registration number on the bow was visible on one of them.

'What's that?' he asked.

'An insurance fraud,' Hammer said. 'It's an *Uttern* boat that was reported stolen from Skottebrygga harbour last summer. The owner was paid 180,000 kroner.'

'Financial motive,' said Torunn Borg.

Wisting nodded.

'It's possible that this case too has an economic motive,' he explained. '2.4 million kroner passed through Torkel Lauritzen's bank account during the days prior to his disappearance.'

Espen Mortensen glanced up from the computer screen and frowned.

'Passed through?'

'Seven deposits totalling 2.4 million kroner on one and the same day.' Wisting went on to give an account of the meeting he had had with Oddmund and Marie Lauritzen. 'Two days later, the money was taken out again, divided into sixteen withdrawals.'

'Who was it who paid in the money?' Hammer wanted to know.

'That we don't know. They were cash deposits over the counter in different banks in Oslo. The videotapes were probably erased long ago.'

'Why haven't we known about this before now? The man's been missing for nine months, for goodness sake.'

'The family didn't find out about it until now. They have, in the same way as us, only looked to see if there have been any movements in his account since he disappeared.'

'But we're talking about a lot of money here. There should have been reports about it in the register of money-laundering or some such?'

'Only if it's reported by one of the bank employees. They don't monitor individual accounts. Each withdrawal is for 150,000 kroner. It's not initially so very striking that an old man comes in and takes out part of his savings.'

'What about the other old folk?' Hammer asked. 'Has anyone paid in money to them as well?'

Wisting shrugged his shoulders. 'You'll need to find out about that as soon as the banks open tomorrow.'

41

Suzanne had still not come home. He rang the doorbell twice, but had to carry the cream and berries back to the car once again. Putting one into his mouth he tasted how soft they had become from being in the warm car. The cream would probably turn sour soon too.

He sat behind the wheel and glanced up at the door while he phoned her. Eventually his call was forwarded to a voice that asked him to leave a message. He munched another berry and started the car. When he was almost home, he called Line's number. She had surprised him with seafood the night before – now he could repay by serving dessert.

Her voice had laughter in it when she replied, so infectious that Wisting had to give a broad smile.

'Where are you?' he asked, hearing conversations in the background.

'At a café down in Stavern. Why?'

'I was wondering if you were at home. I've bought some strawberries.'

'Then we'll drop in. We'll be there in half an hour.'

It took some time for him to realise that she was with Tommy Kvanter, and that she was going to bring him with her. He had distanced himself from his daughter's relationship with the Danish man of her own age, mostly because he had a past and a criminal record. He had chosen to keep his distance, at least until he saw how their relationship developed.

'That'll be nice,' he managed to say all the same as he parked in front of the house.

He placed the cream in the refrigerator and cleaned the berries before pouring them into a bowl and sprinkling sugar over them. Then he took a can of beer from the fridge and put a CD on the stereo system as he walked through to the garden terrace. He stood there with his elbows leaning on the railings and took a large slug, Leonard Cohen's deep voice filling his mind.

It was a warm evening, and a layer of still air covered the town like a blanket. He turned the can of beer between his fingers. In the distance, the church bell rang lazily to mark the end of a late evening service. Accompanied by the melancholy sound from the loudspeakers, the ringing sounded ominous. *That's how it goes. Everybody knows.*

All important cases had a turning point, he thought. A point when something significant emerged and made all the inexplicable pieces of the jigsaw fall into place. He thought he could sense it, that they were reaching that point now.

The breeze caused the flimsy curtains in the living room doorway to move.

There was a noise at the outside door. Line called out that they had arrived and Wisting went in to greet them and shake hands with Tommy. He was wearing a tight, white T-shirt that was stretched at the shoulders. A tattooed serpent's head protruded from the sleeve, colourful and drawn in such fine detail that it seemed to be alive.

He led out to the verandah and covered the table with a wax cloth before setting down the bowl of strawberries and three dishes.

'Do you need any help?' Line asked.

'You can get something for you both to drink,' Wisting suggested.

She gave Tommy one of his cans of beer and took a glass of water with ice cubes for herself.

'Fantastic view,' Tommy commented as he stood beside the railings.

'Yes indeed,' Wisting nodded, pointing out the lighthouse at Svenner for him. 'Will you be travelling out again soon?'

'I'll be at home for three weeks this time,' Tommy answered, turning his back on the sea. 'Then I'll be going out again, but this might be the last time.'

'Oh?'

'Some pals of mine are taking over a restaurant in Oslo. They want me to take responsibility for the kitchen.'

'Oh yes? I thought you enjoyed being a ship's steward?'

'Yes I do, but you get fed up with it. Anyway, I think it'll be good for our relationship.' Tommy nodded towards Line. 'And it will of course cut the accommodation costs in half.'

Wisting simply nodded. He didn't like the thought, but decided not to say anything. Instead he pulled out a chair for Tommy and sat down across from him at the table.

Tommy helped himself first.

'Did you pick them yourself?' he asked.

'I bought them,' Wisting had to admit.

'We have strawberries in the garden,' Line pointed out. 'Mum planted some.'

Wisting craned his neck and looked over at what was beginning to be an overgrown spot in the garden. It was really an informal garden, with just a small lawn at the front, but Ingrid had planted flowers and berries in cracks in the hillside and in the less stony patches.

'You can go and see if you can find any afterwards,' he proposed.

'Have you spoken to Suzanne today?' Line wanted to know.

The question embarrassed him.

'No,' he replied, putting a strawberry into his mouth. 'I dropped by after work, but she wasn't at home.'

'So it was for her you actually bought the strawberries?' Line laughed.

Wisting smiled, shrugging his shoulders. He was caught out.

'They tasted good all the same,' his daughter confirmed, reaching for a refill at the same time as Tommy. He withdrew his hand and knocked over the jug of cream. Line quickly righted it and tried to save some of the contents.

'Sorry,' she said at once. 'That was my fault.'

'It was me who knocked it over,' Tommy said.

'She's always been like that,' Wisting said, using a bundle of napkins to dry it up.

'How do you mean?' Line asked. 'Clumsy?'

'No, you've always taken the blame for things,' Wisting explained. 'Taken responsibility. It was like that when you and your brother played together when you were little as well. You took the blame when anything went wrong.'

Line laughed and changed the subject, but Wisting was no longer listening. His thoughts suddenly turned to the investigation. It was as though something fell into place. He had a feeling that something had opened up somewhere inside him and then closed again. It didn't last longer than a second. It was like having a glimpse of understanding about how things were connected. The feeling of almost grasping something, and then it was gone.

'What did you say?' he asked when he couldn't manage to gather his thoughts after all.

'Do you remember the living room window Thomas broke with his football, I was asking?'

Wisting nodded. 'He gave you ten kroner to say it was you, but then you told tales when I deducted two weeks' pocket money for it.'

'Brotherly love,' Tommy Kvanter commented.

Wisting became serious all of a sudden. What had been said caused him to think about the brothers Ken Ronny and Rune Hauge. He had known the whole time that the story of the police murder was not all it seemed to be. Could it be

194

that Ken Ronny had remained silent to cover for his brother?

He wondered if the same thought had struck Line. She had a serious expression on her face now. Her eyes stared like magnets back at his.

42

He took out the folder from the police murder just as soon as Line and Tommy had left, and withdrew the bundle containing all the statements, reading from the beginning, looking up only when the dim light from the outdoor lamp made his eyes feel tired.

Edgar Bisjord had reported that he had finished work at the scene of the traffic accident at Vestfossen at 03.45 hours. The investigators had worked on the theory that he had been murdered between 04.00 and 04.15. Everyone who had given a statement to the police had been in bed asleep at that time.

Rune Hauge had gone to bed early, as the next day was Monday and he had an early rise. He had just started his apprenticeship at the quarry out at Tveidalen. It appeared that his mother was staying overnight at a friend's house in Larvik, as she had done fairly often after the summer. His brother was out with the car, and Rune Hauge hadn't noticed whether he had come home during the night. It was not unusual for him to come home late. He did not have a job, apart from helping his grandfather renovate the house.

The best alibi was the one given by Daniel Meyer who commuted to Oslo where he lived in workmen's barracks all week, employed by a contractor who was building a large office block at Helsfyr. He got a lift from a work colleague who called for him at his home at 05.30. Theoretically speaking, they could have met Ken Ronny at some place or other along the road, but Daniel had fallen asleep in the car. The driver didn't know the car, and although there had been little traffic, he could not remember any yellow Ascona.

Wisting gazed at the dark horizon, thinking that it never ended anywhere. Beyond the horizon there was always a new one, no matter how far you travelled. The thought filled him with a sense of helplessness as he returned to the papers.

He didn't find anything more that was worth noting, but discovered one more detail. He had thought that Ken Ronny Hauge had been arrested at home at the house in Strandbakken, but an address in Tanumveien had been entered on the arrest report form. He had been arrested at his grandfather's house, where the psychiatric patient Hanne Richter had lived until she disappeared nine months previously.

Christian Hauge's name did not appear on the list of witnesses. Perhaps he had refrained from making a statement in a case involving his own grandson, or the leader of the investigation had considered it unnecessary. After all, the case had been regarded as solved within twenty-four hours. No one had looked for other possible explanations for what had happened. Ken Ronny Hauge had kept his silence and had not pointed the investigators in any other direction.

He leaned his head back, gazing up at the stars. The moon was almost full. He tried to fix his eyes on its uneven surface, but his eyes were drawn back down to the documents on his lap.

Flicking backwards and forwards through the pages he drank what was left in the beer can, then stacked the papers in a neat pile, deciding that he had had enough. He glanced at the clock, wondering whether he should try to phone Suzanne one last time. When he saw that it was past midnight he decided to let things be.

The cat that had been lying lazily in the chair beside him looked up at a sound from inside the house.

He heard it again. He got up and went inside. There it was again. It sounded as if someone was knocking on the front door.

As far as he knew, there was nothing wrong with the doorbell. He unlocked and opened the door slowly.

It was Suzanne.

'Hello,' she whispered. 'I wasn't sure if you'd gone to bed, so I didn't want to ring the bell.'

He let her in, glancing out at the yard behind her. A bicycle was leaning against the garage wall.

'Where have you been?' he asked.

'On a cycle trip,' she explained with a laugh. He realised that she had been drinking. 'A girlfriend and I, but we didn't get very far. We've been sitting at her house all evening. I'm actually on my way home, but I don't think I'll manage to cycle all the way into town. I'd prefer to stay overnight with you.'

He closed the door and pulled her tenderly, carefully, towards him, stroking her in the slightly awkward way he had. She responded by putting her arms around him, letting her head rest on his shoulder and he saw his face in the hall mirror. It looked as if the days gone by since they last saw each other had aged him. New wrinkles were engraved around his eyes and mouth. Silver grey stubble lay like frost on his chin. Then he closed his eyes, pushing her tentatively away and kissing her on the forehead before opening them once more.

'You know what?' he asked. 'I was just thinking about you.'

'Good thoughts?'

He replied by tracing his finger along her face before bending forward and kissing her lovingly.

'Shall we have a drink out on the verandah?' he suggested.

'You look tired,' she said, drawing her hand across his forehead. 'We might as well just go to bed.'

198

Wisting looked again in the mirror. She was right – his eyes were ringed with red, and his face was pale and drawn.

He had to admit that he felt exhausted. However, Suzanne's nut-brown eyes sparkled when she smiled, as she did now, awakening something in him, brushing away all thoughts of the investigation. She watched his hands as he undressed her. Trembling fingers that unfastened buttons and ribbons until her short dress was open and fell from her body. He took her by the hand and led her up to the bedroom.

Line raised herself out of bed and placed her bare feet on the floor. For the first time she had not been completely in the present when she was making love with Tommy. Other thoughts had filled her head, and she had lain awake after he had fallen asleep by her side.

She sat watching him in the half-light. The room was warm and he had kicked the covers off. His body seemed even browner against the white sheets.

She stood up, walking naked through the flat into the kitchen. The moonlight cast a blue, almost ghostly shadow on the buildings outside.

She covered her breasts with her hands when two men emerged from a side street. They didn't look in her direction, but she put on one of Tommy's T-shirts that was hanging over a chair. It reached to her thighs, and the fabric still retained his light, masculine scent.

She sat in front of the computer and turned it on, unsure of what she was actually doing.

The picture of Ken Ronny Hauge filled the screen. He was ten years older than her, and although handsome to look at, it was not any physical thing that attracted her. Something else brought her thoughts continually back to their meeting. A kind of amazement, but she had not quite grasped what it was until now. Could he be innocent? Had he taken the punishment for something he hadn't done?

She began to read the newspaper articles that had been scanned in, although she knew the contents as well as the back of her hand. The evidence against him was as solid as a rock. The policeman who had been killed had noted the car registration number on a notepad that was found in his car, and gunpowder residue had been found on Ken Ronny Hauge's hands. What the police had not been able to find was a motive. Why had Ken Ronny Hauge killed the policeman?

She turned the problem on its head and asked herself why a possibly innocent Ken Ronny Hauge had said nothing. She could actually find only one answer, that the truth was even worse for him.

She took a couple of deep breaths, and was on the brink of phoning her father. He was a good sparring partner when it came to finding new, unusual angles and ideas about deadlocked cases. But she restrained herself. It was the middle of the night, and she hoped that he was sleeping.

At random she searched on *gunpowder residue* in the text archive, but found nothing of any help. She switched off the computer and crept back to the bedroom, took off Tommy's used T-shirt and lay down under the duvet. She snuggled close to him and breathed in the smell of him that she liked so much. Then she sat up abruptly, staring at him and over at the T-shirt she had thrown over the back of a chair.

'What is it?' he mumbled.

'Nothing,' she answered, but it wasn't true. She had seen a possibility. That Ken Ronny Hauge had gunpowder residue on his hands showed nothing other than that he had handled a gun. He did not need to be the one who had fired it. He could have taken it from the person who had used it. From the person he was protecting.

43

It was now Monday 28th June. Wisting felt fully rested for once. Suzanne was still in bed when he left for work. It was the first time she had slept in his bed. He couldn't quite put into words what he felt. In a way it felt good, but at the same time it seemed treacherous. He had allowed her to sleep on his side so that he himself slept on the side that had been Ingrid's.

The morning meeting lasted longer than he had hoped. Everyone wanted to express an opinion about how the investigation had developed in the course of the weekend. He let them all have a chance, but kept his thoughts concerning the police murder to himself. He did not entirely trust his intuition, and he still could not see how it actually linked with the current case.

It was almost ten o'clock when they finished the review and chairs scraped on the floor as they all got up. Wisting sat gathering the papers that were spread across the table in front of him.

Audun Vetti was in no hurry.

'Do you think we'll succeed?' he asked.

Wisting looked at him. There was something nervous about the smile following the question, and a touch of anxiety in his eyes.

'What do you mean?' Wisting enquired.

'Will we manage to solve the case?'

'That's something I can't answer at the moment.' Wisting placed his hand on the pile of papers. 'But it's a case that we can't allow to go down in history as unsolved.'

The Assistant Chief of Police agreed: 'That wouldn't be a good idea.'

Wisting understood that Audun Vetti's concern stemmed from the thought that the applications for the post of Deputy Chief Constable would soon come up for consideration. It would look bad if he was responsible for prosecuting a case that was apparently in the doldrums and without a solution in sight.

Wisting shared his concern, but his own disquiet was for different reasons. The role of the police in society was to create a sense of security by combatting crime. The impression created by the police's energy and determination in an investigation such as this influenced the confidence the public had in the police force. It was the kind of confidence that took a long time to build, but that could be broken down in an instant. Belief in police work was a load-bearing beam in society and perhaps the most important requirement for people's feeling of safety. They could not risk losing that.

It did not happen often, but when really serious cases affected a small community, the same sense of unease sprang up. People began to scowl at one another in the shops, doors were locked painstakingly in the evenings, and children were accompanied on their way to school. Wisting had experienced it several times before and really felt the weight of responsibility. It was their task to reestablish this balance, and so the case must be solved.

Suddenly the noise of hurried activity arose in the corridor outside, someone shouting, the sound of doors slamming and scurrying footsteps. Wisting was getting up from his chair as Espen Mortensen popped his head round the door.

'A corpse has been found out at Stolpestad,' he said. 'Are you coming?'

'A corpse?' Wisting asked.

'In the sea. It's obviously been there a long time.'

202

Wisting took his jacket from the back of the chair and nodded to show that he was ready.

Stolpestad was situated on the western side of the Naver fjord, and had given its name to one of the many family-friendly camping sites that ringed the shallow bay.

They drove through the campsite and down to the shore. Teams of police guards had arrived before them. Two patrol cars were on the grassy plain by the water, and an official was positioned at the entrance to the coast road. He pointed out the direction for them and held back some teenagers who wanted to join them.

A marked path led them through a dense alder grove and over windswept hillocks along the edge of the sea for some distance to the south. Finally they reached a shallow inlet with red and white police tape stretched out.

The first journalists and photographers were already there. Wisting had some questions thrown at his back when he bent underneath the barrier, but did not answer.

Down at the water's edge, a green tarpaulin had been laid over the slippery sloping rock. Sea pinks clung tightly to crevices, heads bobbing in the breeze. A few black birds were circling in the warm air above them, their wing feathers spread like outstretched fingers.

The man who had found the corpse was sitting on a stone, having given a statement to the first police patrol to arrive. He lived in one of the cottages facing the sun above the discovery site. All the newspaper reports about feet washing ashore and the search for more body parts had made him turn his binoculars down in the direction of the pebbles every day. The body had not been difficult to see, lying face-down, swaying in the water.

He had taken a boat hook and gone down, extended it across the water to let the hook sink down on the bundle. Firmly hooked, he had dragged the body towards him onto land. Before fetching a tarpaulin to cover the corpse he had phoned the police.

Espen Mortensen got some help from one of the policemen to fold the tarpaulin to one side. Wisting looked for the feet on the dead body, and saw that the left was missing.

On the other foot there was a white leisure shoe with an orange area on each side with the curved Nike logo. Two days before, a matching shoe had floated ashore near Solplassen.

Mortensen took a few photographs before pulling on gloves and protective clothing. Then he hunkered down and turned the body over.

Hair and parts of the skin had fallen off in large flakes. Parts of the lower jaw were missing and the eye sockets were empty. However, although the face was decomposing, Wisting recognised the features. They had found Sverre Lund.

He stepped closer to the corpse of the retired head teacher and crouched down.

He wondered what the missing eyes might have seen. What had raced through his head when he understood what was going to happen? When the truth, ruthless and irrevocable, dawned on him.

He stood up again. The sun was beating down and water lapped around the pebbles. The birds above them were circling lower, flapping their wings to rise higher before descending slowly, like enormous black shadows.

44

They gathered round the conference table with the curtains drawn. The ceiling projector illuminated the screen with a close-up of the back of the head of a man who had been missing for almost ten months. The hair and skin had fallen off together to expose a gaping, jagged hole in the skull with fractures spreading out in all directions. Small sea creatures had eaten their way through the open wound and left a void. Sticky, brown seawater had run out, solidifying at the bottom edge of the injury.

'Shot in the back of the head,' Espen Mortensen confirmed. 'The bullet has taken parts of the jaw with it on exit. This is officially a murder enquiry.'

'The discovery of the corpse is out in all the news media,' Audun Vetti explained. 'We need to hold a press conference in the course of the day and confirm that this is a murder.'

Wisting nodded. The discovery of four human feet in total had caused big enough headlines in themselves but, now the first corpse had been found, the whole business would blow up. The man who found the corpse had already given interviews to several newspapers. The gist of the coverage in the internet newspapers was much the same: a corpse with a missing foot had been discovered.

'You'll have to make an appearance,' Vetti continued, fixing his eyes on Wisting.

'I've got a lot of other . . .'

'I'll convene it for three o'clock,' the Assistant Chief of

Police swept aside Wisting's objections. 'That gives us a few hours. Can we confirm the identity by then?'

'We have alerted his wife,' Mortensen explained, 'but we need a definite identification before we can release a name.'

'When can we have that?'

'Tomorrow at the earliest.'

There was a short discussion. Wisting concluded it by suggesting that they could say that the police were working from the theory that the corpse was the retired head teacher Sverre Lund, who had been reported missing on the 8th September the previous year. There would be no point in keeping this working hypothesis secret from the media.

'Then you'll turn up at three o'clock?' Vetti demanded.

Wisting nodded. He knew why the Assistant Chief of Police was so eager to share the podium. When there was positive information to be announced to the press, he wanted to be on his own, giving it out in the first person singular. When it concerned an investigation that was not producing results, he wanted to give an account of the police work in the first person plural and have Wisting by his side to refer critical questions to.

'Shall we call off the underwater search?' the Chief Superintendent asked. 'There probably isn't any reason to believe that we'll find anything now?'

Wisting knew that budgetary considerations lay behind the suggestion.

'Let's continue it for the rest of the day,' he proposed. 'We're still looking for four bodies.'

'I've spoken to Ebbe Slettaker,' interjected Torunn Borg, referring to the oceanographer. 'He explained that the discovery of the corpse fits with his calculations of drift trajectories. He's firmly convinced by the theory that the bodies were dumped at sea, and that they have broken loose somehow.'

The Chief Superintendent authorised the further search with a nod.

'This is not what we had expected,' Torunn Borg remarked. 'We thought we were going to find more body parts. That there might be a natural explanation, such as that it was the length of time in the water that caused the corpses to decompose and body parts to detach, but the rest of this body is still intact.'

'I don't think this has a natural explanation,' Mortensen commented.

'But we're not talking about murder victims being dismembered either,' Torunn Borg went on, indicating the screen. 'Why on earth has someone chopped his foot off? Or off the other victims?'

Wisting listened to the discussion as it developed. This was important. He had understood a long time ago that this concerned more than cases of missing persons, that they were dealing with people who had been exposed to something criminal, but all the time he had been asking himself the question why. There were several connections between the victims, but why did someone want them dead? And why should their feet be cut off?

The discussion round the table didn't lead to anything in particular.

Wisting cleared his throat and spoke up.

'We have to assume that this investigation concerns five murders,' he said, putting into words what had not been expressed before. 'We are faced with no suspect, no clear motive and no specific clues.'

What he said in his short summary was cold, harsh and frightening. They were hardly the words that Audun Vetti would choose for the press conference.

'We have to take the five victims as our starting point,' he continued, 'and look for a common reference. Some point of intersection where there is something that affects every one of them. What have we got?' he challenged.

'The secret alert force,' Espen Mortensen replied.

'That only applies to the three men. Moreover, there were other members of that. Why is Carsten Meyer not also among the victims?'

'Maybe he's the culprit?' someone suggested.

Nobody laughed or came up with other suggestions. Wisting noticed that Nils Hammer was not present. He was usually good at coming up with new ideas.

'Where's Nils?' he asked.

'At the bank,' Torunn replied.

He nodded. The money was a clue. What Nils Hammer discovered about the large financial transactions might be important.

'The murderer is himself a kind of intersection point,' Espen Mortensen felt. 'It must of course be possible to make an analysis that leads to some common denominator. To draw up a chart of absolutely all the people in the circle surrounding the victims.'

Wisting agreed. That was a task that they had actually made some progress with. Through interviews with families and other associates they had eventually gathered important information about the victims. The information would have to be at some point subject to more systematic examination, but what they already had was by no means exhaustive.

'We don't know whether such a common denominator exists, do we?' Torunn Borg objected. 'Although obviously there must be a connection among the three men, the two women might be more accidental victims.'

'In what way accidental?'

'They may have seen something they shouldn't have seen. They might have been killed in order to cover up the original crime.'

Wisting got up, walked over to the window and opened the curtains, screwing up his eyes in the strong sunlight.

'What is it that we haven't done?' he asked. 'What have

we not checked? Is there something we haven't seen? Something we could do differently? Is there something we are overlooking?'

He turned to face the people sitting round the table and their expressionless faces. No one could answer, so he declared the meeting closed.

45

Among the notifications on his phone were two unanswered calls from Suzanne and one from Line – neither of them had left any message.

He called Suzanne first.

'Hello,' he said. 'Where are you?'

'At your house,' she replied. 'I couldn't find a key, so I stayed here.'

'Sorry,' Wisting said. 'There's a spare key in the top drawer of the chest of drawers in the hallway.'

'That's fine. I found a book on your shelf and have been relaxing out on the terrace. Will you be calling in at home?'

'I won't manage, and I think it'll be a long day.'

'Yes, I heard them talking on the news about finding a corpse with a foot missing.'

'That's right.'

'Then I'll go home, but you're welcome to drop by if it isn't too late.'

'Maybe I'll do that. I'll have to wait and see.'

'Perhaps I'll see you on the TV?'

'On the TV?'

'They said that you were holding a press conference at three o'clock.'

Wisting glanced at the clock. There were two hours to go.

'It's not certain that I'll be there,' he explained. 'Then I think there'll be more of a chance that you'll see me this evening.'

He tried to phone Line as well, but she didn't reply. He sat down behind the desk, examining his stray thoughts, but everything seemed just as unclear and confusing.

Nils Hammer entered the office without knocking and put a bundle of papers on the table before sitting on the visitor's chair and pulling his snuffbox out of his trouser pocket.

'They're saying on the radio that we've found a dead body that's missing a foot?' he remarked, pinching a portion of snuff into the palm of his hand.

'Sverre Lund,' Wisting confirmed. 'Forensics need a day or two to confirm.'

Hammer placed the snuff under his lip, brushed his hands clean and pulled the papers towards him.

'Almost three million,' he said, withdrawing a printout. 'During the week before Sverre Lund disappeared, 2,950,000 kroner were paid into his account. He took them out the day before he went missing. The same applies to Otto Saga – in his case, 2.5 million. In and out in the course of a few days.'

Wisting leaned back while Nils Hammer explained how cash deposits were made over the counter in banks in Drammen, Asker and Sandvika, and how the money was withdrawn from local banks after a few days.

'Nearly eight million in total.'

'What about Hanne Richter and Camilla Thaulow?' Wisting asked.

'Nothing.'

'One of the staff at *Nordea* bank in Sandefjord remembered that Torkel Lauritzen had been there.' Hammer leafed through his notes. 'He was going to buy a car for his son in Sandefjord. He had asked him about his son, but Lauritzen had difficulty understanding. He had left his hearing aid at home.'

'Lauritzen didn't use a hearing aid.'

'None of his sons live in Sandefjord either. Otto Saga gave the same explanation when he withdrew money in Skien. It

211

made it plausible that the money was not being withdrawn at his own bank in his hometown, since the money was to go to a son who lived in the town. When the assistant began to ask awkward questions, it was convenient to avoid them by blaming his hearing.'

'Can we be certain that they, themselves, withdrew the money?'

Hammer nodded as he flicked through the papers.

'Several of the banks have taken a copy of the identification. The signature and everything else matches.'

'Were they alone?'

'None of the staff can say otherwise.'

Wisting bit his lower lip and gazed out the window. 'Where did the money come from?'

'I'm going to Oslo early tomorrow. I thought I would go round the banks where the deposits were made. Perhaps someone will remember something.'

Espen Mortensen's voice crackled on the loudspeaker: 'Can you come in here for a moment? There's something on the screen you need to see.'

'The screen?'

'From the underwater search. I've got the chief diver on the phone. They've made a find.'

Wisting got up from his chair.

'Whereabouts?' he asked.

'Come in and have a look.'

Nils Hammer was first out the door. Wisting followed him along the corridor and into the crime technician's large office. The venetian blinds were pulled halfway down to block the sunshine and the ceiling light switched off. The only illumination in the room came from the screen of the freestanding computer with the underwater images.

The grey seabed was bathed in light from the powerful lamps on the mini submarine. The barrel and most of the stock of a pistol were protruding from the sludge.

The weapon still appeared shiny in the harsh light.

'It can't have lain there for long,' Mortensen said, taking the words out of Wisting's mouth. 'There's no sign of corrosion.'

Wisting nodded his agreement instead of saying anything. The gun was lying down in a small depression, as though it had formed a little crater when it hit the dregs on the bottom of the sea. The text on the screen stated that they were at a depth of 354 metres.

'It looks like a Colt,' Nils Hammer commented, turning his head to the side. 'Can you get a closer picture?'

Espen Mortensen relayed the question via the telephone. On the screen, the sludge on the bottom swirled up as the mini submarine accelerated. A grappling arm became visible at the lower edge of the picture. The mechanical fingers opened into a claw, grasped the weapon and lifted it smoothly. The pistol was raised from the sea floor, but slipped out of its grip and disappeared out of the picture.

The camera was adjusted, and the weapon once again became visible on the grey seabed. A glossy fish glided by, meandering from side to side before disappearing, like a dying light.

The grappling claw opened again halfway. No one in the room spoke while the operator on board the submersible was working. The hook on the claw locked on to the trigger guard with a sure grip and lifted the gun up to the camera. They could see scratches or other signs of wear and tear. *11.25 m/m AUT.PISTOL M/1914 No* was stamped along the barrel.

'A Colt,' Mortensen agreed, taking a screen printout. '1914 model. That could be the murder weapon.'

'But it doesn't have a weapon number.' Nils Hammer put his finger on the screen where the weapon number would normally be engraved at the end of the pistol slide. 'It doesn't look as though it's been rubbed off either, it's just smooth.'

Wisting leaned towards the screen.

'Perhaps we'll be able to find it on the tube of the barrel or the slider when we get it up.'

'The person who got rid of it never expected it to be found,' Hammer remarked. 'The most sensible thing would of course have been to take it apart. All weapons have a history that allows them to be traced.'

Wisting nodded. Weapons were like fingerprints; no two were completely alike. He had read countless reports from ballistics experts and weapons technicians over the years. He knew that a weapon such as this one had a firing pin stamp, slider, striker and receiver that all left individual marks on the cartridge case in that fraction of a second when the weapon was fired.

He picked up the colour printout of the find that had been made at 354 metres' depth, his thoughts returning to the same thing.

In the police murder of 1991, the analysis of the spent cartridges left behind at the crime scene had led the investigators to believe that the murder weapon was a Colt M1914, but they had never found the actual weapon.

'They're asking if we want it taken up immediately,' Mortensen communicated, with the telephone to his ear.

'Let's get it up,' Wisting requested. 'The site of the find has to be the starting point for a new search of that sector.'

Mortensen passed on the request. Wisting's eyes moved back to the computer monitor, where the grappling claw was disappearing from the picture as the mini submarine prepared to ascend.

46

Eight minutes before the start of the press conference Wisting stood in the cloakroom, wearing his uniform. He fastened the ready-knotted tie and looked at himself in the mirror. His complexion was pale and sallow, and his eyes seemed dull. He definitely needed a holiday and a bit of sun, and he should really phone the doctor.

It would have to be later.

The uniform made him look younger, but otherwise his features resembled many of the old missing men. He was 51, but it seemed that age was taking him by the scruff of the neck and forcing him to his knees.

The press conference was to be held in the canteen on the second floor. Tables had been cleared and extra chairs brought from the conference rooms, but not enough for everyone. The photographers were sitting on the floor and leaning against the walls.

Vetti was the first to enter the crowded room. Wisting took a deep breath, let the Chief Superintendent follow next, and was last to reach the narrow conference table. The Assistant Chief of Police pulled out the middle chair and sat down.

Wisting counted eight microphones with logos from the familiar news media.

He didn't feel comfortable at meetings with the press. It was like wandering about in a minefield, the whole time balancing on the edge of what information would be tactically correct to give out and what might damage the investigation, and what might be offensive to the relatives.

215

At the same time, it also had to do with preserving the reputation and respect of the government service. A press conference was a forum in which it was not possible to check quotations. There would be no opportunity to change or retract statements, and it was all too easy to make a wrong move.

In many ways he saw the media as an entitled participant, although they sometimes made him feel more like a public relations officer than a policeman. The task of the media was to pose critical questions and he, as leader of the investigation, had to put up with the spotlight.

Seen from the police point of view the press conference was a practical arrangement. The need to issue information to the public was met, and the journalists were all treated in the same way. At the same time, it gave the police an opportunity to focus on what they felt might prompt tip-offs. The thinking was also that this kind of common meeting with the press would put a damper on media pressure. Endless questions about whether there was anything new in the case could have a disturbing effect on the investigation. Still, none of the journalists regarded the press conference as an important source of information, and in its way it conflicted with the journalists' requirement for exclusivity. Information was like oxygen to them. A press conference was like kindling an open fire. The case would burst into flames. He knew that, once the lights in the room were extinguished, the mobile phones would start to ring.

A TV reporter at the back of the room was talking to camera, introducing a direct broadcast. How many eyes were on them? The Justice Minister and the Secretary of State were probably standing together in front of a television in the government offices, the National Police Commissioner and her staff would be watching from her office. The Mayor, colleagues throughout the country, old Carsten Meyer in his chair in Kongsberg, would all be watching.

He had also to take into consideration that the murderer would also be watching.

Vetti took a folded sheet of paper from his inside pocket and began with a formal introduction. Thereafter, he gave as concise and unqualified an account as possible, from the events of the past few days to the discovery of the corpse that morning, which was the main reason for summoning the press.

'The deceased has not been identified, but the police have reason to believe that we are talking about 78-year-old Sverre Lund, who was reported missing from his place of residence in the centre of Stavern on the 8th September last year,' Vetti read out, using Wisting's wording.

Wisting scanned the people in attendance while Vetti continued to talk. He let his eye rest for a moment on one of the cameras with its red light, and thought about Suzanne whom he knew would be watching.

'Evidence from the corpse gives us grounds to believe that we are dealing with a criminal act,' Vetti went on in formal terms. 'The cause of death appears to be an inflicted gunshot wound.'

They had agreed to be open about the probable cause of death, although it had not been confirmed. The choice of words *inflicted gunshot wound* revealed that the police had excluded suicide, at the same time as withholding details. Wisting felt he could discern a mixed reaction amongst the journalists. Some seemed grateful for the comprehensive information, whereas a couple in the first row seemed disappointed, as though they already knew the details and had prepared an exclusive presentation. It was probably only a question of time before the headlines were stating openly that the victim had been shot in the head.

Vetti took a sip from a glass of water before continuing.

'One of the central points in our investigations concerns a series of large amounts that were deposited and then withdrawn from the bank account of the deceased a short time before he went missing.' He went on to give a further explanation of the transactions in the accounts belonging to Sverre Lund and the other men.

'Questions?' he invited.

Hands shot up.

'Have you found the murder weapon?'

Vetti passed the question over to Wisting with a glance. It was a manouevre that could suggest that there might be something behind the question. Wisting hesitated long enough for the most experienced journalists to be aware. The question was key, but nevertheless came as a surprise. It was unquestionably information that they would prefer to keep to themselves. A denial might nevertheless be regarded as a lie.

'We don't know what type of gun we might be dealing with,' Wisting explained, evading the question.

He feared follow-up questions, but another journalist started speaking and turned the direction: 'Do you believe that all of the missing men have been murdered?'

'We have, among other things, been working from a theory that there is a connection among the missing men,' Wisting replied. 'Today's development opens the possibility that we may be faced with several murders.'

There was a brisk round of questions concerning the theory of a serial killer. The journalists surpassed one another in their attempts to find smart wording for their questions. Wisting responded by saying that they were keeping all options open.

'What about the two missing women?' asked one of the journalists from the front row. 'Might they have been murdered too?'

Wisting took a little time before giving an answer. The press had apparently found the connection between Camilla Thaulow, Hanne Richter and the three men who were missing. He summarised the connection and stated that, although the link was less definite, it was a possibility that they must also keep open.

'What about the underwater search that's taking place?' another journalist wanted to know. 'Has that brought any results?'

Wisting pretended to look for the face of the person who had asked the question while he searched for an answer that neither disclosed anything about the discovery of the weapon, nor said anything that could cause him to be accused later of lying.

'There haven't been any finds that we can link directly to the case,' he replied, fixing his gaze on the man, whom he recognised as a reporter for *Aftenposten*.

'What have you found?'

'For the most part, different kinds of rubbish. There may be instances of breaching the laws on pollution. We have also found the wreck of a boat that was reported stolen last summer and are going to be following up the connection with a possible insurance fraud.'

'Is it possible to release some of the underwater images?'

'That can be arranged, but I don't know if it's something we can make a priority.'

A red-haired, female reporter by the window spoke up, introducing herself as a representative of NTB, Norway's largest news agency. Wisting didn't catch her name.

'Where did the money come from?' she enquired.

'We have a main focus on that,' Wisting replied. 'But for the moment, we do not know.'

'Could it be the proceeds from a criminal act?'

'As I said, we don't know.'

The female journalist was about the same age as Line. She made a face that Wisting interpreted to mean she did not like the way he had warded off her question.

'How long have you known about the financial evidence?' she asked.

'It was discovered at the weekend.'

'Do you mean to say that there were considerable financial movements in the accounts of the missing persons without the police checking this out earlier? That sort of information must have been accessible through bank statements and so on, surely?'

Wisting closed his eyes for a short spell and put on a patient expression. It was always like this. The first questions were fairly respectful, but eventually the tone became sharper and more aggressive. He was prepared for the question and explained how the investigators had monitored the bank accounts of the missing persons as a matter of routine, but that the history had not been examined until now.

The journalist did not let go: 'Should you not have done that earlier?'

'It is easy to come to that conclusion with the benefit of hindsight.'

'So you admit that you've made a mistake, then?

Wisting realised that he was being backed into a corner and concentrated on not sounding irritated.

'We regard the discovery as a major step forward.'

'But in reality you don't have any clues?'

The journalist tried her best to put words in his mouth. He heard Audun Vetti, in the seat beside him, clear his throat as a sign that they should finish up.

'I'd prefer to say that we are facing one of the most challenging cases we have ever worked on,' Wisting said, giving the woman a smile.

The redhead did not seem satisfied with his answer, but gave him a nod and said no more.

Individual journalists had new questions, but finally they seemed most eager to contact their editors, and Vetti declared the meeting closed. Wisting got up, leaving individual interviews to the Assistant Chief of Police.

47

It took exactly twenty-three minutes for the first interesting phone call to arrive. Wisting stood by the window, having hung his uniform back in the cupboard, his thoughts tossing like a sailing boat suddenly struck by squalls.

He answered brusquely, and stood listening to the man at the other end. His brow furrowed. What he heard confused him further, but it was something he wanted to know more about. They made an appointment and, thirty-two minutes later, the man was sitting in the visitor's chair in Wisting's office.

Karl Edvin Malmstrøm was in his mid-forties, tall and thin, his ash blond, slightly wavy hair combed forward. He wore sandals, khaki trousers and a white, short-sleeved shirt.

'We're staying in a caravan at Gon,' he explained. 'We've done that every summer for the past fifteen years.'

Wisting nodded. The man was one of many who spent their holidays in the area. He worked as an adviser and customer service assistant at *Bien* savings bank in the centre of Oslo.

'I remember both of them, as I said,' he went on, stroking the armrest of the chair with his hand. 'Both Otto Saga and Sverre Lund. It might be that Torkel Lauritzen came to us as well, but was served by another adviser.'

Wisting stopped him and phoned for Nils Hammer. He was the one with responsibility for the money trail, and he wanted him present.

'I'd thought about making contact earlier,' Karl Edvin

Malmstrøm continued while they waited for the other investigator. 'I recognised them from pictures in the newspapers, but it was only when I heard you talking about the other transactions that I realised it could be important.'

Hammer appeared before half a minute had passed. He closed the door behind him, said hello to the bank assistant and sat down on the spare visitor's chair.

Wisting gave a quick explanation of the purpose of the interview, and then asked Karl Edvin Malmstrøm to continue.

The bank assistant took a sheet of paper from his shirt pocket and unfolded it.

'Sverre Lund visited us on Wednesday 3rd September at 11.33,' he explained. 'I got a work colleague to check it before I came here. The exact amount was 345,000 kroner. Otto Saga came in on Friday 29th August at 12.42. He made a deposit of 340,000 kroner.'

Nils Hammer nodded. It agreed with the survey he had carried out.

''There's a deposit in your bank for Torkel Lauritzen's account also,' he added. 'On Wednesday 27th August.'

'Every second Wednesday I have a study day.' The bank assistant folded up the sheet of paper again. 'It must have been another adviser who dealt with it. I can find out who it was.'

'So it was they themselves who deposited the money then?' Wisting wanted to confirm.

'It's not anything unusual,' Karl Edvin Malmstrøm felt. 'Most cash deposits over the counter are to people's own accounts.'

'But it's unusual that old people travel miles to do that, just to take the money out again a few days later.'

'It was a question of discontinued banknotes, as I recall. That could be the explanation.'

'Discontinued?'

'I think that both of them had about 150,000 of the old

222

Camilla Collett notes. In a few days' time, they wouldn't have been able to exchange them.'

Wisting sensed that some kind of understanding was on its way, something that would seem logical and give meaning to the whole thing, but he couldn't quite manage to put it into words.

'On the 5th September the old hundred-kroner notes with the portrait of Camilla Collett became invalid,' the bank assistant explained. 'She was replaced by Kirsten Flagstad in 1997. You could use the old banknote for one year longer, but after that it had to be exchanged in the bank. After ten years it would become invalid. We had lots of deposits like that around that time. There was a lot of discussion about it in the media. We had many pensioners and others who emptied their mattresses and came to us with their savings, but not with as much money as Sverre Lund or Otto Saga.'

'Do you mean that the money would have been worthless if they had come a few days' later?'

'Not necessarily. They could have applied to have them exchanged, but then they would have had to bring them personally to *Norges Bank* in Oslo, accompanied by a written declaration of where they came from and why the money had not been changed previously.'

'Old men with old money,' Wisting said to no one in particular.

'Were there only out of date banknotes?' Nils Hammer asked.

The bank assistant nodded.

'It included two bundles of the old thousand-kroner note with Christian Magnus Falsen, that were still wrapped in *Norges Bank* tape. It looked as though they had never been in circulation.'

Wisting tried to envision the old thousand-kroner banknote with the portrait of the Father of the Norwegian Constitution, but could not remember what it looked like.

'When does that become completely invalid?' he enquired.

'The thousand-kroner note goes out of date in 2012,' the man facing him explained. 'The 500-kroner note with the portrait of Edvard Grieg becomes invalid in 2011, the 50-kroner note with Aasmund Olavsson Vinje went out of date in January last year. I think I read somewhere that there's still a million of them in circulation.'

'What about the 200-kroner note?'

'That entered the series of notes in 1994 and has not been discontinued yet, but a new, more secure version was introduced in 2002, with a broad metal strip at the side of the portrait. I don't think there are any plans to discontinue that one.'

'Did they say anything about where the money came from?' Wisting asked.

The man thought carefully.

'Not directly. It was more a suggestion.'

'What was the suggestion?'

'That it was savings. Sverre Lund said he should have come long before. That it was safer to have the money in the bank, and the kind of things that old people say when they decide to come to us with their money. His hearing was bad, so it was difficult to have a proper conversation. The same applied to Otto Saga. Hearing is one of the first things to go in old people.'

Wisting and Hammer glanced at each other. It was the same excuse they had used when the money was withdrawn.

'Can you remember anything else?'

'One of them talked about the tax authorities and inheritance tax, but I didn't understand the connection. At least, I don't remember it now. Normally I would have asked where the money came from and made a note about it for the person responsible for money laundering at the bank, but it wasn't done. It was obvious that we were talking about old savings, of course. Moreover, he wasn't one of our customers.'

'Did you ask about it? Why he came to you and not to his own bank?'

'No. We're a small, independent savings bank offering personal service in the middle of Oslo city centre. A lot of people make use of us without being account holders.'

'Did they come on their own?'

'I can't say that I noticed anything else. We try to be vigilant when old people come in to take out a lot of money, but in this case we were talking about a deposit.'

'Can you remember what they brought the money in?'

'Envelopes. Sverre Lund had them in a little rucksack, but Otto Saga I think just came into the bank with the envelope in his hand.'

'Where is the money now?'

Karl Edvin Malmstrøm seemed perplexed.

'You explained at the press conference, didn't you, that it was taken out of their accounts again a few days' later?'

'I mean the actual banknotes,' Wisting elaborated. There were always fingerprints on banknotes, and if they were talking about money that had been out of circulation for a long time, it might be easier to discover a print that would tell them where they came from.

'What has physically happened to them?' he added.

'I expect that they've been destroyed at *Norges Bank*.'

'All of them?'

'Some of the notes, as I said, were of extremely high quality and still had their original gloss. Several of them appeared to be perfectly preserved. Not mistreated by the printer, a bank employee, or anyone else. The paper was clean and tight, with no discolouration. The corners were sharp and at the correct angle, with no sign of being rounded off.'

'Are you a collector?'

'Yes. My father travelled a great deal, and I had uncles in the shipping industry. When I was still a young boy I had a large collection of banknotes from all over the world, but I have become a specialist in Norwegian notes.'

'So what did you do with the best banknotes?'

The bank assistant squirmed in his chair.

'I purchased them. It would have been a shame for the notes to be destroyed. Many of them were replacement notes.'

'Replacement notes?'

'When a banknote is spoiled during the printing process, it's replaced by a replacement note,' Malmstrøm explained. 'There's no difference between them and the originals, apart from that the replacement notes are given their own serial numbers. That makes them desirable to collectors.'

'How much might such an uncirculated hundred-kroner note actually be worth?'

'That also depends on what year it was printed. The hundred-kroner note with Camilla Collett, for example, was issued from 1979, but was printed with dates from 1977 onwards. A perfect example from the first year of printing could be worth up to ten times the original value.'

'A thousand kroner?'

'It depends of course on the market and the demand. A rare banknote of a type that few people are collecting will not have a particularly high value, while a less rare example of good quality of a type that is popular to collect can quickly become very expensive.'

Nils Hammer appeared impatient.

'How many banknotes did you transfer to yourself?'

'I bought just over forty thousand.'

Hammer rolled his eyes.

'The first time,' Malmstrøm added. 'In fact when Sverre Lund came five days later, I sold a few blocks of shares in order to redeem some more notes.'

'Do you still have all the banknotes?'

'Not all of them. I have, naturally, helped others to complete their collections.'

'How much have you earned from that?'

'I don't know . . . I haven't added it up, but none of the

banknotes were sold for less than three times their face value.'

Nils Hammer rose abruptly.

'We need those notes,' he said. 'Where are they?'

'At home in the safe, but I don't understand what you want with them?'

'We believe that the money may be the direct reason for at least three murders,' Hammer explained. 'Where they come from will be crucial for our further investigations. A fingerprint examination might well help.'

'But will that kind of examination not spoil the notes? With fingerprint powder and suchlike?'

'Oh yes.' Hammer went over to the door. 'Shall we go and get them right away?'

48

An hour and a quarter later Wisting was driving over the Gamlebrua bridge in Kongsberg. The water level was low and the waterfall not at its most intense, but still an impressive sight. Some people were playing about, paddling in the rapids. One of them got caught in an eddy and was struggling to get out. It was an appropriate picture of how the investigation was progressing, he thought. It seemed as though everything was still swirling uselessly and meaninglessly round and round.

He parked in the same place as the last time he had visited Carsten Meyer, taking a few minutes to gather his thoughts before getting out. The air felt different from down by the coast. It was humid and still, almost oppressive.

Some time elapsed between his ring on the doorbell and the door opening as far as the heavy door chain allowed. Carsten Meyer stared through the gap.

'Is that you?' he asked, glancing up at the street behind Wisting. 'I thought it might be the home help come early.'

'It's me,' Wisting smiled. 'I was hoping we could have a chat.'

'Of course,' the old man nodded. 'Just a moment.'

There was a clanking sound as he released the chain and the door opened wide. Carsten Meyer trudged back towards the living room, supporting himself with a crutch.

Wisting sat down in the same place as before. A new crossword puzzle lay open on the table facing Meyer's chair with only a few of the squares filled in.

'They say it's going to rain,' Carsten Meyer said, looking warily out of the window to the mountain.

'We certainly need it,' Wisting nodded. He hadn't listened to the weather forecast for many days.

'But you haven't come here to talk about the weather, have you?' The old man seemed ill at ease as he moved a cup and a ballpoint pen on the table beside him. He grasped his pipe that was lying in the dish beside the crossword. 'I heard that you've found Sverre.'

'I'm afraid so,' Wisting confirmed. 'There's no longer any doubt that this concerns a crime.'

Carsten Meyer filled his pipe with slow movements, looking at him from underneath his bushy eyebrows.

'How were the five-man group and the rest of the alert organisation financed?' Wisting asked.

Carsten Meyer frowned. His loose and almost transparent skin tightened over his hand as he worked on his pipe.

'We were issued with funds from confidential items in the defence budget,' he explained. 'But it was never money that motivated or spurred us on. It was idealism and personal conviction. We did, of course, have our actual expenses covered.'

'Did the group have any other income?'

The old man facing him struck a match with a clumsy motion and lit his pipe.

'That's something you can read about in Daniel's book,' he replied when he had lit up. 'You would think that most things had been written and talked about concerning the war and the post war period, but there are still lots of secrets to reveal.'

Wisting leaned back in the chair to encourage the old man to talk.

'The contributions from the budget financed only a small part of what we required in order to build an effective organisation in readiness for invasion,' Meyer continued.

229

'The most important supplementary funds came to us from actions taken to recapture war proceeds and compensation for war profits.'

He took the pipe out of his mouth and let it rest in his hand.

'The war was a good time for those who knew how to profit from it,' he went on, putting his pipe back. 'Share prices rose and unemployment went down to almost zero. Prices for goods were very good. Actually it was quite logical, since almost half a million Germans came here and needed to be supplied with most things. Many people became extremely well off through co-operation with the Germans. It was an especially good time for the construction industries that helped the Germans build aerodromes, barracks and railways, or that produced different materials with the help of Russian and Serbian prisoners of war.'

Carsten Meyer took a deep breath, closed his eyes and lowered his head as though he was already tired of the story.

'Many Norwegian war profiteers went free after the Second World War,' he went on. 'Financial compensation from traitors was based on class inequality. At the same time as wanting to punish companies and individuals that had made good money from the war, the wheels of commerce had to been kept oiled. The country had to be rebuilt, and there was little point in punishing the big companies that employed a large number of people. Many of the biggest profiteers went free.'

'But you made sure of fairness all the same?'

'We carried out some equalising actions, as I said, that ensured that we were self-financing.'

'What was that about?'

Carsten Meyer blew a puff of smoke from the side of his mouth that rose in a blue ring towards the ceiling.

'We liberated money that had been hidden away and preserved.'

'How did you do that?'

'We made visits at night to industrialists, contractors, barracks barons and other profiteers. You will perhaps call it burglary and theft but it had to do with confiscating funds from people who had gained financially from the presence of the Germans.'

'Were there no police investigations?'

The old man shook his head.

'We're talking about hidden wealth and black market money. The people whose profits we took risked being investigated as traitors if it became known what had happened to them.'

Wisting sat back with a sceptical expression on his face. What Carsten Meyer was describing was plain theft. The five-man group had been in reality a band of thieves, but Meyer was making them sound like heroes. In a sense they were talking about the perfect crime. Thefts that would never be investigated. Breaking the law in a way that was almost morally justified.

'How much money are we talking about here?' he asked.

'In one place we took out over three hundred thousand kroner from a safe. That's more than five million in today's money. The man we visited ran a cement company in Telemark and was the only person in the area with a cement ship. He had three of them in fact, and had transported all the material for the bunkers along the coast between Oslo and Kristiansand.'

'What did you use the money for?'

'We built training centres abroad. In England and America. In addition, we set up cash reserves so that we had funds available in case of an invasion. None of us made any kind of personal gain.'

'Is there any money left from these cash reserves today?'

Carsten Meyer shook his head.

'I understand what you're driving at. I heard about the money on the news, but we carried out the last action in the summer of 1949. The group was dissolved in 1990. The money was gone long before then. What remained of liquid assets was returned to the Ministry of Defence.'

'Does that apply to your weapons also?'

Carsten Meyer's pipe had gone out while he was talking. Nevertheless, he raised it to his mouth, sucking slowly until his cheeks became hollow.

'Not the personal ones,' he replied, bringing his pipe down to his chest. 'No one asked about those.'

Wisting pulled a printout from his inside pocket with the picture of the pistol that had been found in the depths of the sea. He unfolded and laid it on top of the half-finished crossword puzzle.

The old man put the pipe back on the dish and lifted the sheet of paper. Wisting explained how they had found the weapon.

'Do you think Sverre was shot with it?'

'We don't know, but we're having a problem tracing it.'

'It might be Sverre's own gun.' Carsten Meyer raised his head to look at him. Something unfamiliar had come into his eyes, something glowering and stubborn. 'We were all equipped with weapons like that, but you'll probably never be able to trace them.'

'Why not?'

'It's what they call a lunchbox Colt, made here in Konsberg during the war.' He pointed at the picture. 'It's completely lacking in serial number or any other identification marks. During the war, the employees at the weapons factory smuggled out pistols for use in resistance activities in their lunchboxes.'

Wisting leaned forward.

'Do you have such a weapon?'

Carsten Meyer gripped his pipe, knocking it on the side of

232

the dish before refilling with painstaking movements. He glanced out of the window where the first dark clouds had appeared above the mountains.

'Daniel has taken charge of it,' he replied after a pause. 'He's interested in everything that has to do with the war.'

49

Dark clouds had gathered on the horizon by the time Wisting arrived in town. The air was closer, warm and heavy.

He met two boys and, he presumed, their fathers as he went into the police station. They appeared almost disheartened and excited at the same time, and it was difficult to tell what their complaint was. Perhaps one of them had a bicycle or a mobile phone stolen. Everyday events took place, in a sense, in parallel with the investigation. Other duties did not disappear – they simply piled up.

The other investigators had eaten and left their empty pizza boxes in the conference room. He found a corner slice to chew down.

Torunn Borg passed the open door, popping her head inside when she saw him.

'There's something you need to look at,' she said. 'Come on!'

Wisting followed her along the corridor and into her office. She had laid out grey paper from a roll on the floor, in the way they usually did when they received objects that must not be contaminated prior to being examined in detail by a crime technician.

Four carrier bags and a black plastic bag were lying on the underlay. One of the bags was marked with *FM-kjeden*, a grocery chain that had merged with other stores and disappeared as a trademark.

The contents of one of the bags had been taken out and

lay in a little heap. It was money. Old fifty-kroner bank-notes.

'Where do they come from?'

'From the sea,' Torunn Borg explained. 'Two boys came here with them. They had drifted onto land in a black bin-bag out by Lydhusstranda beach.'

Wisting helped himself to a pair of plastic gloves from a box on the office desk and squatted down to study the find. He was aware of the smell of salt seawater, and many of the banknotes were wrinkled and seemed stiff after they had lain in the water and then dried out again.

Most of the notes were from the 1980s with a picture of Aasmund Olavsson Vinje. He pulled on the gloves and took out a bundle from one of the other bags. These were even older. On the right of the portrait of Bjørnstjerne Bjørnson he found various dates from the 1970s. Several of the notes had been printed as far back as 1966. There were also some notes of a different design and more than fifty years old. There had to be about a million kroner altogether. Money that had become completely worthless.

'Where's Hammer?' Wisting asked, getting up.

'He's still in Oslo. He's got the banknotes from the collector and taken them to *Kripos*. He thought we would get the first reports from the fingerprint section as early as tomorrow afternoon.'

Wisting pulled off the gloves and related the story of his trip to Kongsberg.

'I think we might be getting close to something,' he said, nodding in the direction of the banknotes. 'This is what it's about. Money. They'd become invalid and were dumped in the sea together with the murder weapon and the dead bodies.'

'Could Carsten Meyer have played an active role in this drama?' Torunn Borg wondered. 'The money must have some connection to the five-man group and he's the only survivor.'

235

'Carsten Meyer is an old man with a walking stick,' Wisting said, thinking back to his meeting with him. 'He seems uneasy about something but I think it's more likely that he's afraid he is the next on the list.'

'By the way, we've got the weapon ashore. Mortensen has it in his office. Carsten Meyer is correct. It's an unregistered Colt put together from weapon parts that the employees in the Kongsberg factory smuggled out in their lunchboxes during the war. Apparently there are something like five hundred of them.'

'It's the grandson who has taken over Carsten Meyer's gun,' Wisting explained. 'We need to contact him and find out if he still has it.'

Torunn Borg noted it down as a task that she would take care of.

'The same applies to the other descendants,' Wisting continued, going over to the door. 'All the members of the five-man group were equipped with the same type of weapon. We must locate those pistols. Who still has them?'

There were not many of the investigators left in the police station. Wisting sent the rest home and sat down behind his office desk. The reminder note with the message about phoning the doctor was still lying in the middle of his desk. He took a piece of tape and fastened it in the middle of his computer screen before picking out two of the expensive tablets he had bought in the health-food shop. He swallowed them dry and decided to phone early the next morning. The doctor had his mobile number and would have phoned him if it were anything serious. Moreover, he did not feel quite so exhausted now. He was still tired and out of sorts, but did not feel just as feeble.

The clock above the doorway showed almost nine o'clock, so it was still not too late to visit Suzanne. He would just make one phone call before he finished.

Turning on the computer he searched for the phone

number of Svenn Tollefsen, moving the message from the doctor's surgery to the side of the screen.

Wisting had first met Tollefsen on December 8th 1980. On the same day, John Lennon was shot and killed by a mentally disturbed fan in New York. It was also the day a deranged man had decided to raid the town's branch of *Norges Bank* with a bulldozer.

Svenn Tollefsen had been sitting in the counting house when the whole building began to shake. Wisting had been in the first patrol car to arrive on the scene. By then the bulldozer had become stuck and the driver had given up and run off. Wisting caught up with him a couple of blocks away and an arrest had taken place via the doctor on duty at the closed psychiatric ward. Later, Svenn Tollefsen had stopped counting money and become responsible for security at the bank. It was natural for them to keep in touch.

Svenn Tollefsen commented that it had been a long time since they had contact, before asking what he could do for the police.

'Tell me what you know about fifty-kroner notes,' Wisting requested.

'Well, printed on cotton paper with gravure printing. The watermark consists of a row of portraits, the same as in the main picture. That would be Asbjørnsen, as in Asbjørnsen and Moe of the folktales. The serial number is printed with ultraviolet fluorescence, and there are various microscopic letters in it, among them a hidden N in the rosette on the front. It was upgraded in 2003 with a broad security thread. Almost nobody forges it. There's more to be made from forging the larger notes. To date, over 100 million of them have been printed. The circulation period is becoming steadily shorter. It's not unlikely that they'll soon be replaced by a 50-kroner coin, or simply be done away with.'

Wisting leafed through his notes from the interview with the adviser from the savings bank in Oslo.

'When was it introduced?' he asked.

'The first ones were printed in 1996. Prior to that, we had the *nynorsk* banknote.'

'*Nynorsk?*'

'Yes, with the portrait of Aasmund Olavsson Vinje. He was of course the champion of *nynorsk*, the New Norwegian language, and on that one it was called *Noregs Bank*, instead of *Norges Bank*.'

'And that's not valid any longer?'

'No, it went out of production twelve years ago. The first were printed in 1984. Now it's completely out of circulation. After January last year you weren't able to exchange it either, but it can have a high value to collectors.'

'What about the banknotes that are even older?'

'When Camilla Collett was replaced by Kirsten Flagstad on the hundred-kroner note in the middle nineties, it was decided that old notes would continue to be legal tender for one year after being discontinued, and after that you could exchange them in a bank for a further ten years. In order to clear the situation up, it was also decreed that all old notes could be exchanged in banks up until July 1999.'

'So all old notes had a value up until that time?'

'That's right.' Tollefsen cleared his throat at the other end. 'Is this about the money that the two boys found?'

'Have you heard?'

'It's on the internet. There's speculation about whether it has something to do with the missing men.'

Wisting clicked on to the web pages of *Verdens Gang* newspaper. The discovery of the money was one of the top news items, illustrated by a picture of two boys sitting behind a camping table covered in fifty-kroner notes. He recognised them as the two boys he had bumped into in reception a short time earlier. They had gone to the newspaper before the police. It was probably the only way they could turn the discovery into hard currency.

'Do you think there's a connection?' Tollefsen asked.

'I don't know what to think,' Wisting responded. He had

the information he wanted, and rounded off the conversation with some questions about family and some remarks about the weather.

The sheet of paper in front of him was now filled with dates. He took it with him and let himself into Torunn Borg's office. The money was still piled up on the floor.

He switched on the ceiling light and put on a new pair of gloves to go systematically through the banknotes with the portrait of Aasmund Olavsson Vinje. Some copies of the first edition from 1984 looked in good condition. The bags they had been in must have been tied up well so that water had been kept out. A collector would certainly buy them.

He had jotted down that the old fifty-kroner note had been printed between 1984 and 1996. However, there were no banknotes in the pile that had been printed after 1991. The conclusion was simple: the money must have been kept hidden since that time.

Wisting became thoughtful as he looked out the window. The clouds had come closer and were darker. The sea was churning, and the little boats were heading for shore.

In 1991, Ken Ronny Hauge had shot and killed a policeman with a Colt, or hadn't he? The components of the case were starting to come together, he thought. However, he still could not see in what direction they were pointing. One thing was certain. Something was about to break the surface.

50

'I like that sound,' said Line.

'Mm hmm,' Tommy replied at her side. She could tell by his tone that what he wanted most was to go to sleep.

The rain was drumming steadily and rhythmically on the roof tiles. She stood up and went through to the living room where raindrops were meandering across the windowpane, chased by playful gusts of wind. Down in the street, puddles and little streams gathered and overflowed into one another.

From the living room window she could see the black sea. Flashes of lightning ripped through the night sky out there in the distance, but she didn't hear any thunder. The storm was still a long way off.

She peeped in at Tommy, listening to his heavy breathing. Then she went out to the kitchen and sat at the computer. Ken Ronny Hauge had taken up all her time in the past few days, although she had finished writing up the interview. The possibility that he was innocent had become an obsessive thought. Her deadline was approaching, and she still had three more interviews to do. The first of these was the only woman on the list. Her name was Beate Olsen, who had served fifteen years for killing her uncle. On the evidence of the newspaper reports she emerged as a sly and greedy woman. The actual murder concerned money. Her grandfather owned a company that galvanised metals for use in the shipping industry. Beate was employed in the accounts department, and she had a good understanding of how the business was declining, although the same business had made her grandfather a multi-millionaire. At the time of the murder he was on his deathbed, and there were only two heirs to the fortune: Beate Olsen and her uncle.

The uncle remained a bachelor until he met a woman during a holiday to the Philippines. They planned to marry, but the wedding was postponed when the grandfather's condition worsened and he was admitted to hospital. While he lay on his deathbed, Beate Olsen poisoned her uncle with the aid of potassium cyanide that she had obtained from the galvanising works and mixed into a bowl of sugar. The poison had paralysed his respiratory system and destroyed his lung tissue.

The death had looked like a cardiac arrest, and the case would probably not have been investigated as anything different if internal stocktaking on the same day had not revealed irregularities in the chemical accounts. Several grammes of the deadly powder were missing from the storeroom. A thorough check of the access system showed that Beate Olsen had let herself into the department the previous night. It was a chemist who put two and two together and requested a meeting with the police.

Her stay in prison had turned Beate Olsen into a Christian. She had met Jesus in a cell at Bredtvedt women's prison. Now she was running her own small religious community in Vennesla. Her spell behind bars had enriched her life, and hers was a story that contrasted with the other murderers Line had met.

Her interview subjects had a variety of motives for turning to murder. It was not something she had consciously set up, but it would make more interesting reading. After Beate Olsen she was to interview a gang leader who had served time for a revenge killing in the Pakistani community in Oslo.

The digression brought her back to the police murder. Whether it was Ken Ronny Hauge or someone he was protecting who had committed it, the motive was incomprehensible. There was no relationship between the victim

241

and the culprit. It was an accidental meeting. Two people in the wrong place at the wrong time. Anything else would have been easier to understand.

She left the folder of material about Beate Olsen lie and read the articles about the police murder one more time, picking out some chance snippets here and there. If she continued to let her thoughts revolve around the case there was always the possibility that she would arrive at something that hadn't struck her before.

Finally, she was sitting looking at the interview with the brother that the local newspaper had printed the previous Saturday in connection with the new, large contracts his company had entered.

Rune E. Hauge had started his company with two empty hands seventeen years before, she read. Today he runs a million kroner business.

Another clipping talked about the son who had been newborn when his father started up. Nowadays he worked part-time in the company as well as pursuing his studies, preparing to take over the successful business some day.

Line's thoughts began to wander. She wondered what the E in Rune E. Hauge stood for, and thought that Ken Ronny should really have called himself Ken R. Hauge, which had a somewhat grander appearance.

The storm had come closer while she had sat at the kitchen table, the sound of thunder rumbling in from the sea. Lightning lit up the room in a blue-white flash when she clicked on to the folder with the photographs she had taken out at Ken Ronny Hauge's little farm. In one of them, he was sitting with empty hands on his lap. She liked that picture; it was of the kind that didn't simply provide an illustration, but also told a story. The light was captured in the right way, making his hands appear warm and protective.

She felt she knew Ken Ronny Hauge now, but she knew almost nothing about his brother.

51

The phone rang at 03.40. Wisting sat up in confusion and fumbled for his mobile phone on the mattress.

He answered in a rough voice, listened, said thanks and promised to be there within half an hour.

Suzanne turned over by his side. He'd been dreaming about her and tried to hold on to what it had been about, but the details had already slipped away.

He lay back, closing his eyes for a moment to gather his thoughts. It was pouring rain. The sound echoed through the entire house, and he contemplated simply remaining there. He did not need to go around and look at every single dead body that was washed up by the sea. He could read about it in a report, sit with a coffee and study the photographs that would be lying on his office desk in an hour or two.

A clap of thunder shook the house as he was about to slip back into sleep. Instead, he got up and pulled on the same clothes he had been wearing the night before.

Suzanne sat up, drawing the duvet round her.

'Are you going out?'

He whispered a reply and kissed her on the cheek before he left.

The rain darkened the summer night. He squinted ahead with his forehead at the windscreen. Trees lining the road were swinging and swaying in the wind. Just before he reached his destination, he was overtaken by a police patrol car, the blue light pulsing rhythmically through the driving rain before disappearing beyond a bend.

He had been to Bondebrygga at Nalum a couple of times previously, but had problems orientating himself on all the little side roads that criss-crossed the area where all the summer cottages were situated, taking wrong turns twice before reaching the spot where three police cars were already parked.

Two police officers strode across the long wooden quay that stretched at an angle over the shallow waters of the bay. Farmers and fishermen in the area had used the tidy construction for many hundreds of years, but now it had been turned into a harbour for small boats.

At the far end of the quay, large, hand-held torches swept through the night darkness, streaks of rain drawn across the beams of light. Wisting had an umbrella in the car and considered bringing it out, but threw it aside. A gust of wind snatched the car door when he opened it and almost pitched him out of the car.

The waves were lashing high up on the wooden supports and the quay creaking beneath him. The boats tugged at their moorings like tethered animals. A sudden lightning bolt tore through the sky and illuminated the bay and, in the flash, Wisting saw that several men were gathered at the far end of the quay.

There were five altogether. He wiped the rain from his face as he approached. Four of them he knew from the department for minor crimes. The fifth was a civilian wearing a heavy raincoat and a sou'wester.

'I was going to see to the boat,' Wisting heard the man explain to one of the uniformed officers. 'The kids had been out in it yesterday evening, and they're not all that careful about tying it up.'

Wisting approached the edge of the quay and looked down into the rough waters.

'Where's the corpse?' he asked.

'It was lying right below the bow,' the man with the sou'wester explained, 'but now it's gone.'

'What do you mean gone?'

'Look at the sea,' the man said. 'It must have drifted off while I was waiting for you.'

The policemen cast their lights in the direction the waves were moving.

'What did it look like?' Wisting asked.

The man looked as if he did not understand.

'Was it a man or a woman? Young or old?'

'It's not so easy to say, but I think it was an old man. He must have been in the water for a long time. His face was sort of gone. The skin was hanging in a way and floating in shreds.'

The wind blew in relentless gusts. Wisting gazed into the darkness. He regretted making the journey. A white, crackling flash lit the heavy seas, and the thunder that arrived a second afterwards made the quay shake.

One of the policemen had boarded a boat and was casting his light underneath the quay.

'Over here!' he shouted, directing his beam of light to where a couple of supports were propped on large stones.

Wisting knelt down and leaned over the edge. The points of light were dancing backwards and forwards. He had a glimpse of a human body being tossed about in the waves, the face distorted with empty eye sockets and open wounds.

'Can we get him ashore?'

The policeman in the boat grabbed an oar and tried to hook the corpse towards him, but could not manage. It looked as if the body had snagged on planks of wood that had been placed crosswise to stabilise the framework.

The uniformed policeman put the oar aside and swore. Then he unclipped his equipment belt and passed it to one of his colleagues before jumping into the water. It reached up to his waist, but some of the waves that were rolling towards him were so huge that he had to turn his head to avoid being hit in the face.

He went in underneath the quay, caught hold of one

trouser-leg and dragged the body with him towards the shore.

Two of the other policemen got a tarpaulin ready on the stony beach, a third waded out to help with pulling the corpse ashore.

Wisting took out his torch and shone it down. The face was unrecognisable, with flakes of rotting skin and two pale, violet-coloured starfish clinging to the neck.

He moved the light to the legs. The left foot was missing. Shreds of fatty tissue were suspended where it had been amputated.

'It's one of them,' the man in the sou'wester declared.

Wisting nodded. The dead body was dressed in a tweed jacket and dark flannel trousers, matching the description of Torkel Lauritzen.

It abruptly stopped raining. Wisting glanced automatically at the sky and saw that dawn was breaking.

52

Wisting drove home, had a hot shower, shaved and put on clean clothes. It was half past six when he put on the coffee machine, and thought he would phone to give Audun Vetti an update. Outside, the clouds had broken to let shafts of sunlight through. He drank a cup of coffee before driving to work. The news about the discovery of yet another dead body had spread through the police station. Wisting gathered the investigators for a short briefing just after eight o'clock. They agreed to reconvene at two o'clock for a thorough review of the case.

None of the newspapers had heard about the development before the print deadline, but the news was already out on radio and the internet. Vetti was conducting a telephone interview when Wisting passed his office, using the standard phrases about the deceased not being identified, and that the corpse showed signs of having been in the water for a long time.

Wisting closed his door, sat down at his desk and keyed in the number of Torkel Lauritzen's eldest son.

Oddmund Lauritzen answered immediately. Wisting began by referring to the news reports the other man must have heard.

'On the basis of the clothing, we have reason to believe that it's your father,' he concluded.

The man at the other end of the phone cleared his throat and thanked him for keeping him updated.

'Could you see anything on him?' he asked. 'Was he shot too? Like Sverre Lund?'

'I don't know,' Wisting replied. He could imagine the powerful man with thick, grey hair walking back and forth on the oak parquet in the large villa. 'He's already been driven to the forensics department. I'll receive a report from them in the course of the day. Then I'll call you back.'

Oddmund Lauritzen thanked him again.

'Are you phoning Mathias as well?' he asked, referring to his younger brother. 'Or shall I do it?'

'I'm going to phone him too.'

'Fine.'

'Do you know if your father had any guns?' Wisting enquired.

The man at the other end hesitated before answering.

'He had a pistol, but Mathias has it now.'

'Do you know what type?'

'A Colt, but you won't find it in the weapons register. It was his personal service weapon, but since what he was involved in was secret it was never registered. Mathias took charge of it when Dad moved into the old folks' home. He didn't want to just hand it in. It has a kind of sentimental value for him.'

Wisting ended the conversation by reassuring Oddmund Lauritzen that he would keep him informed, and gave him his mobile number to call if there was anything he was unsure of. Then he sat back thoughtfully. Instead of phoning Torkell Lauritzen's youngest son, he went to Torunn Borg's office and asked her to accompany him.

The cloud cover was denser again when they drove away from the police station. The blue-grey sky warned of more rain.

Mathias Lauritzen was sitting in the same place as the last time Wisting had visited the shabby flat: well ensconced in the chair in front of the television set.

'Which of them is it they're talking about on the news?' he asked, glancing over at his wife. 'Who's been found?'

248

Wisting sat down, explaining why they had reason to believe that the corpse that had been found during the night was his father.

'What about Otto?' he asked, looking across at his wife. 'Is there any news about him?'

'Not in relation to what has happened, but both your father and father-in-law handled a lot of money before they went missing. They deposited almost five million kroner that they withdrew again only a few days later. Do you have any explanation?'

Mathias Lauritzen shook his head as horses do when they want to get rid of annoying insects.

'We've never received a single krone from either of them. I'd no idea they had so much money.'

'We're probably talking about money that's been lying hidden for many years,' Torunn Borg explained.

'Dad didn't talk to me about money,' Kristin Lauritzen said cautiously. 'But I know that he has a lot after selling the house.'

She took a bundle of letters from a drawer.

'Since he disappeared, his mail has come here,' she continued. 'There's just over a million in a high interest account. That's all I know.'

'Why did he do it?' Mathias Lauritzen asked. 'Put in and take out money. What was the point?'

'We think it's about exchanging money,' Wisting replied. 'And that they were sitting with money that was about to go out of circulation, so they had to exchange them for new banknotes.'

'Dad had many secrets,' Kristin Lauritzen said. 'He never spoke about anything to do with the alert force. The money might well have something to do with that though.'

Wisting turned to her husband: 'I understand that you took over your father's service weapon.'

Mathias Lauritzen's shoulders twitched in confusion.

'Was he shot?' he asked.

249

'We're awaiting a provisional post mortem report,' Wisting explained. 'I know that the gun isn't registered, but that's a side issue at the moment. Do you have the weapon?'

'It's in the bedroom,' Mathias Lauritzen nodded. 'I've got it in a box right inside the wardrobe. Kristen, can you get it?'

Kristen Lauritzen remained sitting, saying nothing.

'Kristen?'

'It's not there,' she said abruptly. 'It's not been there for many years.'

'What do you mean?'

'I discovered that when I was looking for your cufflinks when we were going to Trine and Frank's wedding.'

'You didn't say anything?'

The woman with the big hairstyle was silent, biting her bottom lip.

'I thought Trond had taken it.'

'Your son?' Torunn Borg asked.

Mathias Lauritzen's face darkened, as though talking about his son cast a cloud over him.

'He's a drug addict,' he said curtly. 'God knows what he's done with it.'

'Where can we get hold of him?'

Kristen Lauritzen wrung her hands, looking at them anxiously.

'He's in Oslo,' she explained. 'That's all we know.'

Wisting let it lie. He had nothing to gain by blaming them for irresponsibly keeping a weapon.

'What about your father's gun?' he asked instead, directing his gaze at Kristin.

Her voice was hesitant: 'We didn't find anything like that when we cleared the house. He must have got rid of it long ago.'

Mathias Lauritzen agreed: 'He's probably handed it in or something.'

'That would of course have been the right thing to do,' Kristin added, pushing responsibility for the missing gun back to her husband. 'Not leaving it lying in a wardrobe.'

Wisting got up. The purpose of the visit had been to alert the relatives to the discovery of the corpse the night before. In addition, he had some questions. The answers he had received had not been of any help.

Heavy banks of cloud hung in the sky when they left. Torunn Borg drove. The first, heavy raindrops fell on the windscreen.

Wisting had not met Greta Lund before. The old head teacher's widow was completely white-haired with fine wrinkles around her grey eyes that shone white against her brown skin when she raised her eyebrows.

She invited them in for coffee, and they sat round a small table in the living room. Wisting allowed her to talk about the funeral she was planning before coming to the point: 'Did your husband have a gun?'

Greta Lund put down her coffee cup.

'Yes,' she nodded, looking from one to the other. 'He had a pistol. It's many years since it's been out of the cupboard. I don't know what to do with it.'

'Can we see it?'

The old woman got up and went into the house. She came back almost immediately.

The weapon was wrapped in a white cotton rag stained with oil. She placed it on the table and unfolded it. It was identical to the pistol that had been found on the bottom of the sea. A fully loaded cartridge clip lay beside it.

'I'd be grateful if you took it away with you,' Greta Lund requested. 'Then I'll be rid of it.'

Wisting nodded, picking up the weapon. Then he told the old woman in detail about the money her husband had deposited in the bank and withdrawn before he disappeared.

They heard that the married couple had had a tidy and orderly budget, with her taking responsibility for the family accounts.

251

'Do you have any idea where the money came from?' Wisting asked.

He saw that she was searching for an answer. The information about the money unsettled her, as though it was a lover or an illegitimate child that had turned up after her husband's death.

Wisting put the pistol in the glove compartment when they got into the car. They had one more call to make. He wanted to talk to Daniel Meyer about the pistol he had taken from his grandfather in Kongsberg.

Daniel Meyer lived in a small, white house with green decorative mouldings down by the sea. A pennant in Norwegian colours was flying from a flagpole in the yard.

It was raining harder, drifting in torrents from the sea. Wisting turned up his jacket lapels before getting out of the car and ran along the shelter underneath the entrance. He heard the doorbell echo when he rang, but there was no response.

'We should have phoned first,' Torunn Borg said.

Wisting agreed. He rang the bell one more time before going round the side of the house. The garden at the back was bordered with honeysuckle and roses. A rocky crag separated the property from the beach below, but gave little shelter. The wind had swept the tablecloth off the table and knocked over a plastic chair.

He crooked his hands against one of the windows, put his face between them and peeped inside. Daniel Meyer obviously used the living room as a workroom. Reference books and notes lay spread out over the coffee table seemingly without any order or system. Several papers were lying on the floor. A lamp on the wall above the settee was lit, but the room looked abandoned. He knocked on the window without getting any reaction from inside before hurrying back to the car.

53

At two o'clock, Wisting went into the conference room carrying a half-full cup of coffee and found a place for himself at the end of the table.

The provisional post mortem report was on to top of the bundle of documents he brought with him. The corpse was in an advanced stage of decomposition, and the forensic scientists could not specify a definite cause of death. Although the body was decayed it had been concluded that Torkel Lauritzen showed no external signs of violence. The shape of his skull was normal, with no fissures apparent. The arms and legs were not dislocated and had no obvious fractures or injuries in the joints. The same applied to the spine and pelvis. The lungs were described as collapsed, but intact. The lining of the pleural cavity was not torn. The larynx and hyoid bone were uninjured. No foreign matter in the windpipe. No fractures in the thoracic skeleton. The arterial branches showed evidence of significant hardening, but there were no signs of any obvious, abnormal changes in the chest or abdomen.

Wisting was surprised. He had expected the report to describe an injury that could be linked to the use of a gun, but the forensic examination indicated, on the contrary, that advanced cardiovascular disease could have led to death from natural causes.

They had been sitting in their meeting for a quarter of an hour when the message arrived. Wisting had summarised the circumstances surrounding the discovery during the night and the contents of the post mortem report. He

253

was about to give a briefing on the old fifty-kroner bank-notes when the wall telephone rang.

Nils Hammer, who was sitting nearest, took the call, listened, nodded and put down the receiver.

'They've found another one,' he said. 'There's a corpse lying out at Røvika.'

This time Wisting stayed behind. He sent Espen Morten-sen and Nils Hammer to the discovery site, then gathered his papers and went back to his office.

The Røvik fjord was a small arm of the fjord east of Nalumfjorden. As the crow flies, Røvika bay was less than one kilometer away from Bondebrygga quay where the last corpse had been found. The area out by Tvistein lighthouse that they were searching with the mini submarine was situated barely four nautical miles beyond.

Wisting knew the area well. Difficult to reach in a boat, it was enclosed by steep cliffs on land, and islets and skerries that made the seaward approach challenging.

Three years previously, Wisting had worked on a case involving an abandoned sailing boat found anchored at the innermost point of the narrow bay. A trail of blood on board had started a comprehensive investigation that had taken him and Torunn Borg all the way to Spain before they managed to solve a case that involved the smuggling of wanted war criminals.

He lifted the cup to his mouth and sipped the contents. The coffee had gone cold, and he put it back down.

On his computer screen he could follow the progress of the case from the operations log. The person who had reported the dead body was a local landscape photographer who had gone to the mountains around Røvika to take pictures of the choppy sea and the cloud formations out at the mouth of the fjord. The body had been lying twisted on the pebbles in the bay, and he had phoned the police without climbing down the steep mountainside.

The police boat had arrived at 14.23, he saw from the log.

They reported back that it was a female corpse, which had been in the water for quite a while, and that the left foot was missing.

Wisting concentrated on his paperwork while waiting for the log to be updated with new information.

There was one aspect of the case to which he felt he had not devoted enough attention. Incredible though it seemed, they had found four severed left feet. DNA-analysis had confirmed that three of them belonged to Torkel Lauritzen, Sverre Lund and Hanne Richter. Later, the corpses of both Torkel Lauritzen and Sverre Lund had been found, and now probably Hanne Richter also. Otto Saga was still missing, but the fourth foot did not belong to him. It had unknown DNA, and it definitely did not belong to Camilla Thaulow. It had been in the sea for too long.

Wisting looked out the preliminary reports from the time that Otto Saga had been reported missing. He had eaten breakfast at half past eight along with the other residents of the nursing home. Afterwards he was in the habit of sitting down with the newspapers in the common room until lunchtime but, on that day, the newspapers had lain untouched. The staff had let themselves into his flat when he didn't come for his meal. His outdoor clothing was gone, and one of the staff had the caretaker come with him to search the old dockyards and the disused military camp where the old man had worked, and the residential area where he used to live. Three hours later, they alerted the police.

Otto Saga would have been 80 years of age if he had still been living.

In the interviews the police had conducted with the staff at the nursing home he was described as a sociable man who was obliging and had a particular talent for creating a good ambience around him. In the last few days before he disappeared he had withdrawn a little and become anxious. The carers ascribed that to concern about Torkel Lauritzen who had gone missing a few days earlier. The doctor had considered giving him medication, but decided to wait.

Wisting brought out the picture of the severed foot that had been found at Corntin a week earlier. Little grains of sand were sticking to the shoe. The sole had a brown coating of algae. Seaweed and kelp were entangled in the laces. Wax-like shreds and strings of skin were hanging out of the opening.

They still did not know to whom the foot belonged.

It was logged on the screen that the crime technician had arrived at the discovery site. Two minutes later, Espen Mortensen phoned.

'It's Hanne Richter,' he informed Wisting. 'Her left foot is missing. The shoe on the other foot is a white Adidas shoe with three black stripes, exactly the same as the left foot that we found.'

'Can you tell me anything else?'

'She's been shot. There's an entry wound on her forehead.'

Wisting took a deep, slow breath and gazed at the window as he collected his thoughts. Raindrops were running down the glass. Something must have provoked this series of murders; Hanne Richter was the fourth. He could not imagine what had caused the first piece to fall, what lay at the bottom.

'There's not a lot more that I can get done out here,' Mortensen continued. 'I'll take a few photographs and get the body packed up and sent to forensics.'

The phone rang again as soon as he put down the receiver. It was an unknown number, and he hesitated about taking the call. Each time the phone rang, he felt that the case just became more complicated.

The man who was phoning introduced himself as Ragnvald Hagen from the fingerprint department at *Kripos*.

Wisting sat up in his chair, picked up a ballpoint pen and got ready to take notes.

256

'It's about all these banknotes we've received,' the other man explained. He sounded resigned. As though his work duties were routine stuff and bored him.

'Yes?' Wisting said.

'Do you know why they call banknotes circulating assets?'

Wisting did not respond.

'Well,' the man from *Kripos* went on. 'It's because that's just what they do. Circulate. Go from one hand to another. A fingerprint on a banknote usually proves nothing.'

'Have you found any prints?' Wisting wanted to know.

'Of course,' the other man replied. 'We've taken a selective sample, choosing those banknotes that look as though they've been least in circulation.'

'And?'

'There might be something here. We've found the same prints on 43 notes from three different bundles. A whorl patterned thumbprint with fine detail. I don't know how much you understand about prints, but this is quite exceptional. I haven't seen anything like it. It looks as though someone has sat counting the notes before putting them away.'

Wisting swallowed. He felt a sense of eagerness rising, something he had almost forgotten how to feel.

'Do we know who it belongs to?'

'I do at least,' the fingerprint man answered. 'Per Arne Haugen, born on the 23rd February 1952. Lives in Bærum. First registered here in 1982.'

'Porno-Pea?' Wisting asked.

'Some people call him that too.'

Wisting raised his hand to his forehead and rubbed his eyes with his thumb and forefinger. As he had feared, it just became more complicated.

P.A. Haugen, often known as Porno-Pea, was a businessman whose business was pornography. He operated retail sales, magazine publishing and mail order in Norway,

Sweden and Denmark. In the 1970s he distinguished himself as an advocate for pornography in Norway and his sales outlets in Oslo were continually attacked by feminist activists and anti-pornography campaigners. Trade in what at that time was illegal hard pornography led to several police raids and the seizure of a great deal of material. Haugen had served a number of prison sentences for tax avoidance and failure to submit accounts, and for a period was deprived by court judgement of the right to conduct business in Norway. The last Wisting had heard of him was that he had invested some of his wealth in an internet company registered abroad.

'I'll send a provisional report about what we've discovered so far,' the man from the fingerprint department concluded.

Wisting thanked him for the information and put the receiver down carefully before lifting it again to phone Nils Hammer.

54

Line sat at the kitchen table in Tommy's flat, listening to the rain rushing through the gutters. Her eyes were fixed on the computer screen, as they had been through the whole night.

Everything had seemed more logical when she eventually went to bed, than now as she went through her notes once more. All the same, she was still sure that it could not have been Ken Ronny Hauge who had murdered the policeman.

Tommy had been grumpy when she got up, the first time she had seen him like that. When she had gone to bed, in the early hours of the morning, she had been looking forward to telling him what she had discovered. Now she couldn't bring herself to do it. They had quarrelled, and although she actually had to admit that he was right, it was not necessary for her to sit up working half the night and then sleep half the day, she had objected and argued that he had to understand that this was her work. He had slammed the door behind him as he went out. She had watched from the window while he crossed the square in the pouring rain without an umbrella or raincoat. Then she had sat at the computer again.

The company *StoneTech AS* had been established on the first of September 1991 and entered in the companies register a month later. Rune Eiolf Hauge was listed as managing director. According to a state-of-the-art home-page the company supplied, among other things, automated cutting and grinding machinery for the stone industry, and had patented a laser-based cutting technology. The figures in the accounts were substantial, and Hauge himself was good for almost thirty million.

She had discovered that Rune E. Hauge was a tough businessman. Most of her search results appeared in finance and industry magazines. They portrayed him as an enterprising, intelligent man and a forward-looking and determined business owner. However, behind the headlines about success, there were some other stories.

She found readers' comments in which employees talked about irregular payment of wages, a lack of consultation, slow wage developments and an absence of important social benefits. He was accused of using unorganised labour and was repeatedly castigated by the trades unions and the labour inspectorate. He emerged increasingly as a cynical employer without respect for the normal rules of working life.

His private life had also been turbulent. He married for the first time in June 1994. She had found a wedding photograph in a photo archive, in which the bridal couple was pictured with their two-year-old son. The marriage lasted four years. Hauge married again two years later, this time to a woman who had been employed in his company since it started. They had two children together. His address history showed that they had lived apart for two different periods, but that they were living together now in a modern, residential area on the east side of the Larvik fjord.

Line got up and walked up and down the kitchen floor a couple of times. The theory she had formulated was built on speculation and supposition. *StoneTech* had been established at the same time as the police murder at Eikeren. At the same time, Rune E. Hauge was about to start a family. He had been living with the girl who would become his first wife three years later, and who must have been pregnant when they moved in together.

After reading all the material she could find about Rune E. Hauge, she was left with an unfavourable impression – a self-centred, ambitious, arrogant and power-hungry man. They were qualities that contrasted greatly with those of the brother who had been found guilty of murder.

After that September night in 1991, it was Rune E. Hauge who had most to lose from being arrested. He was at the beginning of what would turn out to be a successful fairytale of a business, while his brother was out of work.

She could guess how it all fitted together. Both brothers had been in the car. Which of them had fired the shots, she could not tell, but she had difficulty believing that it had been Ken Ronny. Nevertheless, they had been together on it. Ken Ronny was the one who was brought in. Since there had been no reason to take his brother down with him he sacrificed himself. His silence under questioning and at the trial afterwards had placed a protective veil over his brother, Rune E. Hauge.

Her reasoning seemed sound, but building a case on speculation was like pouring sand into your petrol tank. You could be sure it would break down. She had to find confirmation. She would have to meet Ken Ronny Hauge again. Perhaps she could also find out *why* the young policeman had been killed.

There was a knock at the front door, and she went through to see who it was. Tommy was standing there, dripping wet, with a pizza carton in his hands. Tendrils of black hair were hanging over his forehead.

'I rented a film,' he smiled.

Line smiled back. He passed the box to her and fished a DVD out of his inside pocket. It was a romantic comedy of the type he knew she liked. She managed to give him a kiss on the cheek before he disappeared into the bathroom. She put the pizza down in front of the TV set and went into the kitchen, reluctantly closing the lid on her laptop.

55

Nils Hammer was driving. Wisting leaned his head against the side window and studied the raindrops as they were forced against the glass as they travelled, running into long streams.

It felt good to get away from the station for a while. It gave a breather and the opportunity for reflection without continual interruptions. His thoughts had been circling obsessively round the five-man group and the reverberations their actions in the past might have caused in the present. Without having shared his thoughts with anyone, he had become convinced that the police murder in 1991 must also have been some kind of ripple effect from past events. Possibly he was affected by a sort of mental tunnel vision and allowing his intuition to rule too much.

The windscreen wipers swept from side to side in rhythmic movements as he concentrated on the major developments. His role as the leader of the investigation was to keep an overview.

They took an hour and twenty minutes to reach Høvik. P.A. Haugen lived in an old Swiss style villa that was situated at a vantage point some distance along a *cul de sac*, with an unimpeded view over Drøbak Sound.

The old businessman was exactly as Wisting had imagined him. Apart from his hair now being completely white, he was just the same as in photographs in newspapers and magazines: medium build, suntanned, the top three buttons of his shirt unfastened. Around his neck hung two heavy gold chains that matched a solid gold wristwatch.

'Usually I don't talk to the police without my lawyer present,' Haugen explained as he ushered them into the large house. High ceilings and double doors between the various rooms made it bright and airy.

'But I became curious about what little you said on the phone,' he continued. 'Maybe that was your intention?'

'We are at least hoping that you'll be able to help us,' Wisting replied.

P.A. Haugen threw open the doors leading to an office with red, plump leather furniture and a magnificent oak writing desk. The flooring was made of dark wood, and heavy, burgundy coloured curtains hung at the windows.

'Can I offer you anything?' he asked, opening the top of a patinated globe that camouflaged a drinks cabinet. 'Mineral water, *Farris*, or something?'

They both accepted with thanks, and then sat down in the deep chairs facing the massive desk.

'When you phoned, at first I didn't understand at all,' Haugen elaborated, handing each of them a glass. 'But it seems you have found my fingerprints on old banknotes that were confiscated in connection with a murder inquiry?'

Wisting nodded, watching the man as he walked back to the globe and poured some whisky into the bottom of his own glass.

'I've been following the case,' Haugen went on, sitting down. 'The newspapers are full of it, of course. Only grotesque murders can compare with sex when it comes to circulation figures.'

He laughed at his own witticism and Wisting put on a smile for the sake of politeness. P.A. Haugen appeared to be accommodating, and Wisting had no intention of destroying that illusion. In reality, he represented something that Wisting despised.

P.A. Haugen drank deeply from his glass.

'It sounds completely unbelievable, but I think I can provide you with some answers.'

Wisting remained silent, waiting for the man to continue.

'That said, I don't think that what I have to tell you will help in your murder investigation,' he added.

'What do you know about the matter?'

The big man squinted at them.

'Before I say anything at all, we need to talk about the conditions,' he said.

'What kind of conditions?'

'I need to have a guarantee of no prosecution before I can tell you anything.'

'What do you mean?'

P.A. Haugen leaned his head on the back of the chair.

'This is to do with money,' he said. 'If I tell you what I know, I must have assurances that you can't use what I have said against me.'

Wisting shook his head.

'I can't give such a promise, but in general terms I can say that most of the illegal ways by which you may have acquired the money will now be covered by the statute of limitations. It seems the money has been out of circulation for almost two decades.'

The man took another drink from his glass before dropping his hand and resting it on his stomach.

'I hear what you say. I just don't want my name mixed up in anything. The newspapers are trying to outdo one another in this business, and I've no desire to become a part of it.'

'This is not something that we've any intention of serving to the press,' Wisting assured him, 'but you know just as well as we do that the press will write whatever they want to.'

'Okay,' P.A. Haugen said abruptly, slamming his glass down on the desk. 'May as fuckin' well. This has been a mystery to me for nearly twenty years. I've got over the financial loss and would have been willing to pay it twice over to get to know who was behind it.'

He got up, went over to the wall unit and brought out a thick, hardback ring binder.

The rain was pelting against the large windows, sounding like restless fingers drumming on a tabletop. The enormous fruit trees outside were swaying in the wind. The branches were whipping against each other, the leaves turning inside out in the gusts.

P.A. Haugen laid the binder on the desk and leafed through to one of the last pages. Wisting got up and approached to have a look.

It was a yellowed newspaper cutting from *Verdens Gang*. The date in the right-hand corner stated that it was from Thursday 24th September 1991. The headlines were in two layers:

MILLION KRONER PROCEEDS FROM BANK SAFETY DEPOSIT BOX HAUL

There was something timely about the printed words. It was almost as though he felt it physically. A pressure disappeared from behind his forehead. These were the pieces they needed to bring forth the whole picture.

During the weekend and the night before Monday 23rd September 1991, thieves had broken in to the premises of *Den Norske Bank* at Bryn in Oslo through scaffolding and a window at the back. They had drilled through the floor and down to the vault in the basement, lowered themselves down a hole 40 centimetres wide and cracked open 658 safety deposit boxes. No one was sure how much money they had got away with. The newspapers speculated that it might have been as much as ten million kroner.

'I had just over two million in that vault,' P.A. Haugen explained. 'The only thing I can imagine is that you've come across the proceeds of that robbery with my fingerprints on them.'

The big man went round the desk and sat down again, resting his forearms on the tabletop.

'The case was never cleared up,' he went on. 'It was professionally carried out with military precision. In and out, without leaving a trace.'

Wisting leafed through the pages and found a couple of clippings in which the case was followed through subsequent days. A few witnesses had seen two men wearing boiler suits on the scaffolding, but had not reacted to it. All traces of the culprits stopped at the hole in the ceiling. The drill that had been used had been stolen from a building site in the vicinity. When the perpetrators had been satisfied with their haul, they had pulled down a fire hose and turned on the tap. By the time the break-in was discovered on the Monday morning the bank was full of water that had run down the drilled hole and washed away all traces.

In one of the articles, an Assistant Chief of Police had used the same words that P.A. Haugen had quoted to illustrate how difficult the task of investigating was. At the same time, there was little sympathy available for the many people who had found their safety deposit boxes emptied. One article described how the culprits had left family heirlooms and other valuable items of sentimental value to their owners untouched, while huge sums of money that had been kept hidden from the tax authorities had been taken. Speculation about who was behind the crime was directed towards established, criminal circles in the capital city. Simultaneously, journalists portrayed the unknown culprits in a way that was reminiscent of the glorification in history of the old master robbers Ole Høiland and Gjest Baardsen.

Wisting closed the binder and sat down. He was in agreement with P.A. Haugen. The money that the old men had exchanged came from the safety deposit box haul.

The net of connections was becoming entangled. The safety deposit box robbery had taken place the same night that Ken Ronny Hauge shot and killed a policeman at

Eikeren. That was his motive for choosing to shoot his way out and later keep silent about everything that had to do with the case. Ken Ronny Hauge was one of the men behind the bank raid. The E18 was the quickest route out of the capital, but the main road through the countryside was a natural choice to make if you wanted to avoid the busiest traffic. Chance events caused it to go wrong, and the young policeman was murdered so that another crime was kept hidden.

It was such a logical chain of events that he wondered why none of the investigators in the two cases had seen the potential connection before. They had probably been reported side by side in the newspapers, but without the information Wisting now possessed there had been no apparent correlation. Without something to link them, there was very little to suggest that these two serious crimes might be connected. They took place miles from each other. The investigators in the bank robbery were looking for a professional gang, and the police murder appeared to be an isolated action by a young, confused man who had never been arrested previously.

P.A. Haugen interrupted Wisting's train of thought: 'Who was it?' he asked. 'Who was it who emptied the safety deposit boxes?'

'I don't know yet,' Wisting replied, getting up from his seat. 'But I think we're close to finding the answer.'

'When can I have it back?'

'Do you mean the money?'

The other man nodded.

'I don't think you should count on getting it back.'

'What do you mean? It's my money, isn't it, with my fingerprints on it.'

'You were the one who didn't want your name mixed up in anything,' Hammer reminded him.

'But that's something different.' P.A. Hauge frowned. 'What are you planning to do with it? Take it yourselves?'

267

Wisting gazed at the big man for a long time in silence before quietly explaining that they were only talking about a small sum of money that they had, as a matter of fact, come across.

'We'll have to come back to a possible distribution when the case is solved,' he concluded, mainly so that the other man would drop the subject.

P.A. Haugen gestured with his hand as though to signify that the money meant nothing to him.

'Did you find anything other than money?' he asked.

'What do you mean?'

The man at the desk exposed a gold tooth at the back of his mouth when he grinned.

'I had some pictures lying in that safety deposit box too,' he laughingly responded. 'Of a private nature, if you understand what I mean.'

'I understand,' Wisting replied, shaking his head. 'We haven't come across anything like that.'

P.A. Haugen got up and walked round the desk to accompany them out.

'I'm almost more interested in getting the pictures back than the money,' he said, walking ahead of them to the doorway with rolling movements.

'You'll be hearing from us,' Wisting rounded off the discussion, thanking him for his assistance without offering a handshake.

Outside, the wind had become stronger, whipping the rain against his face. Wisting lowered his head between his shoulders, pulling his jacket tightly round him. For the first time in this investigation, he felt that he could see the outlines of a solution.

56

Neither of them spoke for the first two minutes back in the car as curtains of rain drummed on the roof and blurred the windscreen.

'The police murder,' Nils Hammer said abruptly, 'took place at the same time as the bank safety deposit box robbery.'

Wisting nodded and repeated the theory he had reasoned out during the meeting with P.A. Haugen.

'I've read up on the old case,' he rounded off, explaining how he had requisitioned the documents dealing with the police murder. 'I think that Ken Ronny Hauge is covering up more than that other crime.'

'That one or those ones that he's taken part in,' Hammer added.

Wisting nodded again, becoming thoughtful. In its character and execution, the bank raid resembled the crimes that the five-man group had carried out during the post-war period, punishable offences that *might* be morally defensible. The culprits had helped themselves to money that was probably the proceeds of other punishable activity, leaving behind valuable jewellery and personal possessions.

'Military precision,' Hammer remarked, as though reading Wisting's thoughts. 'That's what it said in the newspaper cuttings. The raid was carried out with military precision. How old were Torkel Lauritzen and the others in 1991?'

'About 60 years old,' Wisting answered. 'Lauritzen was still working as the personnel manager at *Treschow-Fritzøe*.'

'And Otto Saga was still head of the Air Force officer training school in Stavern,' Hammer went on, gripping the steering wheel more tightly. 'It wasn't closed down until 2002. And Sverre Lund was still the head teacher at Stavern school. They were all still working.'

Wisting bit his bottom lip. The chaos of possibilities that had opened up made him feel faint. He suddenly felt unbearably tired and exhausted, and realised that he had forgotten to phone the doctor that day as well.

'How much did it say that the haul from the safety deposit box robbery was?' Hammer continued. 'Up to ten million? That fits well with the money that the old men exchanged. It's their share of the haul!'

'The five-man group was shut down in 1990,' Wisting reminded him, rubbing his eyes. 'And although they were in good physical condition, I can't quite see it. Grandfathers working together, with one of their grandchildren, on what would be described as the coup of the times.'

They remained sitting for a while, throwing theories back and forth, without any result other than the conviction that they were close to something significant. They still didn't quite manage to grasp what was in the knowledge they possessed.

Wisting leaned his head against the window again. The sound of the wheels on the wet asphalt made him sleepy, but the feeling that there were small, significant details still overlooked prevented him from dropping off.

The police station was empty when they arrived. It was almost nine o'clock and most of the investigators had done more work than he could impose on them. He himself had been awake since Torkel Lauritzen's body had been found beneath Bondebrygga quay at Nalum eighteen hours before.

He made a quick visit to his office to look through his messages, without finding anything of interest, before going home.

It had stopped raining. The water was lying in puddles on the uneven surface of the yard in front of his house in Herman Wildenveysgate. Dry branches had broken off the tall birch tree beside the driveway and were strewn across the stone slabs.

Heavy clouds darkened the summer evening. He let himself in and switched on the light and the radio to break the silence. Then he suddenly felt hungry. There were still a few cartons of yogurt in the refrigerator. He ate one at the kitchen worktop, then helped himself to another and brought it with him into the living room. The bundle of documents dealing with the police murder was lying on the coffee table. Without quite knowing what he was looking for, he sat down and began to leaf through them.

It didn't take him long to find it.

In the hunt for possible accomplices, the social circle round Ken Ronny Hauge had been interviewed and had to account for their movements on the night the murder took place. The person who was regarded as having the best alibi was Daniel Meyer. Wisting remembered reading that before. Daniel Meyer was a weekly commuter and lived in workers' accommodation in Oslo. A colleague picked him up from his home at 05.30 on the morning of Monday 23rd September, and they had driven together to the city.

The interesting thing was where in Oslo Daniel Meyer was living and working. At interview it had been logged that he worked for a contractor who was building a large office block on the site of the old match factory at Helsfyr. Wisting could envisage the red brick buildings in the east end where underpaid factory workers had laboured under life-threatening conditions. At the beginning of the 90s, that had been Daniel Meyer's place of work. Almost wall to wall with the bank that had been the scene of one of the most spectacular robberies of the time. Through long working days Daniel Meyer had been able to study how customers had come and gone, what the work routines were, and how the bank was constructed.

Wisting swallowed as something fell into place, a sense of how the police murder and the safety deposit box raid were connected.

He turned the pages to find Daniel Meyer's colleague who had given him a lift. He confirmed the alibi but had nothing to mention, apart from Daniel Meyer being, as usual, very tired. He dozed in the car all the way to the capital city.

The distance from the scene of the murder at Eikeren to his home in Stavern was not more than a hundred kilometers. Even though the roads then were worse than now, it was possible to drive it in an hour and a quarter. The policeman had been killed between 04.00 and 04.15. It would have been possible for Daniel Meyer to get back to Stavern in time to be picked up by his work colleague. It could have been part of an already planned alibi for the bank raid.

Wisting hugged the papers he was holding to his chest and laid his head back in the chair.

They were getting there, was the last thought he managed before he fell asleep.

57

It was still raining when Wisting awoke. At some time during the night he had moved from the chair in which he had fallen asleep to the settee.

The roof of his mouth and his lips were dry after sleeping with his mouth open. He licked his lips, grunted and sat up. The clock showed that he should have been at the office half an hour earlier. He had slept for almost ten hours, but did not feel rested.

He thought about lying down again, but remained seated, trying to collect the thoughts he had fallen asleep with. They seemed even more vague than on the previous evening, but nevertheless he managed to assemble them so that they emerged in a logical way. It was Ken Ronny Hauge and Daniel Meyer who had committed the bank robbery almost twenty years previously. Probably Daniel Meyer had planned it, inspired by his grandfather's tales of heroic exploits during the post-war period. The opportunity must have presented itself as he became familiar with the bank's routines and saw how he could enter from his work on the scaffolding at the building site.

However, although Wisting now had an understanding of the factual circumstances surrounding the police murder, he had difficulty comprehending its direct connection to the case he was now investigating.

His starting point had to be that the money the three old men had exchanged was part of the proceeds of the robbery. It had lain hidden somewhere or other until the passage of time meant that it had to be exchanged if the entire booty

273

was not to be lost. The fifty-kroner notes had already become too old and were simply dumped in the sea, together with the murder weapon. What he did not understand was why the old men had to pay with their lives. And what parts were played by the mentally ill woman Hanna Richter and the carer Camilla Thaulow? As though these questions were not enough there was also the fact that the feet of the murder victims had been chopped off. What could the meaning of that be?

He sighed heavily before gathering up the papers from the police murder into a bundle and going through to the kitchen. He took the last yogurt carton from the fridge and decided to phone Line in the course of the day to see how she was getting on. He went through to the bathroom, undressed and had a shower. The water heated up quickly. He closed his eyes and leaned back into the jets of water. They still didn't have anything tangible, he decided. They still needed to find proof.

After his shower he made a plan for his working day, put on clean clothes and left in his car. Instead of driving directly to the police station, he swung off the road at Agnes and drove down to Daniel Meyer's house by the sea.

The pretext for talking to him was the same as the last time he had driven down the gravel path. He wanted to ask about the pistol that his grandfather had entrusted to him. It would be the start of a conversation that might move the investigation forward.

There were no other cars in the yard in front of the house. Perhaps Daniel Meyer had put his own car into the garage, or else he was not at home again.

Wisting parked, got out and slammed the car door behind him. He scrutinised the windows as he walked to the door, but there was nothing to indicate that anyone had heard him arrive.

The pennant on the flagpole was flapping in the wind. A seagull took off from a rocky outcrop and struggled upwards with its wings against the wind. The doorbell did not produce any response.

Wisting went round the house and peeped in through the verandah window. On the inside, everything seemed untouched since his last visit. Books and notes lay across the coffee table in the same way. The single wall light shone on the wall behind the settee. That meant that Daniel Meyer had not been home for twenty-four hours.

Cold rain was driving obliquely in from the iron-grey sky. Wisting pushed his hands deep into his trouser pockets, strode across the small patch of lawn behind the house and up onto the sloping rock that divided the property from the sea. The waves below him churned up murky sand and gravel on the beach. He stood watching the waters before straightening up against the wind and taking out his phone. He called the operator and asked to be connected to Daniel Meyer's mobile phone. He went back to the front of the house while the phone was ringing and tried the door handle. Locked. The phone rang out, and no one answered. He turned and went up to the post box that was situated on the driveway. He picked up two newspapers and glanced at them – today's and yesterday's editions, and the local. The case he was working on dominated the headlines. The day before, the money trail was the most important news, while today the headlines read *Two new corpses discovered*. Those were the body at Bondebrygga quay the night before and the other that had been found at Røvika. The photograph was credited to the landscape photographer who had reported the discovery.

The newspapers were getting wet in the rain, and he replaced them in the post box. Then he went down to the rear of the house again and up onto the verandah. He tried the door. It was locked too, but he pulled on it a couple of times and felt how ramshackle it actually was.

It was an old-fashioned lift and push door that was locked at the frame with a simple hook-type latch. Weather and wind had caused movement in the woodwork, and an attempt had been made to fill the gap between the door and the frame with a rubber strip.

Wisting looked about and caught sight of a barbecue utensil hanging on a hook beside the gas barbecue. He took the fish slice, pressed it under the door and lifted it up. It was easier than he had thought. With a little jerk he jacked the hooked latch up and out of its keeper, and then the door was open.

'Hello?' he shouted into the house as he took his first step inside.

He received no answer.

'Hello,' he repeated, calling out that he was from the police before going from room to room, just to confirm that they were empty.

He stood facing the coffee table that Daniel Meyer used as a home office. In the main, there were copies from various reference works and printouts of old newspaper articles that had been stored on microfilm. Working notes looked as though they were connected to his book project. It appeared, however, that the work had been pushed aside. Several articles about the case he was investigating were lying in the middle of the table. On top were printouts of internet reports about the money trail and how the missing men from the five-man group had exchanged large sums of cash. Wisting leafed through the collection of articles and also found an account of the old fifty-kroner notes that the boys at Lydhusstranda beach had found. Right at the bottom were much older newspaper cuttings on which the paper was yellowed and the date 1st July 1999 was noted in ballpoint pen.

Washhouse burned to the ground was the headline. The photograph that illustrated the piece had been given a larger space than the actual text. It showed the black, burned out shell and a chimneystack that were left after the intense blaze, and a couple of firemen coiling up hoses. Wisting skimmed through the text. It had to do with an abandoned, small farmstead out at Brunlanes. He had to look back and forth between the description of the place and the picture before he understood that it concerned the place where Ken Ronny Hauge had gone to live after being released from prison. Now he recognised the ruins from the fire in the picture as well. Parts of the chimney were still there by the sea.

Wisting put the cutting back into place with the others. He did not know what it might mean, but Daniel Meyer must obviously have seen it in connection with the new clippings.

He looked around and discovered that he had left wet footprints on the floor. He didn't quite know what he had expected to find, but for one moment imagined that Daniel Meyer was lying dead in one of the rooms.

He thought about whether he should look for the pistol since he was in the house, but decided instead to leave. He had no legal grounds for going in. The man who lived here might be suspected of having participated in the murder of a policeman almost twenty years previously, but the case had not yet expired under the statute of limitations. He had no right to ransack his house.

He went out the way he had entered. The sliding door was more difficult to lock than to work open, but he managed. Wet prints on the parquet were all that gave away the fact that someone had been inside, and they would soon dry up and disappear.

58

The corridor in the investigations department was strangely empty. Wisting went down the corridor with its open doors and vacant offices. Computers had been left without anyone having logged out, and at several of the desks there were half-empty coffee cups, as though the investigators had abandoned their posts in a hurry. Not even the girls in the criminal proceedings office were sitting in their usual places.

Further down the corridor he heard excited voices coming from Espen Mortensen's crime technician room.

Silence descended when Wisting entered. Everyone turned to look at him, before turning their eyes again to the computer screen that was broadcasting pictures from the bottom of the sea outside Tvistein lighthouse.

A woman was standing on one leg, her arms to the side and her head inclined backwards as she moved her body slowly and rhythmically. The picture on the screen reminded Wisting of a ballet performance.

The woman was Camilla Thalow. Her body rocked backwards and forwards in the light from the powerful lamps of the mini submarine. She was dressed as described in the police bulletin that had gone out a week before: long dark trousers, a white blouse that was swaying in the water, and a pair of white training shoes.

Round the ankle of one leg there was fastened a steel wire that stretched down to the grey sea floor. At the other end, it was tied to something that resembled the axle of a car that functioned as a weight.

The mini submarine manouevred in a circle round the dead woman. Little fishes were frightened and rushed off, but came back again right away to nibble small pieces of flesh from her face and wherever the skin was bare.

The camera zoomed to the wire around the one leg, and Wisting could see how it chafed and cut into the skin.

He realised that this was how the other bodies had been placed at the bottom of the sea, but the underwater currents had pulled and torn at them, and in time the foot had been separated from the rest of the body.

The severed feet were not part of a lethal plan, but the result of something that had gone wrong for the murderer.

The explanation appeared so simple that he had to wonder why he had not seen this solution earlier.

The office staff and those who were not participants in the investigation left the room. Wisting stepped closer to the screen. The aspect that had been most bewildering and puzzling in the case was now explained. There was a logical explanation for why and how a total of four severed feet had washed ashore. That part of the mystery was solved. It was no longer something he needed to brood over.

'Congratulations,' Hammer said, pushing a portion of snuff under his lip. 'It's the needle in the famous haystack. I really didn't believe we were going to find anything.'

'We did find the pistol,' Torunn Borg protested.

Hammer shrugged his shoulders.

'I don't know if two needles are easier to find than one.'

'The leader of the search says that they have seen a lot of other scrap iron too,' Mortensen explained. 'Chains, wire and other objects that are lying on the bottom and could be used for the same purpose.'

'Could it give us anything?' Wisting asked, pointing at the wheel axle on the computer screen.

'Perhaps,' Mortensen replied. 'We can certainly find out what type of car and what model we are talking about, but more than that I don't think we should hope for.'

One of the ladies from the criminal proceedings office was back.

'There's a psychiatrist phoning and asking for you,' she said. 'He called yesterday as well. Can you take the call, or shall I ask him to phone back?'

'A psychiatrist?'

'I think his name is Terkelsen. He's phoning from Furubakken.'

Wisting recogised the name. It was Hanne Richter's psychiatrist.

'It's to do with the case,' the office lady added with a nod at the screen.

'I'll take it in my office,' Wisting answered, walking quickly back.

He sat down at the desk, feeling out of sorts. His head ached and his muscles and joints were sore. He noticed how his body was rallying. He was sweating and freezing at the same time. It felt like the start of a cold, but he was afraid that it might be something more, that the listlessness he had felt these last weeks might take a turn for the worse. He lifted the telephone, closed his eyes and announced himself.

The man at the other end began by referring to Wisting's visit to his surgery at the psychiatric clinic five days previously. His speech was long-winded, slow and with a mournful tone.

'One hears all the time that one shouldn't hesitate to make contact with the police, although you yourself may not think that the information you have is particularly relevant.'

'That's right.'

'That the police may nevertheless be able to use the information, and that, in conjunction with other information, it may be valuable.'

Wisting leaned back in his chair, remaining silent while the psychiatrist came to the point.

'Well,' the other man continued. 'I have of course been

280

following the case in the newspapers and on the television. It can't be avoided, and recently there has been a great deal of discussion of these banknotes. I don't know if it has anything to do with the case, but there was one thing that emerged from my discussions with Hanne Richter that might be of interest.'

'What was that?'

'I had put it down to paranoia at the time, but in light of everything that has come out since we spoke last, I'm no longer so sure. It doesn't need to have been a delusion.'

'What did she tell you?'

'She talked about there being money inside the walls of her house.'

'Money inside the walls?'

'In the walls of the living room.'

Wisting's grip tightened on the receiver. He saw with his mind's eye how the wooden lining along the living room wall in Hanne Richter's house was broken up and spread all over the floor.'

'Can you elaborate?' he invited.

'Not really,' the other man responded. 'I noted it in a sentence during my last conversation with her.'

'How had she found it?' Wisting enquired. 'What had she done with it?'

'As I said, I assumed it to be a sign of worsening psychosis, and didn't attach further importance to it. As I remember the discussion, she had a notion that the money was placed at her house by the same mafia organisation that abducted her and put a radio transmitter in her body. It was a new aspect of the conspiracy against her.'

Wisting asked a few more questions, but eventually had to give up. When he ended the call, he nevertheless felt that what she had said about the money was not a part of the madness that ravaged her. Seen in connection with everything that Wisting now knew, it seemed sensible. The money that Hanne Richter had talked about must be the proceeds of the bank robbery. It had lain hidden behind the wooden panelling in the house that actually belonged to Christian Hauge. That was where Ken Ronny Hauge had been arrested on Monday 23rd September 1991. What was it he had read in the old investigation documents? That Ken Ronny Hauge had no permanent employment, but was helping his grandfather to renovate the house?

The investigators who arrested him had looked for the murder weapon, but never found it. Obviously, it had lain hidden behind the wall, along with the money, until someone took it out again last autumn and started off a deadly series of events.

He felt they were getting closer. During the first week, the questions had simply been swarming, making the case more complicated every day that went by. Now the answers were coming.

He got up abruptly and gathered the other investigators for a quick meeting. He shared his thoughts and theories with the others. Halfway through the presentation they started to nod their heads, but they continued listening without interrupting.

'Ken Ronny Hauge,' Torunn Borg said aloud, almost to herself. 'Of all the names that have been mentioned and the people who've been referred to in this case, he has to be the one who's most capable of murdering five people.' She got up and approached the little worktop to fill a glass of water. 'All the same, it's not enough. We only have circumstantial evidence. We have nothing to prove that he has killed any of them. We have nothing to link him to any of the murder victims.'

'The three old men were friends of his grandfather.'

'Yes, but we need more than that to make an arrest. We need to prove that, in some way or another, there was contact between them a short time before they disappeared.'

'The money is a connection,' Espen Mortensen pointed out. 'If it's right that the money has been hidden behind the living room wall at Hanne Richter's house we should be able to find Ken Ronny Hauge's fingerprints there.'

Torunn Borg shook her head and walked over to the window.

'I don't rightly know how we can build that up into evidence,' she said, drinking from her glass. 'The only thing we have is third-hand information from a crazy woman's psychiatrist. In addition, it was probably Ken Ronny Hauge who built the wall. His fingerprints would be no more than another piece of circumstantial evidence. If we had actually found his fingerprints on any of the old banknotes it would have been a different matter.'

'Okay,' Wisting said. 'What we need is a definite connection between Ken Ronny Hauge and one or more of the victims. How can we find that?'

'Perhaps the answer will come from there,' Torunn Borg said, pointing outside with her glass of water to the police station entrance.

The others looked at her but, when she didn't explain further, they got up and went over to the window. A bent old man was being helped out of a taxi. His hair was thick and grey and he was wearing a grey overcoat with a belted waist. He supported himself with a stick as he walked to the entrance.

'Who is it?' Wisting enquired.

'Advocate Storeggen,' Torunn Borg explained. 'He has Parkinson's disease and lives out at the nursing home. When I went round conducting interviews with the residents he had as little to contribute as the others, but he also said that he had client information that he would have to consider whether he could divulge.'

Wisting's eyes followed the man. Despite his gait being affected by his illness, he appeared purposeful and determined.

59

Wisting received the retired lawyer down in the reception area and went up in the lift with him to his office. The man slackened his belt when he sat down in the visitor's chair, but kept his overcoat on. His fingers trembled, fumbling with the buttons. His hands were wrinkled and covered in liver spots, with blue-black veins beneath the skin. His breathing was laboured.

Wisting stood looking at him while he settled in the chair. Underneath his coat, he was wearing a dark suit with white shirt and tie. He was newly shaven, but the bloated skin of his face had made the task difficult. He had probably had help from one of the carers, but nevertheless he had several little nicks on his chin and throat.

The lawyer must have been approaching ninety. He had been an independent and self-reliant person all his life, but old age had most likely made him dependent on help for the most everyday things.

'Coffee?' Wisting offered.

'Yes, please,' the old man nodded. 'I'd like that.'

Wisting had to go through to the conference room to find a couple of clean cups and a pot that was not empty. When he returned, he noticed how the slightly nauseating smell of an old person had filled the room.

'One of your staff was out at the nursing home on Sunday,' Storeggen began as Wisting poured. 'She asked about things that had to do with Otto Saga and Torkel Lauritzen. And about Christian Hauge.'

Wisting filled his own cup and sat down.

'I don't know if it means anything to you,' the lawyer continued, 'but you can best decide that for yourself.'

'What do you know?' Wisting enquired.

The man at the other side of the table cleared his throat.

'Christian Hauge came to me a year ago, wanting help to write a will, or at least discuss the possibilities for one.'

'Who was to benefit?'

'It was of course the grandchildren, Rune Eiolf and Ken Ronny. I assume you know the story. Christian Hauge's daughter drowned herself because of her despair and shame after Ken Ronny murdered a policeman at Eikeren. But there was also another heir. An unknown descendant.'

Alf Storeggen bent forward with difficulty and took hold of his coffee cup. His hand shook as he lifted it, and he chose to put it down again.

'Who was that?' Wisting asked.

'Kristin Saga. She's married to Torkel Lauritzen's son and is called Lauritzen as well now.'

Wisting sat back in his chair. Yet another piece falling into place. The missing DNA match. They had compared the DNA profile from the severed feet with the profiles from the surviving relatives, but had not found that any of them matched Otto Saga. This was the explanation.

'Are you sure?' he asked nevertheless.

'Christian Hauge was sure at least. He told me about the group of friends and their close relationship, and how it had become a bit too close.'

'Did Otto Saga or any of the others know about it?'

The old man shook his head.

'I don't know, but I doubt it very much indeed.'

Wisting closed his eyes for a moment. He tried to collect his thoughts. All of the murders could be regarded as a chain reaction that started after Christian Hauge died. He could not see, all the same, how what he had just learned could take the murder investigation forward, with the exception of solving the identification question.

285

'I didn't ask about how large a fortune it concerned,' the lawyer continued, 'but suggested leaving it as a secret. If she had lived more than half a lifetime believing in one father, then I thought it would be best to let her live the rest of her life with the same belief. And so it was. She inherited nothing. It would only have created ill feeling.'

'So she didn't receive what was rightfully hers?'

Storeggen shook his head.

'There was never any will written, but I didn't know at that time how much money we were talking about. If I had known that, I might have given different advice.'

Wisting cocked his head.

'Was it so much money?'

'According to Torkel, there was talk of around two and a half million in loose notes. Any possible bank deposits would be in addition.'

Like a kind of inbuilt reflex, Wisting's hand searched for one of the pens on the desk. Without being fully conscious of it, he could sense that the conversation was about to take a dramatic turn.

'Did Torkel Lauritzen tell you this?' he asked cautiously.

The old man nodded deeply, stretched his hand out again to the coffee cup and tried to raise it to his mouth.

'It was a couple of days after Christian Hauge died. The grandson had come to Torkel with almost two and a half million kroner. It was his grandfather's legacy.'

'Which of the grandsons?'

The lawyer nodded again and put down his coffee cup.

'Ken Ronny Hauge,' he explained.

'Christian Hauge left Ken Ronny Hauge two and a half million?'

The other man nodded: 'In cash.'

'Why did Ken Ronny Hauge go to Torkel Lauritzen with the money?'

'The problem was that there were lots of old banknotes

286

that had gone out of circulation. He wanted help from Torkel to exchange them.'

'Why could Ken Ronny not exchange them himself?'

'Ken Ronny Hauge had killed a man, of course. It was seventeen years ago, but although his prison sentence had been served, he would never be finished with it. He was also sentenced to pay the widow and children compensation and damages. It sum was a million kroner at that time, but with interest it had become an insuperable amount. It would never give him the chance to get back on his feet. The cash had to be kept outwith the distribution of the estate, otherwise the enforcement officer would have taken everything. Torkel felt he had to help out. If nothing else he owed it to Christian Hauge, for old times' sake.'

Wisting put pen to paper and wrote KEN RONNY HAUGE in capital letters. He felt he understood everything now. The plan Ken Ronny Hauge had probably spent years of his life concocting. A murderous plan.

The old man coughed into his hand while pressing his eyes together as though they were sore.

'But you know all of this already,' he said, clearing his throat.

'What do you mean?'

'Not the paternity, but the fortune in cash. I expect that you have investigated all this earlier.'

Wisting shook his head.

'It's the first time I've heard of it.'

Alf Storeggen's hand curved round the handle of his walking stick. His breathing was constricted, and there was a gurgling sound. Wisting saw that something was making him uneasy. His eyes darted back and forth, as though his thoughts were jumping about.

'I can't believe that,' he mumbled.

'Have you told this to the police before?'

Storeggen shook his head so that the loose folds of skin beneath his chin quivered.

'Not to the police.'

'To whom, then?'

'I was ill when Torkel Lauritzen disappeared last autumn,' the lawyer explained in a rough voice. 'Pneumonia. I couldn't manage to do much, but eventually after a few days and Torkel hadn't been found, I told this to one of the carers who promised to take it up. I thought it might have significance for your investigations.'

'Who did you tell?'

'Camilla Thaulow. The one who's also gone missing. Did she really not say anything?'

'I haven't heard about it before now at least.'

The old man shook his head.

'Why did she not say anything?' he mumbled to himself.

Wisting bit his bottom lip, thinking about the woman who had just been found at a depth of over 300 metres, and who had lived her whole life with her mother. The only man she had met had become an expensive experience, swindling her out of all her savings. What Alf Storeggen had told her was valuable information. In some way or other, she may have decided to make use of it herself.

Alf Storeggen leaned on his stick and got ready to leave. Wisting stood up and felt his dizziness return.

'I'll get someone to drive you home,' he said, picking up the phone. He ordered a car and went round the desk to help the other man out of his chair.

He accompanied the old lawyer out of the police station and stood waiting until he was sitting inside a patrol car. The wind had changed direction, and he thought he could feel it: it was as though it carried with it the taste of something promising.

288

60

Line emerged from the shower, dried herself and wiped the steam off the mirror before wrapping the towel round her hips. She took out her make up and spent almost a quarter of an hour before she was happy.

She had a dress in her bag that she had not used, and tried it on before pulling on a pair of jeans and a T-shirt instead.

Her morning had been taken up by reading up on miscarriages of justice. She had found more than she had been aware of, and more than she liked to think about.

In front of the computer screen again she looked at the picture of Ken Ronny Hauge. She had not made an appointment, but would take the risk that he would be at home. If not, she would wait to see if he turned up.

She took out the expensive *Hasselblad* camera, checking that the memory card was empty and the battery charged. She went over to the window and took a few trial photos with different shutter speeds of the grey weather before packing it away in her bag.

As early as last night, she had decided how she would begin the conversation with Ken Ronny Hauge. She would provoke a reaction from him. *I think you're lying*, she would say, adding: *I think you're innocent*.

61

There were six people round the conference table. William Wisting sat at the end. He had broken into a cold sweat and had to concentrate to keep his focus. Torunn Borg, Nils Hammer and Espen Mortensen were sitting to his right, while Chief Superintendent Anvik and Assistant Chief of Police Vetti were on his left.

'I think it happened like this,' Wisting began, going on to give a chronological summary of all the events and how this had led him to pinpoint Ken Ronny Hauge as the perpetrator. Daniel Meyer had also played a part behind the scenes, but they did not know exactly what.

'This has involved converting the proceeds from an old robbery into legal tender,' he concluded, laying his hand on the summary report he had distributed. 'The methods used have been more cynical than we have ever seen before.'

The others sat in silence.

'What do we do now?' the Chief Superintendent asked, glancing towards the Assistant Chief of Police who had the responsibility to prosecute. 'Is there enough to make an arrest?'

'There's nothing I'd rather do,' Vetti replied. 'But I'm afraid it's not enough. We don't have anything specific.' He held up the report. 'In reality, this isn't anything more than a working hypothesis. The division of roles between Ken Ronny Hauge and Daniel Meyer is unclear. Were they working together all the time, or was Ken Ronny Hauge operating alone?' He dropped the report on the table. 'We have no proof. There's no technical evidence to link him to either the money or the victims. We can't risk anything coming undone now. We need to have a completely water-tight case.'

Wisting scowled across at him. Vetti was right, but the reason for making an arrest was that there was a justifiable suspicion about a person. It was not necessary to be certain of being right. Evidence could come to light during the further investigation, in the shape of the lies the arrested person might become entangled in or discoveries made while searching his car or home. What they risked if the worst came to the worst was not getting support for a request to remand him in custody. For the Assistant Chief of Police, that would be a setback that would not look good beside his application for the post of Deputy Chief Constable.

Vetti cleared his throat: 'I want us to do the rounds one more time. See what we can turn up. Perhaps bring him in for questioning as a witness so that we can get him later for perjury. Possibly charge him with avoiding inheritance tax. But it's too early for a murder indictment.'

He got up and went to the door, as though to avoid any discussion.

'What I mean is that we must not be in too much of a hurry,' he concluded as he left.

The Chief Superintendent got up as well, nodding in satisfaction that the case was progressing towards a solution, before he too left the room.

'What'll we do?' Nils Hammer asked when the investigators were left alone at the table.

Wisting felt tired and unwell, almost faint. He got up and went over to the worktop to fill a glass of water.

'We'll go for a drive,' he said. 'Then we'll see if we manage to stir up something or other that we can use.'

Crows took off from a densely growing field and flew low across the meadow as Wisting drove down towards the little farmstead at the water's edge. The spot had a somewhat deserted appearance. Junk and rubbish were lying in heaps, old car parts, bottles with peeling labels, bricks and pieces of cement. A rusty cast iron stove with a gaping hole in its side was leaning on the wall of the house. The last time he had been here, the mess had given the place a certain charm. Now it gave the property a gloomy character. Perhaps it was the effect of the weather, or perhaps it was what he now knew.

Wisting parked in the middle of the courtyard and remained sitting behind the steering wheel. His dizziness had worsened, and he needed to concentrate before getting out.

The rain had made the area between the main house and the barn very muddy, and water was lying in puddles. A dog lifted its head as they slammed the car doors. It had sought shelter from the rain under a garden table and yawned before lying lazily down again.

Wet grass washed their shoes as they strode up to the entrance door. Flakes of old paint fell off when Wisting knocked. There was no response from inside.

The wide barn door was open and banging in the wind behind them. They went over to the large building and peered into the semi-darkness inside.

'Hello,' Wisting called out, without getting any answer.

The room inside was fitted out as a kind of car workshop. It smelled of motor oil and old steel. An American car was sitting close to the wall on the left hand side with its bonnet up. Around it were car parts, welding lights and cutting tools scattered all over. The shape of another car was outlined under a blue tarpaulin in the middle of the room.

Wisting took a couple of steps into the large building, but stopped. The tracks from wet car tyres were showing on the rough concrete floor, leading to the car that was covered over. He glanced at Hammer as they approached. Hammer pulled away half of the tarpaulin to reveal a small, black

Peugeot. It was wet from the rain, and drips from the undercarriage were falling on the floor.

'Hello?' Wisting repeated. It was an effort to shout. Blood was pounding in the veins behind his forehead and he had to close his eyes to get a grip on himself.

'He can't be far away,' Hammer said, pointing at several footprints on the dusty floor made by whoever had circled the car to pull the tarpaulin across. The prints were drying, and impossible to follow.

'Ken Ronny Hauge!'

This time it was Hammer who was shouting. A bird living beneath the roof trusses was startled, flapping its wings until coming to rest again. Otherwise, it was completely quiet.

Wisting turned to go outside again, but came to a halt. Over by the east wall was a cylinder of wire cable. A length of about two metres had been cut off and lay coiled up. Beside it was a box containing wire clamps.

He squatted down to pick up the cut length and examined it. The steel seemed acid resistant. The diameter looked to be the same as on the wire that had held Camilla Thaulow firmly to the bottom of the sea.

A gust of wind rattled the corrugated iron overhead. Wisting put the steel wire down carefully. Analysis of the alloy in the steel could connect it to the murder of the missing nurse, the kind of evidence they were looking for.

He straightened up and felt dizzy again. The slightly too quick movement caused light red spots to dance in front of his eyes. He supported himself on a partition wall, shook his head cautiously and felt the blood pumping hard through his veins. His whole body felt weak and he closed his eyes while he took a couple of deep breaths.

'Oh, fuck,' he heard Hammer swear behind him.

Wisting opened his eyes. Hammer stepped over the wire cylinder and approached a pile of old hessian sacks lying against the wall. There was a foot sticking out of one of them.

293

Hammer pulled the hessian sacks to one side. A swarm of flies flew up. The body was lying face down, the back of the head a large, open wound. Wisting could see the crushing injuries in the skull. Hair and blood stuck together had hardened into a dark crust.

Hammer swore once more and turned the dead body round. It was Daniel Meyer. His face was distorted and stiff, with a startled expression. His eyes were opened wide and his mouth half open, as though he had been in the middle of a scream.

Wisting felt himself break into a cold sweat, swallowing to keep the nausea at bay.

'He's here somewhere,' Hammer said, taking a couple of steps back. He looked around before taking out his mobile phone.

'I'm calling in reinforcements,' he said, walking towards the open barn door.

Wisting took some unsteady steps after him. The clammy air inside the barn was not reaching his lungs. He concentrated on breathing in deeply.

Hammer put his phone to his ear, standing in the middle of the door opening. At the same time, Ken Ronny Hauge leapt on him from the side. Wisting watched it happen like a slow-motion animation. The attacker had a wire cutter in his right hand. The blow struck Nils Hammer on his right shoulder and Wisting heard something break. The mobile phone dropped to the ground as Hammer fell to his knees, twisting round and raising his left arm to ward off the next blow.

Wisting's body would not obey. He tried to gather his strength to jump on Ken Ronny Hauge and knock him over, but instead felt his legs give way. He staggered, groping for something to hold. The sounds around him faded as he gasped for breath. His last thought was that he was fainting, and then his eyes flickered and everything went black.

62

The rain stopped as Line drove in front of the small farm-stead out by Helgeroa. She hooked her bag with the camera and notebook over her shoulder and got out of the car. The place appeared desolate and abandoned.

She knocked the door of the main house at the same time as calling out Ken Ronny Hauge's name. There was no response. She took a couple of steps back down the broad stairway and looked around. The doors into the barn he used as a workshop were closed and car tracks across the muddy courtyard suggested that he had just driven off.

An empty drying rack stood in front of the house. Gripping one of its bars she gave it a shove. The rack moved round half a turn. She had really decided to wait in the car if he was not at home, but if he had just left, he might be quite some time. She decided to drive to Nevlun-ghavn and buy an ice cream and come back later. Walking towards the car she suddenly noticed the dog lying under the garden table where she and Ken Ronny Hauge had sat the first time she had visited him. It got up and arched its back before sauntering over to her.

She patted the dog behind the ear and said a few words to it. Its wet fur smelled unpleasant.

The dog yawned and sat down as Line looked around, wondering how Ken Ronny Hauge could have left the dog untethered.

Then she caught sight of him. He was standing in the clinker-built boat down by the quay, and he had spotted her as well. He raised his hand in greeting before disappearing into the cabin, popping up again almost immediately and jumping ashore. As he walked towards her he grabbed a wheelbarrow that had been lying beside the boathouse, pushing it in front of him.

She went to meet him, leaving the dog to return to his spot beneath the garden table.

'Good to see you,' he said, putting the wheelbarrow aside. He was wet from the rain. His dark hair lay flat and his white T-shirt was plastered against his body so that the muscles were outlined against the thin material. 'Is there something else I can help you with?'

'I wanted to talk to you,' Line smiled. 'Have you time?'

He smiled back, nodding.

She followed him into the main house and into the kitchen from the hallway. It was a big room, as so often in old houses, with log walls and beams across the ceiling.

Ken Ronny Hauge pulled the wet T-shirt off and threw it onto a chair before going over to a large ceramic sink and washing his hands with a bar of soap that was lying on the worktop.

Line tidied a bundle of old newspapers away, sat down and put her bag with the camera on the kitchen table in front of her. She opened it while she scrutinised his tanned body. He was more powerfully built than Tommy, his back broad and with no hair, unlike Tommy.

He took out a towel from below the worktop to dry his hands and hair as he entered the adjoining room. When he returned, he had put on a long-sleeved jumper.

'What were you thinking about?' he asked, sitting down opposite her.

Line swallowed and met his eyes.

'I think that you haven't been honest with me,' she said.

The smile of the man at the other side of the table stiffened.

'What do you mean?'

'I think you're innocent. I think that it wasn't you who killed the policeman that time in 1991.'

Ken Ronny Hauge gave her a strange look, as though she had said something to hurt him and he was considering how to react. Rainwater was dripping from the roof onto the weatherboard outside the kitchen window. Line held eye contact and waited for the tipping point to arrive. He would either dismiss her, or he would begin to talk.

He shook his head. 'Who else could it have been?'

'Your brother?' she suggested. Her voice had become unsteady.

'Rune?' Ken Ronny Hauge laughed. 'He's much too cowardly for anything like that.'

'Who was it then?'

Ken Ronny Hauge got up abruptly, went over to the worktop and filled a glass with water.

'Let it be!' he demanded.

Line did not give up.

'The evidence pointed to you,' she said. 'It won't benefit you to argue against it, but I don't believe it *was* you. There are possible explanations for how the gunpowder residue came to be on your hands. Transfer of contamination, for example. I think you were driving the car, but I don't think you fired the gun.'

The man on the other side of the room leaned against the worktop and watched her. Rainwater was still dripping outside the window as the silence between them became uncomfortable.

'You're mistaken,' he said eventually.

'It was you who hid the gun afterwards,' Line continued. 'That's when your fingers became covered in gunpowder residue. There was no way back. If you told the truth, you would have been found guilty as an accomplice anyway. It might have given you a couple of years less, but at the same time you would have dragged down your brother who was soon to be a Dad.'

Ken Ronny Hauge went over to the window, pulled back the curtains and looked out before standing beside the worktop again.

'Now I think you should go,' he said.

Line shook her head.

'I want to know the truth.'

Wisting blinked. It felt like waking from a deep sleep. He could not manage to gather his thoughts, and remained lying without moving. His head was aching and he felt sick.

He took time to collect himself and become aware of what had happened. Raising himself carefully on his elbows, breathing deeply and looking about, he found that he was still in Ken Ronny Hauge's barn in semi darkness. Only a few narrow strips of daylight came in through gaps in the wall.

He grasped a shelf as he pulled himself upright. His whole body was shaking, and he retched without vomiting anything up. His face felt stiff as he stroked his hand over his chin. When pieces of dried blood fell off he realised that he must have had a nosebleed.

'Nils,' he called out tentatively, but got no answer.

A glance at the bundle of hessian sacks by the wall was enough to confirm that Daniel Meyer was still lying in the same place.

The barn door was closed with the civilian police car right inside. He felt in his pockets for the keys and his mobile phone, but both were gone.

The car was not locked. He sat inside and swore when he discovered that it was a leased car with no police radio. He checked whether the keys were still in the ignition and swore again when they were not.

The barn door would not open, even with all of his body weight on the panels. It must have been bolted on the other side.

He rested his head on the door panels and peeped into the

courtyard. He saw no one, but there was a car in the yard outside the main house and he screwed up his eyes to see better. There was something unpleasantly familiar about it.

'Line,' he groaned.

His heart was beating anxiously in his chest, and he was afraid he would faint again. He filled his lungs, controlling his breathing carefully. He was fighting against the panicky feeling of fear that came creeping over him and would paralyse his ability to think logically and rationally.

Slowly he regained control. His eyes searched the room while he found his bearings. There was a single door at the side of the double barn doors. He tried the door handle but that was locked too. He found what he was looking for among the tools that were scattered over the floor, a crowbar. His head swam as he squatted to pick it up, and he forced himself to remain standing, gathering his strength before applying it to the doorframe.

Line moved away uneasily. Ken Ronny Hauge went over to the window again and looked out, as though he was waiting for something. Then he turned round and picked up a packet of tobacco that was lying on the worktop.

'It was a bad idea to take part in this interview,' he remarked as he started to roll a cigarette. 'I've changed my mind.'

'What do you mean?'

He licked the paper and finished making the cigarette before replying: 'I'm taking it back. I don't want you to write about me.'

Something in his voice seemed threatening. Line watched him while he placed the cigarette in his mouth and lit up. She suddenly thought that she could see on him how the years in prison had made him bitter, hardened and intransigent.

'Do you not want to read it first?' she asked.

He shook his head, took a drag and exhaled a cloud of smoke towards the ceiling.

The article was one of her best, both from a linguistic point of view and content-wise. With the help of literary expressions she had managed to describe the intense atmosphere she had experienced at their first meeting. Now he seemed simply cold and indifferent, and she realised that her first impression had been wrong. Nevertheless, she had no intention of complying with his request.

'I don't think the editorial team will go along with that,' she said.

He picked a speck of tobacco off his tongue and inhaled again. His gaze met hers. There was something frightening about it. His eyes had contracted into narrow lines.

'Do what the fuck you want,' he said, taking the cigarette from his mouth. 'Just get away from here.'

He took a few steps towards her, leaned over the worktop and reached for the ashtray to stub out his cigarette. He stopped in mid-movement. Outside, a man was staggering out of the barn. His face was bloody, but Line recognised him at once.

'Fuck!' Ken Ronny Hauge bellowed.

Line opened her mouth, but suddenly understood how completely wrong she had been about Ken Ronny Hauge. Fear gripped her with paralysing force. Her chest tightened, and it felt difficult to breathe.

Her father hesitated in confusion outside the barn before walking unsteadily across the yard.

Line acted without thinking. She grabbed the camera that was at the top of her bag and swung it at Ken Ronny Hauge's head with all the strength she could muster. The lens came off and fell onto the table. Ken Ronny Hauge wobbled. Line got up and hit him again, this time with so much force the camera-housing cracked open. Ken Ronny Hauge fell across the table and slid to the floor. Several gurgling sounds came from him before he lay motionless.

Her legs were unsteady. She tripped on the man on the floor, put her hands out to stop from falling and dashed outside, her heart banging in her chest. The metallic taste of blood filled her mouth. Tears ran from her eyes and made it difficult to see clearly.

Wisting squinted in the daylight, taking deep breaths of the salt air. At last his head was clearing.

The door to the main house was suddenly thrown open and Line came running towards him. He opened his arms and embraced her, but had to sit on the ground.

'What has happened?' she demanded, squatting down in front of him.

He did not have the strength to explain.

'It's just a nosebleed,' he said, wiping his face with his hand.

'Are you on your own?'

Wisting shook his head and looked around.

'Nils is here somewhere. He was struck down.'

'My God . . .'

'Where is he?' Wisting asked. 'Where is Ken Ronny?'

'In the kitchen.' She gave a quick account of what had happened. 'He might waken at any moment.'

'Phone for help,' her father told her. 'He's deadly dangerous. He murdered them all.'

A perplexed expression came over Line's face, but she did not wait for an explanation.

'My phone is in there,' she nodded towards the main house. 'Where's yours?'

'I don't know.'

She was about to get up to fetch her mobile phone when Ken Ronny Hauge appeared in the doorway, blood running from a wound on his face. In his right hand he carried an iron bar that hung by his side. He approached them with quick strides.

Line got up, thoughts racing through her mind like a flock of terrified birds. She looked about wildly but the only weapons she could see were two oars leaning against the wall of the barn. They were bigger and longer than the iron bar Ken Ronny Hauge had armed himself with.

She grabbed one and ran at him, but he warded her off and counterattacked. The force of the iron bar's blows reverberating along the oar meant she could hardly keep hold of it. She had to take a few steps back, and was about to be trapped against the wall of the barn when her father moved unsteadily to take up the other oar and Ken Ronny Hauge turned on him. Line raised her oar like a lance in front of her and tried to push him over, but he skipped away from each attempt, again forcing her backwards.

When he lifted the bar to strike again Line threw the oar at him. Ken Ronny Hauge lost his balance and fell, the iron bar slipping out of his hand. He got hold of it again and was about to get up when they both noticed smoke leaking out of the main house.

Line hit him across the back with the oar. It was as though it woke him up. He scrambled to his feet, threw away the iron bar and ran inside the house as flames burst through the windows and door.

Line looked on, emotionally exhausted.

'Have you got the car keys?' Wisting asked her, nodding in the direction of his daughter's car.

'They're inside the house,' she said.

The flames changed colour and character as they licked fiercely over the kitchen window. She could see Ken Ronny Hauge's outline inside as he fought the fire.

Without hesitation she ran into the house and found her way to the kitchen. Orange and red flames, with deeper shades of blue and green and sporadic tentacles of violet, twisted and turned. Ken Ronny was hitting them with the towel he had used to dry himself but the waves of fire only became more intense.

Inside, she could see how she had struck Ken Ronny Hauge with the *Hasselblad* camera. When he fell forward his cigarette had shot out of his hand, hit the lace curtain at the window and landed on the pile of old newspapers and magazines.

She took a few steps into the smoke-filled room and pulled her bag towards her. Ken Ronny Hauge paid no attention to her, but gave up his struggle against the flames that had taken hold of the dry wood. Throwing the towel away he dashed further inside.

Line ran outside again to her father.

'What about Ken Ronny?' he asked as the panes of the kitchen window exploded into pieces.

'He's still in there.' She handed him the phone. 'You do it!'

He keyed in the emergency number, announcing himself in a steady voice when the operator responded. He gave a brief summary and said what assistance was required.

The conversation seemed to renew Wisting's strength. He looked towards the house where the flames now had a better grip. Long, ice blue tongues were leaping out through the smashed windows and eating their way up to the second floor.

He could not understand what Ken Ronny Hauge was doing in there, but could not simply stand watching. He ran into the burning house with adrenalin pumping through his body, his eyes and throat stinging in the smoke.

The fire had spread extensively. Dry wood around the hallway leading to the kitchen sparked and burned, red-gold flames were being sucked out into the porch and climbing the stairs to the second floor. The angry noise was deafening. The fire stood like a terrifying wall, preventing him from venturing further into the house. He was about to turn when he caught sight of Ken Ronny Hauge standing at the top of the stairs with a suitcase. The man hesitated for a moment before starting to walk, not managing more than three steps before putting his foot wrong. He stumbled, fell and remained lying in the middle of the staircase, in an unnaturally twisted position.

Wisting held his arm in front of his face to protect himself against the heat, took a few steps up the stairs and tried to drag him down, but could not manage it. He could not fill his lungs with enough air.

Line appeared behind him and placed her hand on his shoulder. He stepped aside to let her past. Together they managed to pull Ken Ronny Hauge down the remaining stairs and into the yard. Black clouds of smoke billowed around them in the courtyard but they were safe.

Wisting lay on his back gasping for breath. Ken Ronny Hauge coughed and twisted round.

'There's a pair of handcuffs in the glove compartment of the police car,' Wisting told Line, pointing to the barn.

Line ran in while Wisting dragged Ken Ronny Hauge to the drying frame. When Line came back he cuffed him firmly. Behind them flames stretched upwards, sparks crackling as they rose in the smoky air before dying and falling to the ground. For a moment Wisting felt like one of them. Burned out.

63

Twenty minutes later, the courtyard was full of emergency vehicles.

An ambulance drove off with Nils Hammer. The dog patrol had found him on board the boat, fastened securely with steel wire to a metal drum. The doctor who examined him was optimistic.

Line was sitting in the back seat of a police car with her legs outside and Wisting stood beside her with a rug over his shoulders. The fire crew had overcome the flames, but there was almost nothing left of the house. It was smouldering a little here and there, but they were about to roll up their hoses.

Wisting stepped over the charred remains of the log walls into the ruins. Debris from the furnishings was scattered everywhere in a confusion of blackened and twisted rubbish. Settees, tables, chairs, shelves, worktops, cupboards, and drawers – everything charred by the flames and dripping wet from the firemen's hoses.

He found the suitcase at the bottom of what remained of the staircase. The heat from the fire had forced it open. Wisting kicked at it with his foot. The contents had been consumed by the flames, but all the same it was not difficult to work out what had been inside. When he cleared flakes of ash from the top the original contents were easy to identify: bundles of banknotes.

He squatted down, trying to pick up a bundle, but it disintegrated between his fingers. So, this was what it had all been about. Money.

He brushed his hands and got up again. The investigation was drawing to a close, he thought.

Through the shouts and crackling on the firemen's portable radios, he heard the familiar sound of his mobile phone. It was lying on the garden table together with the keys to the police car. The dog glowered at him from his position underneath it when he picked them up.

It was the doctor.

'I've been trying to get hold of you, but have of course seen from the news that you've been busy these last few days,' he said.

Wisting mumbled an affirmative reply, but didn't know if he had the energy to listen to what the doctor had concluded after studying all of his test results.

'That's exactly what I wanted to talk to you about,' the doctor continued. 'You are overworked. You risk a breakdown and becoming completely burned out if you continue at the same pace. How are you feeling, anyway?'

Wisting supported himself on a patrol car without answering.

'Exhausted and weak?' the doctor suggested. 'Lacking energy?'

Wisting confirmed this.

'Have you had dizzy spells?'

'That too.'

'Well, I've already written out a sick note for you. What you need is a long holiday. Relaxation. Do you think you can manage that?'

'Yes,' Wisting responded.

He received some practical advice before rounding off the conversation. Then he put his arm round his daughter, pulled her towards him and laid his head on her shoulder. The layer of clouds above them was about to break. The sun would soon shine through.

EPILOGUE

Wisting sat down to a breakfast of fried eggs and coffee on the terrace. Before he began eating he leaned back and gazed out across the sea without looking at anything in particular.

Two weeks had passed. He was feeling better and fitter. He wakened feeling more rested, and had regained a great deal of his energy. His days were filled with tasks that he had postponed for too long. Gardening and basic maintenance in the big house. The evenings had been long and warm, and he had spent them with Suzanne, eventually feeling his shoulders relax and his strength returning.

He breathed in through his nose and filled his lungs with the salt sea air that the breeze brought ashore.

When he had finished eating, he pushed his plate away and unfolded his newspaper. He leafed through the crime reports, as he had done every day for the past two weeks, but then stopped and had to turn back through the pages. He recognised a picture of a burned out building. The editors must have searched deeply through the archives before putting it into print. It was the same photograph as the one Daniel Meyer had torn out of a newspaper more than twenty years previously and that had been lying amongst all of his notes.

Wisting began to read. A former fellow prisoner had reported to the police that he had set fire to the washhouse on the farm out in Helgeroa on the orders of Ken Ronny Hauge. Assistant Chief of Police Vetti gave an account of the police's theory that Ken Ronny Hauge and Daniel Meyer had been together on the safety deposit box robbery in 1991. Ken Ronny had hidden the haul and let Daniel Meyer believe that the money had gone up in flames while he was in prison. Eventually when the newspapers were describing how the exchange of the old banknotes was part of the case of the severed feet, Daniel Meyer realised that he had been deceived. His confrontation with Ken Ronny had resulted in his death.

He drank some coffee and read on. The remainder of the article was a review of what had emerged in the media coverage in the days following Ken Ronny Hauge's arrest. The newspaper quoted *Verdens Gang*, which obviously had access to Hauge's police statement. The plan to convert the old proceeds from the robbery into legal tender had been concocted after his grandfather died. He had seen how he could use a fictional distribution of inheritance as the pretext to get help from his grandfather's old friends, an inheritance that had to be kept secret to avoid questions from the authorities.

It was never the intention that anyone should die, Ken Ronny Hauge was quoted as saying. Torkel Lauritzen had been the first victim. He had become unwell after the last sum of money was taken out of the bank in Sandefjord and died in the passenger seat of the car. From fear that the whole plan would collapse Ken Ronny had decided to dump the body at sea. The course of events was largely confirmed by Audun Vetti, who established that the cause of death was most probably cardiac arrest, but that there could all the same be consideration of charges of desecrating a corpse and failure to discharge the obligation to give assistance.

The ballistic investigations confirmed that the other victims had been shot with the pistol that was found on the bottom of the sea. The final analyses had also confirmed that this was the weapon that had been used to kill the policeman at Eikeren. In his statement, Ken Ronny claimed that it had belonged to Daniel Meyer's grandfather.

It was strange to be a passive spectator in an investigation in which he himself had taken a leading role. Wisting took a gulp of coffee, and was leafing through the paper to the television pages when there was a knock at the front door.

'Hello,' he heard Line shout.

He called back to let her know where he was.

Line sat down in the chair opposite.

'How are you feeling?' she asked.

'Fine,' he smiled. 'I've just eaten. Do you want anything? Coffee?'

She shook her head.

'They've found the last corpse,' she said.

Wisting raised his eyebrows.

'They just announced it on the radio,' she explained. 'A dead body has been found in the sea outside Hummerbakken. It was missing a foot.'

'Otto Saga,' Wisting declared.

'Ken Ronny Hauge's not so silent this time,' Line continued. 'He's admitted all of it, except the police murder.'

Wisting nodded. They would probably never find out what had really happened on that dark September night in 1991 but, like Line, he did not believe that Ken Ronny Hauge was necessarily the one who had fired the fatal shots.

'It'll be a strange trial,' Line went on. 'To stand accused of the murder of the man who actually was guilty of the murder you yourself served sixteen years in prison for. The worst thing is that I don't think any of it would have happened if it hadn't been for the punishment he got that time. I don't believe he really was evil. I think it was jail that made him like that.'

Wisting drank his coffee. 'How's your interview project going?' he asked.

'I'm going to Bergen,' Line replied. 'That's actually why I've popped in to see you. I'm leaving this evening.'

'To Bergen?'

'I've had the deadline extended. I had to find a new interview subject, of course.'

'Who is it?'

'Maybe you can remember the case. Trond Furebø. He was found guilty of murdering a prostitute and a journalist who wrote about the case.'

Wisting tried to think back, but didn't think he remembered it. That was how it was, far too many cases.

'Did you get yourself a new camera?' he asked.

She shook her head.

'I've borrowed one from the editorial team.'

The cat came creeping over, interrupting the conversation about the investigation and what had happened out at Helgeroa two weeks previously. It jumped onto Line's lap and settled down.

Wisting got up, and went into the kitchen for a couple of slices of boiled ham. He tore them into pieces and threw them down on the terrace.

'You're spoiling him,' Line said as the cat jumped down.

Wisting smiled. She was right, but he didn't see any reason why he should stop spoiling the tousled cat.

'When are you going back to work?' Line enquired.

Wisting went over to the railings. 'Soon,' he said, looking towards the horizon. He could make out banks of clouds in the distance.

For more William Wisting,
turn the page for an extract from
Closed For Winter.

1

Swirling sheets of fog drifted inland, settling on the wet asphalt and forming blurred haloes around the streetlamps. Ove Bakkerud drove with one hand on the steering wheel as the surrounding darkness drew in. He particularly enjoyed this time of year, just before autumn leaf-fall.

This would be his final trip to the summer cottage at Stavern, to nail closed the window shutters, drag the boat ashore and shut the place for winter. He had looked forward to it all summer long; this was his holiday. The actual work took no more than a couple of hours on Sunday afternoon, and the remaining time was at his disposal.

He swung off the main road and rolled onto the crunching gravel, the car headlights sliding over the briar hedge bordering the road all the way to the parking place. The dashboard clock showed 21.37. He switched off the ignition and emerged from the vehicle to inhale the fresh tang of salt sea air, listening to the waves boom like distant thunder on the shore.

The rain had eased and harsh blasts of wind were gusting to disperse the fog. The Tvistein light swept the landscape, glimmering across the rocks.

As he wrapped himself more snugly in his jacket, he stepped behind the car to haul the shopping bags from the boot, savouring the prospect of rare steak for dinner and fried bacon and eggs for breakfast. Man's food. Thrusting his free hand into his pocket to check for the keys he ascended the path to his cottage on the rocky outcrop. A slight incline, and then the entire ocean stretched before

315

him. His sense of the enormous panorama filled him, as always, with a special feeling of peace.

The cottage had been a simple, red-painted wooden cabin, without insulation and damaged by dry rot, when his family bought it almost twenty years earlier. As soon as he had sufficient funds he demolished the entire structure and rebuilt, and gradually he and his wife created their own little paradise. From the years when he had spent all his free time on construction work, this location had become his place to relax, breathe out, and take things easy. A place where time meant nothing and where the hours could pass according to the dictates of wind and weather.

Placing the shopping bags on the flagstones fronting the cottage, he took the keys from his pocket. The lighthouse beam struck the exterior wall and Ove Bakkerud froze and caught his breath. His grip tightened on the keys, his mouth felt dry and goose pimples spread from the nape of his neck to his forearms.

The bright lance from the lighthouse again cut through the darkness, confirming that the door was ajar, its frame shattered, the lock tumbled to the ground.

Glancing around, he perceived only darkness, though a noise, a twig snapping, rose from the undergrowth. Further off a dog barked; then nothing but the wind rustling through autumn leaves and waves breaking on the shore.

Ove Bakkerud stepped forward a few paces, holding the top edge of the door to push it open. Fumbling his way towards the light switch, he turned on the exterior lamp and the ceiling light in the hallway.

He and his wife had discussed the possibility of something like this, having read accounts in the newspapers about gangs of youths breaking into cottages to rampage through the furnishings, as well as more professional outfits ransacking entire communities of summer cottages in their search for valuables. Nevertheless, he could not believe his eyes.

The living room had taken the worst: drawers and

cupboards lay open, contents strewn over the floor, smashed glasses and dishes, and settee cushions scattered across the room. Everything saleable was gone: the new flat screen television, stereo system and portable radio. The cabinet where they stored wine and spirits was completely bare, a half-empty bottle of cognac the only item left behind. It felt as though their special place had been violated.

He stooped to lift the ship in a bottle, usually displayed on the mantelpiece but now lying on the floor, a large crack disfiguring the glass. Two of the masts had fractured. He recalled the many hours he had watched his grandfather's calloused fingers transform the tiny fragments into a fully-rigged ship. The moment the craft was installed inside the bottle, his grandfather had pulled the threads to hoist its sails.

His voice trembling, he phoned the police and introduced himself.

'When were you last at the cottage?' the operator enquired.

'Two weeks ago.'

'So the burglary took place after the 19th September?' Ove Bakkerud suddenly felt totally drained. 'Do you know if they've broken into other cottages?' the police officer asked.

'No,' Ove Bakkerud replied, gazing through the window and spotting a light at Thomas Rønningen's cottage in the distance. 'I've just arrived.'

'We can send out a patrol to have a look in the morning,' the police operator continued. 'Meanwhile it would be best if you disturb things as little as possible.'

'Tomorrow? But ...'

'Will you be at this number? Then we can phone when we have a car available.'

His mouth opened in protest, to demand that the police come immediately with dogs and crime scene technicians, but he held his tongue. Swallowing, he muttered a thank you and drew the conversation to a close.

Where should he start? He headed for the kitchen to fetch a dustpan and brush before remembering the policeman's admonition to leave the crime scene undisturbed. Instead he peered down at the living room window of his neighbour's cottage.

He was wondering about that light being on, since Thomas Rønningen rarely visited during autumn, having enough on his plate with his successful Friday-evening chat show. All the same, he had taken time off to celebrate the opening night of the season in August, sitting beside Ove Bakkerud at the barbecue pit drinking cognac, telling stories about the events behind the scenes before, during and after each broadcast.

A shadow flitted across the window.

Perhaps the burglars had broken in there as well. For all he knew, they might still be there. Stepping swiftly towards the doorway, he picked up the torch from its usual shelf. The police might well adjust their priorities if Thomas Rønningen was involved.

The footpath's descent to the sea curled between dense undergrowth and the impenetrable branches of crooked pine trees. Shining the torch beam on glossy tree roots and pebbles did not prevent him from scraping against pine needles and twigs.

On this side, the brightly lit cottage windows were too high for him to look in. Zigzagging the torchlight over the terrain, he approached the steps leading to the front entrance, where a blast of wind caught the door, slamming it against the verandah railings. The intense silence sent shivers down his neck and spine when he realised that he was completely defenceless.

The torch beam shed light on the doorframe, revealing similar evidence of a burglary. However, this time there was something more. The edge of the door was spattered with blood.

The William Wisting Series

A WILLIAM WISTING MYSTERY

CLOSED
FOR
WINTER
JORN LIER
HORST

'UP THERE WITH THE BEST
OF NORDIC CRIME WRITERS.'
MARCEL BERLINS, *THE TIMES*

WINNER · THE NORWEGIAN BOOKSELLERS AWARD

Inspector William Wisting has witnessed grotesque
murders before, but this is something new. Then more
corpses are discovered on the deserted archipelago,
while dead birds fall from the sky...

WINNER: Norwegian Booksellers Prize 2011

'A very engrossing crime novel.'
Edinburgh Book Review

The William Wisting Series

A WILLIAM WISTING MYSTERY

THE HUNTING DOGS

JORN LIER HORST

'ONE OF THE MOST BRILLIANTLY
UNDERSTATED CRIME
NOVELISTS WRITING TODAY'
JOAN SMITH, *SUNDAY TIMES*

WINNER - THE GOLDEN REVOLVER TOP NORWEGIAN CRIME NOVEL 2013
WINNER - THE GLASS KEY TOP NORDIC CRIME NOVEL 2013

Years ago William Wisting closed one of Norway's most widely publicised criminal cases. Now it is discovered that evidence was planted and the wrong man convicted. It is Wisting's turn to be hunted.

WINNER: The Glass Key
(Nordic novel 2013)
WINNER: The Golden Revolver
(Norwegian crime novel 2013)
WINNER: The Martin Beck Award
(Best crime novel in translation 2014)

The William Wisting Series

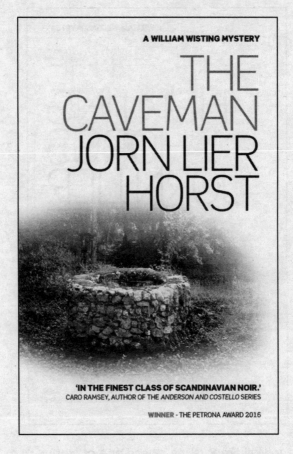

A WILLIAM WISTING MYSTERY

THE
CAVEMAN
JORN LIER
HORST

'IN THE FINEST CLASS OF SCANDINAVIAN NOIR.'
CARO RAMSEY, AUTHOR OF THE *ANDERSON AND COSTELLO* SERIES

WINNER - THE PETRONA AWARD 2016

Only three houses away from William Wisting's home, a man has been sitting dead in front of his television set for four months.

WINNER: The Petrona Award 2016

'The finest class of Scandinavian noir.'
Caro Ramsay

The William Wisting Series

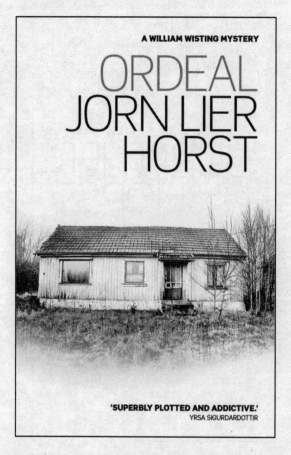

A WILLIAM WISTING MYSTERY

ORDEAL
JORN LIER HORST

'SUPERBLY PLOTTED AND ADDICTIVE.'
YRSA SIGURDARDOTTIR

This time, the only way Wisting can solve the case is to cut across important loyalties and undermine public confidence in his own police force...

'*Ordeal* kept me engaged to the end and I cannot wait for the next.'

Yrsa Sigurdardottir